NOCTURNE

LISA ST AUBIN DE TERÁN

NOCTURNE

———— • ————

HAMISH HAMILTON · LONDON

HAMISH HAMILTON LTD
Published by the Penguin Group
Penguin Books Ltd, 27 Wrights Lane, London W8 5TZ, England
Penguin Books USA Inc., 375 Hudson Street, New York, New York 10014, USA
Penguin Books Australia Ltd, Ringwood, Victoria, Australia
Penguin Books Canada Ltd, 10 Alcorn Avenue, Toronto, Ontario, Canada M4V 3B2
Penguin Books (NZ) Ltd, 182–190 Wairau Road, Auckland 10, New Zealand

Penguin Books Ltd, Registered Offices: Harmondsworth, Middlesex, England

First published 1992
1 3 5 7 9 10 8 6 4 2

Typeset by DatIX International Ltd, Bungay, Suffolk
Filmset in $11\frac{1}{2}$/13 pt Monophoto Garamond
Printed in England by Clays Ltd, St Ives plc

A CIP catalogue record for this book is available from the British Library

ISBN 0-241-13148-0

For Alexander

The sun to me is dark
And silent as the moon,
When she deserts the night
Hid in her vacant interlunar cave.

Since light so necessary is to life,
And almost life itself, if it be true
That light is in the soul,
She all in every part; why was the sight
To such a tender ball as th'eye confined?

Milton, *Samson Agonistes*

CONTENTS

I
ALESSANDRO

In Alessandro's village, one of the things a boy grew up for was to be old enough to go to the fair. It didn't visit their village – if it had, things might have been different – but it settled on foreign soil, on the alien territory of San Severino some two miles distant, beyond the old customs house that was sinking into the mud on the riverside. It came in early June, as regularly as their own *festa* of the Madonna del Campo. Every year Alessandro watched the ox-drawn convoy arrive and depart, a procession of horses, caravans, carts and cages. The caravans rattled and lurched along the unmade road, scattering chips of faded paint and flakes of rust.

'You be good now, or your uncle will sell you to the fair,' mothers all over the village threatened disobedient children. It was said that the fairman did buy children, and it was well known that he exhibited human curiosities, but there was no rumour of a hoard of children. It was obvious to Alessandro that there were spells involved; spells that could turn an ordinary child into the famous spiderwoman.

Before, after and during the fair's arrival, there was endless conjecture. Did the freaks revert by witchcraft to normal people at night? Was the thin shaggy camel a real animal or the object of a curse? Perched above the village on an overhanging rock, squeezed between thorn bushes and broom, Alessandro and his friends watched the travelling fair make its slow, lumbering progress to San Severino. It was impossible to see through the windows of the caravans or inside the cages. The latter were draped with what must once have been striped awnings, tied down against the wind and the rain and faded by the sun. Each bandaged cage bore a crudely carved wooden crest announcing its particular freak.

There was Nando *il Nano*, the smallest dwarf in the world. There

3

was a fat lady who was said to be so immense that she never left her caravan but had a special grille at one end of it through which she could exhibit herself. She was said to sit in overlapping folds like forgotten dough that has overflowed its bowl. Even the bags under her eyes were said to hang and puff over her cheeks, and her arms stuck out like two fat thighs. Some of the older men in the village fantasized about the fat lady. Alessandro did not share their fascination with her or with her colleague, the bearded lady. His own village, after all, could boast the Signora Elena, who had a fully grown moustache and what could easily, with some careful shaving, develop into a respectable beard. The Signora Elena kept the school, and although Alessandro had left at the age of twelve, her ugliness was still compounded for him by memories of her cruelty. It seemed absurd to pay to see her like at a peep show. His eldest brother, Marco, told him that the bearded lady at the funfair had as much of a beard as their uncle Bernardo and that it grew in tufts from her chin and ears and sideburns. He claimed to have seen her back as well and said it sprouted hair in patches like burnt summer grass.

At the top of his own list of what he would like to see when he finally got to the fair were the dwarf and the spiderwoman, the strong man and the camel. Then came the caravans themselves, the moving houses with their trails of smoke and their tired dray horses. What attracted him least, and what he most feared, were the monkeys. He had seen them from afar, year after year, clutching the pommels on the Spanish saddles of the fairman and his family and followers-on. Dressed as cowboys and Indians, gypsy dancers and glittering stars, the troupe rode through the village every year, churning up the dust with their ox-carts as they dragged the dismembered carousel from one site to the next. They knew there was little money to spare for a funfair, with wages at five lire a day. To pay to enter the fairground was a big decision. So the exotic cavalcade was all important; it reminded those who were reluctant to go what they would be missing, and tempted the rest with hints of illicit treats.

How many monkeys belonged to the fair Alessandro didn't know, but there were always three of them running loose as it passed by.

4

They scratched and scurried across the humped tin roofs of the caravans, screeching and gibbering at the heat under their wizened hands. They waved at the crowds, they gave shrill screams and then turned somersaults and laughed. They beckoned with their tiny fingers, beseeched with their sad popping eyes. They reminded Alessandro of dying babies. They looked like his own shrivelled brother who had died of diphtheria clawing at the air, gasping for breath.

Alessandro had been much younger then, he was still at school. One morning he had stopped to look into the wooden crib on his way to see his mother in her semi-quarantine behind the kitchen. The little larder she was living in was almost windowless. It was so dark he didn't see at first that his mother was not there. She must have gone out beyond the village to do her business. The sick baby was alone. His dying brother was almost as big as the cradle he lay in. His feet touched the rough chestnut panel at the end. His face was pale but blotchy and it moved through a cycle of colour that ended in blackberry stain. Before the illness, they had played together, Alessandro was teaching the little one to walk. From the cradle the dull eyes cleared, flickering recognition. The shrunken hands grasped for him. They caught his cuff and then clawed with a grip far stronger than his own. The eyes grew desperate, the fingers clutched, while the rasping, screeching air battled through the closed throat.

There had been talk of taking the baby to the fever ward in Castello. Neither of his parents would allow it; there was no safety beyond the boundaries of their village. Between the priest and the midwife and the other women, the baby would heal or die, and either live there on their outcrop of rock or be buried in the cemetery beyond it. Alessandro had torn his cuff away from his black-faced brother and run away, but in his dreams, long after the baby died, he still came grasping after him, reaching out to drag him down into his airless underworld. The monkeys clawing at the sunlight from the patchwork roofs of the convoy filled him with a similar kind of dread.

The villagers used to fantasize about the funfair; they would

5

gather in groups and arouse each other with speculations on its erotic possibilities. The boys used to fight over whether it was actually a circus or a funfair. The village elders called it a circus, yet the hoardings and the billboards clearly named it a fair, Maestro Rossi's Funfair. It was lettered along the sides of the carts and painted on to the reins of the horses.

'It's a circus because it's got animals and freak shows. My father says that's what makes a circus, the animals.'

'A circus has a tent and a ringmaster, the Signora Elena said.'

'Well, she should know, she's in training to join it. But what about Maestro Rossi, he's the ringmaster, and a tent is stupid, why would it need a tent?'

Sometimes Alessandro would fight and sometimes he would let the matter drop. Most of the boys of his age in the village had not been to the fair either. They worked eleven hours a day in the fields and still had chores at home, so it wasn't easy to get away. Those who had defied their parents were beaten for it on their return and then treated like heroes. Alessandro wasn't afraid of his father's beatings. He had suffered them often enough before. But he knew that if he went, his mother and his sister would suffer more than he would. It was hard enough to see his mother's tears, without being the cause of them. His father was a fierce man with inflexible standards. He ruled his house more strictly than his neighbours did. He made his sons work harder and obey more readily than any of the other boys. He was a proud man with a pride that often choked him. There were times when he would have liked to soften, but his pride kept him bound rigidly to principles that were not entirely his own. It was only after Alessandro left school, in the summer of 1934, that his father became a disappointed man. His hopes died with his sharecrops and he withdrew behind a barricade of silence and debt. He and his sons worked their way out of this misfortune, but their father never recovered. He became, in the course of a few months, an old man. His hair turned grey, his hitherto straight back bowed.

By the time Alessandro was fourteen, the balance of power in his home had shifted into his mother's hands. She had lived in cowed subservience for twenty-five years. She had waited patiently during the last two years for the moment to come. She had carried eight children in her womb, and watched with almost silent grief while four of them were carried away from their cramped kitchen to the cemetery. She did not blame her husband for the loss of her babies; she knew that he grieved for them too. She did blame him, though, for refusing to share their death with her, and for refusing to share their life. He was like a stranger. The man she had known and married was smothered somewhere inside the other's grim, humourless shell. Hardship, she felt, was no excuse for turning sour; everyone's life was hard. They lived in an area traced and retraced with fine lines of calamity. Their lives were like a woman's leg marred by clusters of broken blood vessels.

For all that, life was something to be savoured. She wanted her sons to understand that. She wanted her daughter to as well, but she knew that the message was, in some ways, fraudulent for a woman. Girls grew up to be domestic animals from the age of eight. Her daughter's dowry would be a stock of fond memories of stolen moments. The mother kept her living children in a silent conspiracy against her husband. She helped them to undermine his petty tyrannies and to cover up their misdemeanours to save them from his rage.

She had rarely complained in her marriage; unlike some of her neighbours who wailed and ranted. 'You won't change an ox into a mule,' she used to say. Secondo, her husband, was a good man in his way. He worked, and he drank wine only with his meals. He never came home drunk and beat her senseless as Graziella's husband did. Secondo measured his blows. He never gambled and he observed all the rites of the Church, attending mass every Sunday with the old women. When he was tired or worried he became angry, and when he was angry he found fault with and punished his wife and children. The days were long out in the vineyards and the cornfields and he often went home like a wounded animal, finding its way back to its den by instinct.

Sometimes, in the hours before his day began, on summer days lying in his wide iron bed listening to the larks rising in the fields

7

beyond the village, memories stirred in him. He remembered being a boy high up in the woods of Zeno Poggio, raiding birds' nests at dawn. Everywhere he went, a trail of younger brothers and sisters would follow him, begging him to show them where the nests were. Esmerelda, with thorns and brambles tangled in her thick hair, was his favourite. Esmerelda had been like his shadow; a quick, appreciative shadow that had made a shrine of him. At some point this worship had become a weight, but he didn't know when or how. It began with a sweet taste and a warmth. Eventually the taste had turned sour and her warmth to a dull stare lit by the occasional flicker of betrayal and defeat.

Remembering, he recalled the sweet scent of broom flowers in the month of May, and the sweet scent of Agostina, his wife, lying under the branches of bright golden petals, exhausted from a morning of hoeing corn, yet always ready to respond to his clandestine kisses. For years after their marriage, it was in May that their children were conceived, always in May to be born in the earliest spring; calling the midwife out in frost or rain. How had his slender, willing Agostina become the dumpy, bitter body by his side? How had the evenings when he hurried home to her from the fields, to play with Marco and baby Elio and talk over his plans with her while she baked the evening *ciacia* on her stone griddle, turned to the grim silence of his home now?

Secondo had felt his heart contract when Alvaro the first baby died. Carrying the coffin to the *camposanto* had seemed to trap his grief within him, and his heart had never regained its elasticity. It was as though what little humour he had salvaged from the rigours of his upbringing had been buried in the white casket with his son. He often wondered if he could retrieve it, or somehow revive the light inside his house. He felt that his home was like the pipe he smoked, something he had filled for pleasure and then tamped down and set fire to. His pipe was stale now, but he still smoked it although the smoke was choking him. The stale smell and the taste of ashes were in his mouth. His children were growing away from him like shoots on an olive tree. Circumstances had frostbitten his own sap; the new shoots were taking over.

8

One night early in June after the best of the broom flowers had faded from the surrounding hills but before the fireflies had begun, Secondo sat and brooded into the reciprocal smoke of his low kitchen fire. It was hot, much too hot for a fire, but the supper had to be cooked and they had no money to spare on paraffin. He watched Agostina sweating as she twisted the gnocchi-dough between two fingers. She was smiling to herself. Outside, through all the sounds of village life funnelled through the narrow stone streets, she heard the distant hurdy-gurdy of the travelling fair. She heard the sound of pasta being kneaded next door and she heard water splashing against the enamel bowl on the steps outside her house. Marco would be washing. Beyond, in answering trickles, she heard the sound of water being rationed on to skin. She heard the Poesini girls laughing and banging the spoons as they laid the table for the eighteen Poesinis to squeeze around the pot and eat. She heard the slap of Maria Teresa being chastised. She heard the louder slaps and cries of Giuliana and her husband enacting their nightly ritual of wrath and sex. All over the upper village, mothers and sisters were calling their families in to eat. The bells of Santa Maria in Alto were ringing to signal the end of the empty mass that no one had time to go to. The swifts were swooping and gliding through the cool fissures between wall and wall of their houses. There was a distant sound of sweeping as the housemaids swept the courtyard and steps of the *padrone*'s villa, filling the street with dust that rose through their own one small window and settled in a thin layer of powdered *noblesse oblige* on every stick of their rustic furniture.

Like all the women of the village, her hearing was tuned to decipher the world around her. Enclosed as she was for most of the day, drudging over her cooking and mending, she had learnt to recognize every new note and whispered endearment that grew out of the dank grey stones. The noises that passed through the village that evening, though, were so loud that even La Giuseppina di Franco who had been half-dead and half-deaf for the last decade must have heard the travelling fair. There was the lowing of oxen, rising to a bellow that echoed through the entire valley. There was the sound of horses' hoofs, the dragging of machinery, grating across the dirt road like stones dragged down the riverbed, crashing and thudding and rattling all the window shutters for miles around. There were monkeys chattering like gangs of children. There were the shouts and 'whoa's' of the ringmaster, the rattling of caravan wheels, the jolting and banging of signs and drums, and all competing to be heard above the excited yelping and betting of the local crowd, which was both cheering and jeering the funfair on its way.

Agostina dipped her hand into a small heap of flour and then back into the warm dough absentmindedly. She had made every meal she prepared so many times that she did not need to think how to cook. The ingredients were few, the recipes even fewer, so she prepared their meals mechanically, stealing the time to daydream. The sounds of the fair prevented her from slipping into a daydream that evening. She thought instead that for once Elio would be able to go to the fair, and so would his brother Alessandro. Secondo had given up on discipline, his growling was a hollow growl that they all recognized as such. This year, all the boys would get to the fair. She smiled for them, for their victory and also for Secondo's defeat. The boys would have to walk to the market at Castello and take something to sell. Chicken, rabbits, barley and corn were no good. Poor people like them had their own, and the *padrone* never lacked for food. She herself had never lacked for food, there was just never any money. The year that the weevils ate their corn, they had been short of food. They had been forced to eat chestnut bread all winter. Did that count as hunger, she wondered? It was more boredom than hunger. She wondered if Elio would be able to catch a hare. There was a market for hare. Best of all were the woodcocks from the crest of Zeno Poggio. Some families would pay a small fortune for a brace of woodcocks. The season was wrong, though. The birds would be breeding and they were precious. Elio could wind up behind bars if he got caught there. It would have to be a hare, and maybe some *porcini* mushrooms if the Madonnina saw fit to send down some rain during the coming week.

*

10

Agostina had twice watched the cavalcade pass by in its white dust cloud. The first time must have been in 1933. It was the year her mother died. Her mother had given birth to twenty children and reared fifteen. Her mother had a straight back as erect as the Fascist officers who showed off their uniforms in the village square when they came to serenade Rosanna Mariangeli, the prettiest and the luckiest girl in the whole valley. Other girls married into drudgery or were ruined by the arrival of illegitimate children. A baby in your father's house was the worst thing that could happen to a girl. Not all of them survived the family beatings. The mouth of her cousin Nunzia hung open with its gormless smile for that reason and Rosina of the hill, the woodman's daughter, had grown lopsided from her father's kicks. Poor Rosina, she lost the baby, too. At least little Nunzia had her son to comfort her through all her days of slavery in her brothers' kitchen. Rosina had nothing, she was to be pitied almost as much as Agostina's own sister-in-law, Esmerelda, who had lost her babies and the words in her mouth.

The first time Agostina saw the cavalcade, it filled her with sadness. She saw it as a procession of all life's potential passing her by as she stood on the lip of stone overhanging the road. The colours, the whinnying, the clashing of wheels, the whirling white dust and the confusion all terrified her. Her three sons and her daughter were nearby: the boys were with the other boys pretending not to know her. Elena, her daughter, was fascinated and afraid; she clung to her skirts, half-burying her face in the darned cotton apron. Agostina felt her loins ache with the old familiar dragging feeling of her monthly time making her body heavier than it should be. Then she felt a nagging pain which spread across her groin. There were caravans passing underneath her. Cat-like animals dressed in bright jackets were darting along their roofs, running on two legs and talking to each other. She saw them waving their miniature fists at her, chiding her. Where did these demon cats come from? Where were they going? She wanted to ask Marco, her eldest, or Elio, her favourite. The boys were out of her reach, lost in their chanting, rocking backwards and forwards on the trampled grass.

11

The convoy continued to rumble by, laden with unimaginable surprises. The fair was not new to her even though this was the first time that she had seen it; her mother had told her about the fair during the Great War of 1916. It had arrived in Castello and set up its ground in the fields by the river outside the city wall. Her mother and her married sisters had all seen it, complete with wild animals and booths, painted horses, swings and carousels. Every Saturday the city sent an ox-cart to their village to haul the wives of soldiers into town. In Castello they were given a subsidy to tide them over until their husbands returned from the Front. Women who had never been past the flax ditches at the edge of the village were paraded down hours of dusty roads and taken into town. They made friends and found lovers. The countryside was riddled with deserters. Every alleyway in Castello was lined by boys on the run, running into the official traps like rabbits into nets. There were boys in the woods and men who came out only at night to steal food who fared better than the town boys. Perhaps they too were drawn to the fair. Perhaps they thought it was worth a court martial and death to see the hump-backed horses and the clowns.

Agostina's mother could talk for hours about the fair. She would sit and shell peas or scrub clothes or mend shirts or knead dough, but her mind played continually over the fairground she had seen and all its miracles.

'Imagine a horse as big as our house, with one hunchback and then another, imagine the rift between, a valley fit to plant corn. Imagine hair like thin hay shorn across its sides and a face like Albertino's grandfather but with even bigger lips, moving and munching and staring, and stopping only to make a fountain spray from its mouth. Imagine three such beasts with flags and slippers and ribbons everywhere. More ribbons than Assunta has to sell in all her shop. Imagine cats that talk and stand on two legs like wood sprites. Imagine all the colours of all the fields around cut into strips and floating in the air, wrapped in burnt sugar and wine. Imagine a woman with a hundred legs crawling inside a room. I didn't see her, mind, but La Marisa di Beppe did, she paid money – she spent her egg and her bean money on it so there was no supper for days at her house, but she said, when you see a woman with a hundred legs it takes your appetite clean away. Eh ... these are things that you have to see to believe.

'If it weren't for the war, I wouldn't have known myself, but we women have all seen this fair and there is music in a trunk with a handle. Who can tell if this is good or bad magic, but it's magic and that's for sure.'

She had six sons away fighting, of whom one was dead and one missing. Her daughters-in-law were afraid to go into Castello to claim their pensions, suspecting that by leaving their village they would be bringing bad luck and even death on their absent husbands. So it was the older woman who travelled on the convoy of young widows and wives. The fair had turned her mother's world upside down. She never quite recovered from the sight of it. For years afterwards, she would carry her pails of goods backwards and forwards across the fields, claiming to have seen the most marvellous sights behind this or that tree, this or that stone. When the worst months arrived, she would hitch her skirt with all the other women and work out in the smothering sun helping to bring in the sharecrops. Every harvest she was visited in her dreams by the hunchbacked horse. She swore that this horse talked to her. In her old age, strapped by arthritis to the strict bounds of her cottage and her meagre plot of land, she used to talk to the hunchbacked horse, describing her life, reliving all its highlights as she recounted them to her imaginary companion.

Her mother had enjoyed her life. She had worked hard, so hard that her back had bowed and her joints had grown deformed and there was little comfort in her old age. She worked until the very afternoon when a massive stroke struck her down as she tied up her rows of tomatoes. She always called her husband *babbo*. When he was away with the woodmen, she talked about him to their hordes of children, and since they all called him *babbo*, she did too. That afternoon, when the stroke felled her, she called out across the parched earth to him.

'O *babbo*,' she called, 'would you believe this.'

'What? What are you talking about, woman?' he asked, fondly,

13

because there was only one woman in his life and that was still his resilient wife with her thinning hair and her locked joints and her commentary of nonsense. 'What?' he repeated. Then he waited, and getting no reply he was afraid of the silence. His house had been a prattling house ever since they had set it up together. They had shared and gossiped over all their chores. 'What?' he called again, not wanting to turn round; wanting to be reassured by a quick answer and another round of chatter. 'Would I believe what?'

She had believed so much. She believed the accounts of all her neighbours. She believed every snippet of gossip and malice and every fiction that grew out of the straggling hamlets around their own. She had believed what she saw and what she imagined of the wartime fair. She believed in crates of Siamese twins and dwarfs in bottles. She believed in giants, witches, miracles and spells, she believed in so much, but he had only ever believed in her and in the children that they had made together out of the darkness of every day. So he never did believe that she just called out and died. He never accepted that she would not return, and he whispered the soft words that they had never stopped saying to each other even in their old age. He whispered into the night, and sometimes so keen was he for an answer that he found himself listening out for the words of the hunchbacked horse he had never believed in.

Agostina had been so excited by the passing of the fair that she could hardly see or breathe. This was not helped by the choking dust, but it was mostly her desire that blinded her. This was the fair that her mother had talked about. Here was the famous hunchbacked horse; somewhere, concealed by dust, were the giants and the dwarfs and the woman with a hundred legs. Her mother had known how to live her life. She had laboured and struggled more than even Agostina herself, but their tiny cottage had been filled with laughter and understanding. It had always sounded as though the key to her happiness lay with this fair.

'You see,' she used to say, 'it arrived as a curiosity, a transitory thing, but it stayed for three years. The Government requisitioned their horses and sent them off to the Front. The Draft Board used to go round sometimes and flush out the caravans and tents, but most of the fairpeople were of the sort it would have been difficult to drill. You didn't even know if they were men or women. Like the bearded lady, for instance; a lot of people said she was a man. Maybe, but we all saw the pair of ripe melons that grew on her chest. I don't think the Draft Board would have felt at their ease with that kind of bustline stuffed into their army uniform. Then take the dwarfs, yes, they qualified by age, but they would have made our army the laughing stock of the Front if they had been drafted.

'So they stayed. They had no choice. Their horses were requisitioned, their oxen too. What could the hunchbacked horse do by itself? The owner had a nervous collapse. His hair fell out, and then his teeth. He used to sit for hours and cry. He said, until he came to Castello he had lived entirely off fish eggs and wine. Poor man, we were hard put to find a chicken's egg in those days. Imagine in the town how a bunch of gypsies fared, a bunch of pirates stealing off the land. There were hundreds of deserters competing for every mouthful. There were fights. Some of his people went to prison. We were sorry for him, but what luck, what a piece of luck for us, I mean, three years of the fair being always there. Every time we went in for our war pensions, we knew when the queue finally ended we could go and see the field of wonders outside the city wall.'

If Agostina's mother were alive, she would have been jostling through the boys, elbowing them out of the way with the swollen ends of her thin bones. She would be cheering and clapping on the edge of the overhanging rock. Agostina felt her own life was wasted. She did not enjoy things; she hardly felt things any more. She had long since withdrawn into her being. As she stood on the ledge looking down on to the road, she was distressed to find herself as empty as a winter gourd. Here was the fair, the famous fair, and all her excitement left her with was a sense of loss as it passed by. It seemed like a procession of lost opportunities mocking her and her drudgery. Thinking of her mother, she realized that she had made so much more of her life, although the circumstances had been almost the same. She had not turned her cottage into a grim

15

shrine to defeat. Her mother had known how to nurture and sustain not only her husband's love but also her love for herself. Agostina looked down at her own children: three shorn heads and a pair of tight plaits. They must do better than her. They must learn the language of pleasure, and speak it, and know it so well that they never forgot to speak it all their lives. She realized that she must help them in every way she could to escape from the dark passage of her emptiness. She would encourage them to find happiness, and maybe, when they brought it near her, some strands of it would rub off on her.

She heard the bell of San Crescentino tolling the Angelus. The monks would all be in from the fields. The confraternity was about to eat. All the village was about to eat. The crowd dispersed, leaving only a few boys staring after the dusty convoy. One day, she decided, she would send the boys to the fair. She would slip Marco some of her own savings and tell him to take his brothers. By grieving for what they had lost, she and Secondo had forgotten to appreciate what they had. Now they had dulled each other's edges, rubbed away each other's feelings. Her life had slipped by unnoticed. It had not made the glamour of the fair, it had spilt away like a glass of stale wine. Her boys were nearly men: even Sandro was eleven years old and nearly as tall as his brothers. She wanted to chip the cement from around her mother's coffin and pull out the drawer that held her in the *camposanto*. She wanted to say,

'Mother, o *mamma*, is there any way I can get back in touch with my life? I have only the cut cords of my children. I feel confused and sad. I know you are dead, but I feel that even so you are more alive than I am.'

She wanted to go to Secondo, lost in smoke, and say a kind word to him, or reach out and touch his shoulder. She knew that she was capable of neither. Words shrivelled in her mouth and movements of tenderness towards him were beyond her. One day, though, she would send the boys to the fair. She would defy Secondo for them. From now on she would live through her children. 'I'll be a flea on their backs,' she thought. She made her way up the winding steps to their doorway. She didn't like fleas, she wanted to be something else but she couldn't think of another thing to replace it; whenever she needed a word she always asked Alessandro. This evening she was shy to do so. She wasn't used to ideas and words troubled her.

That night she lay in bed listening to the dogs barking all along the valley. She was still searching for the word for the thing she would be. Maybe when her sons returned from the fair they would bring that too, the word that would give her shape, describe her and let her be something new. She would wait. She was tired of all her emptiness. Ever since her babies had started to die, she had been tired.

—— II ——

It seemed that his name predestined him to darkness. Alessandro did his military training in the north, at the barracks of Desenzano on the shore of Lake Garda. Every night they woke him there in the barracks, shaking him roughly.

'Eh, wake up, it's your time again.'

It was dark where they slept. The dormitories were all long windowless blocks of concrete with an open grid under the roof for ventilation. It was January when he first went north and the frosts took control of every night.

'Mezzanotte . . .'

Voices whispered and called to him from all over the room. He had never slept alone before, and he missed his brothers' warmth beside him. The frost had climbed into bed with him, making his coarse army blanket lie in uneven ridges. He wasn't afraid of the other conscripts; he was used to fighting and good at it. And he was a big man who seemed much older than his nineteen years. He had the wide shoulders and broad frame of his mother's family. By day he would have gladly taken on any number of his tormentors, but it was night time and there was nothing but darkness, his vulnerability and their taunts.

He was a long way from home. He knew exactly how far to the minute and the hour, just as he knew the distances from his village to every other small town. He had left school at twelve like everyone else, but from the time he had met Valentina, he had studied the geography of the heart. Every time her father's travelling fair moved on to a new location, her absent lover worked out a way to her. He had a map and a set of railway timetables for the whole of Italy. Every time she fell within his radius, he would set off for the station, walking in long strides with the dawn. Then he would buy

18

his ticket and travel however many hours it took to reach her. Sometimes he would travel all day and all night just to spend an hour with her. His brothers said he was mad. They did not understand the nature of love. How could they? How could they know that the inside of Valentina's mouth was the elixir of life.

This town though, Desenzano, was too far. It fell beyond the boundaries of possibility. It was eight hours to Milan, then another two to Brescia, and still another local train to this part of the lake. If the fair had camped here with its carousel and its candyfloss and its bearded lady, it would have been too far to come. Valentina. He conjured up her sweet face in his thin cold bed. Valentina.

'Mezzanotte. Mezzanotte!'

A rain of objects landed on his frosted blanket. He wondered if it would be like this back home. What would the weather be doing to the olive trees? A frost like this would kill them back down to the ground. There was a lot of talk about starving in the village, especially now with the war. His father said that no one had ever starved there. They were just hungry and life was hard. They lived in a monotonous pendulum between work and sleep. Well, not even that, for there was Valentina and all the hours between. His father was a disappointed man. Everyone said so. He had grown bitter. He had twice lost his crops when his neighbours had not, and the shock had stayed with him. It was as though the key that wound him up to life had rusted.

A small sharp object hit him on the side of his head just above the ear. He let out an involuntary cry.

'I got him. Did you hear that? I hit him.'

The voice betrayed itself, as most of their voices did, each clinging to its own dialect. Three years of Sundays in pursuit of a travelling fair had taught him to differentiate quite well between one region and the next. It was the Genoese conscript with the scabby head who had spoken. After the first few days, Alessandro's fear had given way to frustration. It was bad enough to be stuck out in barracks at Desenzano without having to put up with these pointlessly sleepless nights. He couldn't even concentrate on Valentina with all their howling and nonsense.

19

'Mezzanotte, Mezzanotte, Mezzanotte,' they chanted. When he lay still and ignored them, they taunted him even more. Theirs was a game, a play that needed finishing. Every night their teasing had to be brought to a conclusion before anyone could sleep.

'Mezzanotte . . .'

When he didn't respond they pissed on him.

His brother, Elio, had been called up in September 1940, but he had already escaped into the hills to avoid it. Everyone knew that. He'd never been interested in politics. Elio lived for his accordion. He used to play at the local dances, and every evening, when there was nothing on, he would sit and play for hours. When he joined the Partisans, he took his accordion with him, but they sent it back the following week with one of their runners. They said they were trying to hide and that wasn't easy with the sound of an accordion carrying across the hills. Alessandro often wondered whether Elio would have joined if he had known that. He came back in November when they were gathering the olives in.

'I hear you've been called up, brother,' he said.

'Eh, what's to be done?'

'You can come with us. I'll take you back tonight. We need people we can trust. You don't have to be a Socialist, there are loads of deserters in our band.'

Elio was full of notions that afternoon, and full of speeches. If he had told his younger brother of a way to keep seeing his sweetheart, he might have followed him. The conscripts were being sent north, while the Partisans remained in the hills near home. But Partisans couldn't travel round after a fair. The Fascists checked every dwarf and every trunk of their equipment. He didn't want to die for his country, and particularly not for another country whose remoteness fell over the edge of all his maps and timetables, but he would die for Valentina. He would live and die for her. His life was dedicated. Both families opposed the match. It was a question of time, though; the war was changing everything. He hoped that it might change his father's attitude. His mother was already nearly on his side.

The confusion continued in the barracks. If he responded, when the inevitable orderly came in he would be blamed and his leave would be cancelled. As yet, he had had no leave, but he would soon be due a weekend pass. He smelt the sour smell of piss again. And he felt, intuitively, an arm somewhere near him. If he reached out, he could break it. He clenched his fists, he wanted to see Valentina more than that. He banished the stench of humiliation from him by imagining the long curve of her thigh. Her skin smelt of hot sand and had a faint rubbery taste. His tongue stirred across her olive skin. They were olives that would never be dried by frost. He rubbed his face into his own hand the better to remember the touch of her flesh.

Voices howled and then stopped, silenced by outside intervention. There was a scuttling in the dark and then for the space of a few seconds all was still. Even the watchman had returned to his camp bed. Every night had been the same during these first long weeks of his training. The orderly would arrive, angry at being dragged away from his drink and cards. The dormitory lay in seeming peace. Everyone was kicked awake and went through a false show of waking up, then a roll was called; he would wait for his name, hearing it now in Desenzano in a way that he had never heard it before. In his village it was a good name to have. His father and his grandfather and all his brothers and uncles carried it with some pride. It was true that his father was now a disappointed man, but his losses had not been due to any fault of his own and he had borne them like a man. No one had ever laughed at him before, and Alessandro was too big to be bullied. It was in the barracks that his name had first appeared strange. He waited for it under the dazzle of the bare light bulbs:

'Gavarini Massimo.'

'*Presente.*'

'Linate Davide.'

'*Presente.*'

'Marrioti Mario.'

'*Presente.*'

'Mezzanotte Alessandro.'

'*Presente.*'

The soldiers were impatient to fight. The Alpine Units were being moved out. It made them restless and bellicose. Every night

21

they woke Alessandro Mezzanotte at the midnight hour. He wanted to talk to them, to explain that he had a girl in a travelling fair whom he had to meet up with. Nothing else was worth bothering about. Their taunts were as nothing to him. How could he make them understand? Her hair was thick and black and always carried traces of the smell of burnt apples and candyfloss, rosemary-flower water and the grease of the carousel. Her voice was hurried, as though she was always breathless from running to him. Her hands were small and delicate with surprisingly square tips to her fingers as though they had been designed by a mason who had changed his mind before he finished the job.

He had first seen her when she was only fourteen. The fair had come to San Severino, the village next to his. He had been with his two elder brothers and spent a whole evening there. Having virtually no money to spend between them, he and Elio had wandered around the tents and stalls, feasting on the colours and the novelties. Marco, their eldest brother, was there with his girl. They were *fidanzati* and could thus be seen together. The few lire that Marco owned all went on rides and candyfloss. Alessandro remembered, set against the dusk and crowned by distant woods, a cameo of Marco and his girl mounted on a painted horse; she in front, side-saddle in her long skirt, he behind, astride and laughing. As the hurdy-gurdy music rose and fell, the horse followed until it seemed to remain suspended in the air. Alessandro felt a pleasure so great it took his breath away. That night, Elio pushed him along the broken road home.

'What's the matter with you,' Elio grumbled. 'You're behaving like a halfwit. Everyone was staring at you.'

Alessandro kept his silence and stumbled on. He was fifteen. He had been working in the fields for three years. It was June and the Indian corn needed hoeing and the hemp and potatoes. The next day, he and his brothers made a line with their father and worked their way through the weeds. They finished early, and under the pretext of going bird-nesting Alessandro slipped away by six o'clock. He was going back to the fairground, pulled by a power beyond himself that he didn't recognize until later as being the plaited threads of desire, destiny and love.

22

He found Valentina crouching on a stone by the dwindling river. She was wearing a cotton slip that the water had moulded to her flesh. As he watched her, he felt all the veins in his body tighten and seem to gather around his heart. A woman emerged from a caravan wedged between willow trees and broom.

'Vagabond, urchin, scum!' she shouted at him and pulled Valentina away, out of his sight. He heard the shrill voice of the gypsy woman berating the girl in a dialect he could not follow.

Early next morning, he went egg-hunting, poaching and gathering as he never had before. He found four black truffles and a clutch of partridge eggs, half a dozen blackbird's eggs and several fig-leaf trays of wild strawberries. He sold them at the gate of the *padrone*'s villa for a fraction of their worth, but there was nowhere else to sell them on a working day. Valentina served the candyfloss. She claimed that she had always served it and therefore that she must have been doing so on his first evening at the fair. It disturbed Alessandro to think that he could have walked past her several times and failed to notice her. Perhaps that was why the smell of stranded sugar would, for him, forever remain in her hair. Even during the war when there was no sugar and no floss, he detected the scent of its pink stickiness. There would never be a time or a place to say any of this at the barracks.

The night before, the orderly had said that if there was one more disturbance, the entire dormitory would lose its leave. A boy in Brescia, the nearest town, had gone berserk and attacked his Commanding Officer with a bayonet and tried to kill him. It was rumoured that the boy had been shot like a cow in an abattoir. Alessandro didn't know if it was true, but he understood. If anyone did anything stupid to stop him from getting back to Valentina, he too would go mad and he would kill someone. Perhaps that was what he needed to make his comrades understand; not the love but its violence.

His father always said that friends were people who helped you when you needed them, in which case Massimo Gavarini was a friend. Alessandro was a big man and a good fighter and if not for

Gavarini he could have easily killed the Genoese conscript when he finally decided to stand up for himself and stop the heckling about his name. The scabby Genoese was not the most guilty, as Alessandro knew by then, but he was the most recognizable of the gang. They were down on the bare piece of land at the far end of the camp and out of sight of their officers. There was a high fence loosely hemmed with barbed wire which made an angle with a concrete shed, providing the only privacy anywhere on the camp. Batch after batch of conscripts discovered this shielded triangle and settled their scores there and traded their cigarettes and their secrets, pounding the earth as hard as a herd of goats. One of the soldiers had access to a girl in Brescia. He was offering to fix up some of the boys with her for a commission. He had a couple of photographs, one that he showed for free, and another that he was charging so much to see and so much to touch.

Alessandro found the Genoese there, queueing up for a touch.

'Eh, you with the scabby head,' he called.

The Genoese turned to stare at him, together with most of the others, regardless of the condition of their scalps.

'Yes, you Genoese, I want to talk to you.'

The Genoese boy turned his deep-set eyes away from Alessandro and back towards the shuffling queue ahead of him. One corner of his mouth was caught in a smile. Some of his comrades were smiling more openly, tickled by Alessandro's sudden presumption. A tall, unnaturally skinny lad with huge fists and elbows began to move his arms like folded wings and clucked like a hen.

'Co co dé, co co dé.' He left his place in the queue to perform a little dance.

The others laughed. Alessandro stood, unruffled, while he waited for the ritual to wind down, then he repeated, 'Eh, Genoese, I want to talk to you.'

The chicken dancer, who came from Milan and assumed some airs of leadership on this account, said roughly, 'Scram. We have nothing to say to you.'

Alessandro shrugged in a noncommittal gesture conveying both apology and defiance. 'Eh, *Dio buono*,' he said, 'that's good, because I have nothing to say to you. I was addressing scabby head there.'

24

The gangly lad, who had taken it upon himself to be master of ceremonies, put on a puzzled expression. 'Does anyone understand this bumpkin? Does anyone know what he's saying? Is he talking to us?' He strutted around, twisting his mouth and wrinkling his nose and raising an eyebrow, now at this conscript and now at that. They giggled and shook their heads. Half of them, with accents and dialects far thicker and less generally intelligible than Alessandro's, were relieved not to be the subject of the baiting. These last laughed more loudly than the others.

'We don't understand, eh, I'm really sorry but we don't seem to speak the same language. Perhaps you could hop back to your hills and bring out your hairy mother and, ah, get her to translate for you.'

Alessandro remained calm, it was in his nature to be calm. His father was a more volatile man, but Alessandro himself was impervious to scorn. He settled scores sometimes because he saw that they needed to be settled. In the absence of any apparent anger on his part, the tension was low and a spirit of raillery prevailed.

'Alas, the regions have curbed conversation. I had another language in mind. I take it you understand fists in Genoa, or are you too mean to ever take your hands out of your pockets?' Alessandro moved up towards his man and struck out at him with a small tap on his arm. The Genoese boy stared round in wonder.

'Do you believe this boy?' he asked, inviting his team to support him. Alessandro moved around, holding his elbows in against his sides. He touched the Genoese again, slapping the brittle fabric of his uniform. Unclenching his fists, Alessandro invited him to join him in the ring.

'Co co dé,' the Genoese jeered, 'look at him flapping his elbows like a chicken.' But something had changed, the boys were stepping back. They liked a fight better than a joke. The Genoese liked a fight too, but best of all he liked to join in a brawl with his mates.

'Come on,' he invited them, 'let's teach this brat a lesson.'

'Go on then,' their gangly leader told him. 'Go on, teach him. We'll watch, won't we boys.'

Everyone was surprised by what followed. The Genoese boy was

25

surprised because, although he wasn't keen to fight, he wasn't expecting to be beaten. The gang was surprised because they thought they had a mother's boy in Alessandro, they had set him down as a coward, not the potential killer he showed himself to be. Alessandro himself was surprised because in the thrashing he gave the Genoese he discovered a hitherto unknown anger in himself. What surprised him most, though, was his friendship with Gavarini, who was to be the best friend he ever had. It was Gavarini who interceded and saved the Genoese boy's life.

They sent the Genoese boy away encased in plaster. They took him in a Red Cross van. After they had cleared his kitbag of belongings out of their dormitory, no one referred to him again. It was as though he had never existed. His narrow space was claimed and used by the others like neighbouring teeth growing into a gap. Alessandro was treated with a reverence which he ignored. He wasn't proud of himself. If anything, he was ashamed. Not only had he damaged the scabby boy, but he had failed to know himself.

He had always thought of himself as a simple boy, nothing more or less than the boy who looked back at him from the corner of the mirror that lived at the end of the plate rack over their stone sink at home. He thought of himself as Alessandro Mezzanotte, and of Alessandro Mezzanotte as a tall boy with broad shoulders and mid-brown eyes the colour of ripe hazelnuts. His face was wide and oval, his skin was white, his cheeks grew ruddy with both heat and cold. His hair was dark brown and curled away annoyingly from the grease and cream he used to try to tame it. His beard was thick and needed shaving every day, while his brother Elio and his father never shaved more than three times a week. His nose was long and fine, a Roman nose, bending slightly at the bridge as though it had once been broken. His neck was thick and rather short. His forehead was high and handsome (according to both Valentina and his mother). His hands were the wide splayed powerful hands of a peasant. He saw all these things in the scrap of mirror. He had seen them day after day while he shaved. When he went to see Valentina, he saw them more, studying himself to discover why she loved him and how he could keep that love.

26

From the moment that he broke the Genoese's bones, he didn't like to look in the mirror any more. He shaved unevenly, avoiding the sight even of his own chin. Mezzanotte was no longer a boy's face in reflection, nor was he just a lover governed by his sensuality. There was someone else in there, someone he had never met before. It was someone he didn't understand. Every time he stepped out of his low camp bed, this other self was there too, he was there in the latrines and in the drill. He was there in his dreams and must also have been there every time he made love to Valentina. His other self had been inside his lover and lingered there, tasting her juices and sniffing her hair.

Unless he came to know himself, his whole self which must include this unknown other half, he could not honestly say that he loved Valentina with all his heart. He might just love her with half a heart and the other half be ready to spring in some unaccountable way. The other half was cunning and sly, so sly that it had lain dormant for nineteen years. Would Valentina love his other self, he wondered, and if she did, why was she ready to love a stranger? If she did not, then half of him would wither.

Every night he tried to dream his way out of his labyrinth of worries and back into the clear channel of his love. He found himself thinking more and more about his paternal grandfather, living still in the small stone tower above Zeno Poggio. The old man had two sheep and a mule below in a tiny dark stable next to a cupboard full of tools and wine and corn. Upstairs, Alessandro's grandparents lived in a single room, a small black square of ingrained smoke. His grandmother worked continually. She always seemed to be pounding something. She would pound ashes, dough, clothes, salt or his grandfather's gnarled feet.

Upstairs again was his aunt Esmerelda. This aunt was as dark and dried out as everything else that hung in their kitchen. She looked as though generations of soot had settled on her, grafting into her skin, hair and clothes. Under this dull veneer only her eyes shone brightly. Esmerelda was deaf and dumb so Alessandro never knew what it was that the expression in her eyes was trying to convey, but he was convinced that she was trying to say something.

27

He had never believed that she was entirely deaf, it seemed to him she was merely hard of hearing. He had often observed her smiling at things said in such a way or in such a light that she could not have lip read them.

It was rumoured that aunt Esmerelda had had any number of illegitimate babies in her youth and that each one had been swaddled and carried the four hours to the orphanage in Castello and left screaming in the stone repository outside the convent wall. It was rumoured that as a girl his aunt Esmerelda could speak, but that she went deaf and dumb after a beating her father had given her when she first fell pregnant. It was also said that she ran away and hid in the woods one summer to bear her last child, and that she kept it a secret until the weather turned, living off berries and nursing her infant under the chestnut trees. Then her father found her and took the child away and she never spoke again. It was also said that she was dropped as a baby and had been damaged ever since; and that at the age of three she fell through the shutters at the top of their tower and lay in a coma for more than two nights.

Whatever the truth, her shrivelled, silent presence invited gossip and conjecture. What interested Alessandro most about his aunt was not the stories, but the look in her eyes. Whenever he visited his grandparents he would sit on the dipped stone around the hearth and try to fathom what the bright gleam meant.

'Eh, enough of your thinking, boy,' his grandfather would say, 'what a child for troubling his head! Have you ever seen the like, Anna?' he would ask his wife. Then he would turn back to his youngest grandson and say, 'Two words of advice, my boy: no thinking and no masturbation. Both a waste of time, both wear you out. Thinking is just masturbation of the brain, the more you do it the more you want it, and when you get a chance to pause you're just exhausted. If the good Lord had wanted us to think for ourselves, he would have made it all a lot easier.'

Alessandro had heard that advice dozens of times. He wondered what the old man would say if he could see him now, trapped between those two pet evils. He was still ten days away from a pass and the nights were long and lonely in the barracks. Sometimes he

28

heard the distant crack of gunfire. From time to time, planes flew over their camouflaged camp. Once there was some desultory machine-gun fire. Valentina had promised to marry him, nothing else was as real. The fair was coming to Gardone del Lago soon, and he would run to meet her and take her down to the water's edge and spend every moment of his leave either inside or astride her. Perhaps her loveliness would banish his new knowledge, or perhaps like a balm it would help him to accept himself. Meanwhile, he fondled himself from lights out to reveille. He fondled himself in his sleep and all through the dark hours before the dawn. The parts of his gun, grenades, drill fatigues, were all pasted together for him on to pages of worry and unfulfilled sex.

January turned to February and the frost gave way to drizzling rain. The triangle of ground at the end of the camp became a patch of mud. There was talk of fighting, of being sent to the Front. Leave was cancelled and then reallotted and then cancelled again. The fair that should have arrived at Gardone del Lago for St Valentine's Day was refused its permit to travel into the militarily more delicate areas of the north. They would not be allowed so near to the Swiss frontier. The fair and its caravans and personnel had been checked and searched scrupulously both by the Fascist civil authorities and the military forces and nothing untoward had been found. Nonetheless it was halted and turned back to reap whatever meagre harvest it could from revisiting its summer haunts. Valentina wrote to tell him that they would be an hour outside Bologna in the first week of March. Alessandro pinned his hopes there, seeing nothing but that date and his desire to see Valentina again.

Already when he closed his eyes to conjure her up, he saw nothing but her mouth, the nape of her neck and the tops of her thighs. He began to worry that he would not recognize her any more. His longing was consuming her. His photograph of her, the small, worn, black and white photograph that he had sewn into a secret pocket of his shirt, had disintegrated under the strength of his sweat. This was something he had not dared own up to. He felt if he told Valentina she would misinterpret the loss. She might think that he had not looked after the photograph. She hadn't wanted to give it to him in the first place; she had few enough belongings in the cramped corner of her caravan. Virtually all that she owned she kept in a small beaded bag which was one of the few legacies left to her by her mother. Although Alessandro had often seen Valentina's father, with his grey moustache bushy and curly like the horns of a mountain goat, his wild eyes and his high leather boots, he had never seen her mother. He had no idea where she might be, or indeed, whether she were dead or alive. Valentina often talked about her, but any questions on his part were met with a fierce rebuff. It was a mystery that no one seemed anxious to solve.

He had thought at first she must be the gypsy woman who had screamed at him down by the river. Theoretically, it was possible for his future mother-in-law to have been any of the women in the fairground troupe. She could have been a dwarf, or the bearded lady, or even the crabby so-called spiderwoman with her unnaturally long arms. Or she could have been dead and buried outside any one of the little towns that sprawled across the map from Rome to Chiasso and from Rimini to Savona. Or she could have been ill and hidden in one of the other caravans or carts. Most likely, though, Valentina's mother had run away and abandoned her husband and daughter. Whatever the reason, she appeared only in Valentina's conversation and only as a woman so full of virtue as to be virtually a saint. She was the donor of all that was good or nice. According to Valentina she looked very much as she did in the lost photograph.

'I don't want to give it to you,' Valentina had said.

'But you can see yourself whenever you want. You'd transform my life if you let me have it. If you knew how I miss you, you wouldn't turn me down like this.'

'Everyone says I look like my *mamma* in it.'

'I'll never lose it, I promise. I'll keep it with me all the time, and when we're married you can have it back. How about that?'

She had agreed reluctantly, and he had sweated it to pieces and now he was so excited about her that his memory had started to

30

play tricks, distorting her image in such a way that her lovely face was fading.

There had been more of a real sense of the war when he was at home. The planes flew over his village regularly and once a week there was a procession with a band. There were Partisans in the hills and commentaries on the wireless. Boys in every part of the parish were packing kit to leave. And other boys would be home on passes, flaunting their uniforms. Boys deserted and were hunted in the woods. Then there were the secrecy and excitement of the black market, the rare coming and going of army trucks and all the bird calls of the Partisans who were creeping around the woods beyond the village. Bands of deserters from further afield used to roam through the valley, thieving and sleeping rough. Things happened in his village. By comparison everything seemed strangely sheltered in the barracks, as though they had all been called up and forgotten there.

A package arrived from home. There was a pair of huge misshapen socks knitted by his grandmother wrapped around a slab of stale chestnut bread. His brother Marco sent him a packet of cigarettes and a letter. He took the half-sheet of lined paper and read:

Dear brother,

      Gelsomino's son has returned from Albania without his right foot. He sends his best wishes to you, as do we all, especially *la mamma* who cannot sleep at night for worrying about you. The winter has been a hard one. We fear for the olives. Everyone says the war will finish in the spring, meanwhile, be brave.

           Your brother Marco

Alessandro threw the socks and the bread away so that the others wouldn't laugh at him. He felt a twinge of guilt as he thought of his ancient grandmother trying to pound the wool into shape and then struggling for days with the needles and thread. Nobody in the family, though, kept his grandmother's socks; they all unwound the wool and kept it in skeins to use again. It was well known in the village that she could neither knit nor weave. She had come originally from across the hills and his grandfather had tamed her. His brother told him to be brave. Was it bravery to sit and play

31

cards with Gavarini every night? Gelsomino's son had lost his foot, while at Desenzano all that got lost was small sums of money and his treasured photograph.

By the time they were through their tenth set of *briscola*, Alessandro had grown sad about his letter. He wanted to go home and to cry, and he wanted to see Valentina again.

'Gavarini, I tell you, I'm forgetting what she looks like. How will I manage to remember her again?'

'For the love of God, go and give her one, you'll soon remember both what it feels like and what she looks like.'

'Gavarini, don't make fun of me. I'm in love with her.'

'*Ai, si,* love!' he said, looking across disdainfully at Alessandro's mournful face. 'Listen, just keep hoping that girl can remember *your* face. There's a lot of temptation in a fairground and you know once you get below the waist one face is much like another.'

Alessandro lunged across the table, dropping his cards. Gavarini leant back, avoiding him.

'I'll kill you for that.'

'Sure you will,' Gavarini said calmly, folding his hand of cards away. 'You'll kill everyone. You're so strong, you could be Il Duce's secret weapon.'

Alessandro's face set hurt and angry.

'O, Mezzanotte, Mezzanotte, I'm sorry I teased you again, but you're so easy to tease and I had a terrible hand. Now we'll have to start again. Come on, look into the future and you'll see that it's not worth falling out over. You and I are friends, and don't you forget it.'

The days dragged on monotonously. Alessandro had a miniature crystal ball that Valentina had given him. Sometimes he tried to look into the future, but each time he saw nothing. At nineteen years old it was hard to imagine that that would be his future: a sightless blank. There was no hint in the barracks that any of them would die. He wanted to go home, little realizing that they would take him there, scarred and mutilated, without his eyes. They would take him back to his village, but he would never see it again.

II
STEFANO

III

Mara Altini had married beyond herself. Some of the girls from her class in Castello had married below themselves, choosing to follow their hearts to obscure bakeries or ironmongers dotted across the parish. Idle aunts measured the jumps in hierarchy during the long hours of the afternoon when they sat under the ancient plane trees of the cathedral square, criticizing a world that had chosen largely to ignore them and knitting socks and balaclava helmets to ward off the onslaught of incomprehensibly modern times. They watched the girls from Mara's class, some of whom were their goddaughters or nieces, marrying up and down across the social plain.

'Girls are like gravity,' they agreed, 'they go down; they seem like so much chaff on the wind and then they all sink.'

'Not all, remember, Maddalena Betterelli married the Marchese from Lazio, and if that wasn't marrying above herself I don't know what is. That little picture-framing shop was all her father had and she had seven brothers to come before her.'

'And Mara, your own Mara? She's feathered her nest so well she doesn't even need you to bottle her fruit.'

No one saw that Mara Altini was adrift but herself. Her marriage seemed to her like a series of tests which she kept failing. Try as she might to learn the correct responses, the questions altered and the rules shifted so that she felt at a continual disadvantage. She loved her husband and yet she seemed unable to prove to him, beyond any reasonable doubt, that this was the case. He needed proof, it was his business to find and sift it, discarding any that failed to stand up to cross-examination. Her lack of expertise in this emotional courtroom disappointed him. More and more his disappointment emerged as silence. Meanwhile, Mara struggled to please him, to appease him and to prove that she was not the negligent, thoughtless wife he accused her of being. His silences lasted for days and sometimes weeks. During her many hours of solitude, Mara studied the mosaics of the floor and felt her own nervous system fracture and fragment like the centrepieces of the four main rooms of her apartment. All her own pieces were held together by a loose grout provided by the daily kindnesses of Fabrizia, her housekeeper, by the closeness of her own baby son, by the occasional penetration of something from the outside world and by her rare moments of peace with her husband.

No one saw Mara Altini fragment, she kept her falling apart to herself, wrapped in the loose cotton cardigans she liked to wear. Her husband saw her pliability as a good sign and continued to hammer away at the last rocks of her resilience. Had she spoken out and explained that these rocks were not only the last of her opposition to his absolute will, but also the last vestiges of her sanity, he would have stopped perhaps, because he loved her and it was not his intention to drive her so far within herself that she would never return. Mara wanted to explain her disintegration to him, but he was a busy man and he was always too busy recounting her mistakes to be able to listen, so the small mosaic chips of her personality were pounded into sand and banked up to become the island she lived on surrounded by quicksands. She had married beyond herself, she knew, because out of reach and almost out of sight were her husband and her small son, Stefano. It was in her fourth year of marriage that the intervening, unforgiving and unforeseen currents of the quicksands sucked away her new baby, the frail watery creature who had lived inside her for five months and then slipped away from her womb.

'It was a girl,' the doctor told her. 'There'll be others. Now sleep.' Would those other girls come in her sleep? Would her own lost one find her there? Would her husband come to her in her sleep and find in this woman whom he loved above all others something at last that was not tinged with disappointment? Would Stefano manage to creep into her arms and nestle there, hidden by the dark from the harsh house rules? Sleep held out its own arms and offered not only rest but hope.

*

36

Weeks passed, and the doctor called in other doctors, who diagnosed a virus. The term was too loose, too vague, to satisfy her husband. He insisted on further tests. Mara was wrapped and unwrapped in a hospital blanket and carried up and down the stone stairs to her room. There was talk of *la nonna*, the sleeping sickness that had hit Castello in an epidemic sixty years before. Weeks passed and his gentle bedside patter changed from coaxing to chiding. The longer she stayed asleep, the more he suspected her of shamming. Once a day, she surfaced and fulfilled her bodily functions in a dream-like state. Every day, her husband, the *onorevole* Edoardo Altini, would hurry home from the county court in order to be present at the moment of his wife's momentary awakening. Having poured out endearments to no avail, he resorted to his particular brand of bullying. Sometimes his son crept up behind him and listened to him through the door. He would try to memorize some of the spells his father cast on his sleeping mother so that he could neutralize them later.

'There's a limit, Mara, to how long this unauthorized sleeping can go on, you know. I suppose it amuses you to make me the laughing stock of my profession, but you may as well know that I refuse to succumb to your blackmail and sabotage. It is quite clear that this dereliction of your duty is indicative of the true way you feel towards me, not to mention Stefano, who also has a right to your time and attention. Your behaviour is nothing but cowardice.

'Tomorrow morning you will wake up, do you hear me, you will wake up, and get up like a normal human being!'

Months of tomorrows passed and still Mara slept on as though bewitched. Gradually, Edoardo Altini resorted to the weapon that had been so powerful during the early part of his marriage: silence. He ignored his wife while she ignored the world. The love he had felt for her began to die, shrivelling away at the edges like an autumn leaf battered into winter. Something fragile at the centre remained, but the rest was lost, condemned to die by his own intransigent standards. He was a criminal lawyer, soon to be a judge; he had never made any allowances for himself and he refused to corrupt those around him by making allowances for them. Unable

37

to cope with her withdrawal, he perfected his own, hiding away the last of his vulnerable emotions. Gradually, he invested all his energy in his profession and in the education of his son, determined, as he often told his brother Andrea, to make it up to the boy for the difficult start life had dealt him. Where he had failed with his wife, Edoardo Altini was determined to succeed with his child: he would allow no softness to rot the boy.

During the first year of her illness, everyone believed that Mara would recover. The housekeeper, Fabrizia, who had kept house for the old widow Altini for more years than anyone could remember and for Mara ever since her marriage, explained the situation daily to the neighbours.

'Mara's not really ill at all, she's just sleeping. She's very, very tired and the miscarriage has drained her, but she'll be hale and healthy again before the spring is out.'

Month by month Fabrizia shifted their target, accommodating the extra weeks of her mistress's hibernation. It was Fabrizia who nursed her, changing her bed linen and daubing her smooth brow with rose water. It was Fabrizia who tied the floppy bow around Stefano's neck every morning and packed his snack box and escorted him to the nursery school behind the church, leaving him like a forlorn crow to roost with the other black-smocked children huddling in the courtyard. And it was she who brought him home, eternally hopeful that the day would have roused his mother finally from her sleep.

His father forbade him to sit with his sleeping mother, he had told Fabrizia that the less contact there was, the better. Fabrizia worked for the *onorevole* Altini because she had worked for his mother. She and the old widow Altini had spent many happy decades together during which she had seen Edoardo grow and harden like a special kind of cement. He was a legacy from someone she had loved and she cared for him to the best of her abilities, rolling out his tagliatelle and pounding his veal as diligently as she had his mother's before him. Fabrizia had hoped that he would soften when he married Mara. She did her best to help and protect his child bride. Fabrizia saw Mara suffer but she didn't see how

38

much until it was too late. In the hope that he might help her to recover, she guided Stefano to his mother's bedroom in strict defiance of his father's orders. She allowed the child to sit for hours in the darkened room, breathing in the scent of almond soap and summer petals with the inevitable mustiness of locked-away things. He would put his face to his mother's almost lifeless cheek and feel the light warmth of the breath from her nostrils.

Sometimes, on Thursdays and Saturdays, when he accompanied Fabrizia to market, their progress through the crowded cobbled streets was hampered by the number of people who stopped to stroke his dark curls and to look at him as though they had not seen him for several years.

'Dear God, how he is growing,' they would murmur and then, 'Poor little lamb' or, 'Poor little innocent'. Sometimes, turning away from him, they would add almost tearfully, 'What a crime!'

Stefano knew that one day his father would be a judge. He was often told so, both by his father and by his father's friends; so one day his father would deal with whatever crime the people were referring to. Instinctively, Stefano began to feel like a criminal. From his earliest childhood he had been aware of trying to hide things from the law: from his father. He began to practise deceit. He ceased to mention his mother. His teacher told him how birds decoy predators from their nest. He thought of himself as decoying trouble from his mother's nest. It seemed to work; for three years she lay in her semi-comatose state in her high carved bed. His father was made a judge and was given the power to lock people away for ever.

Beyond the city, but clearly visible from the hills around it, were the mountains of the moon. Most years there was snow there, and those who could spare the time went skiing there. When he was seven, his uncle Andrea took him skiing with his own family. He returned to Castello bursting with stories to tell Fabrizia and to whisper to his mother. He had learnt to ski and won a prize and fallen in love with snow. During his absence, disaster had struck: he ran up the grey stairs to his mother's room to find that she had gone. She was locked away somewhere, banished beyond the city walls to some foreign place too far to reach on his own. Fabrizia would take him there, twice a year on the train. His father, the Judge, as he came to be called by all and sundry, insisted on referring to Mara in the past tense, as though she had died during that white week in February when Stefano had ski'd on the mountains of the moon.

The avenue of poplars that led to the convent hospice where Mara lay immured stood out like a causeway across a swamp. It was raised from the flat marshy fields around it in such a way that the sentinel trees gave the impression of having crawled up its banks, survivors from a battle. All the trees were old and mutilated; gnarled scars turned each poplar into a veteran amputee. The first time Stefano saw them it was spring. There were skylarks hovering low over the fields and then rising above the mist in sudden bursts of song and mottled wings. The poplars were covered in blood-red shoots that grew like a frenzied celebration of life itself. The taxi from the station had left him and Fabrizia at the main convent gate. The driver had refused to take them any nearer, so they had the long dank avenue to negotiate. Twice a year he would visit his mother there, and twice a year he would see the trees. Every autumn would find them with their newly grown limbs slashed back to engorged stumps. It seemed to Stefano that the trees were like the hopes of all the sick patients who lived inside the convent walls: they would rise only to be destroyed again and again, slashed back with relentless regularity. He came to dread his visits, walking the gauntlet of that avenue of hope and slaughter, always hoping for a flicker of recognition from his sleeping mother and never finding it in the long hours spent in vigil over her pseudo-coma.

Sleep had enslaved her; it had stolen her life. Every day as the sun went down, at different times depending on the season but always in the twilight hour, his mother awoke. He had witnessed her arousal many times, and the nuns said that her behaviour never differed. She stirred in her bed after twenty-four hours of almost total immobility. She opened and closed her mouth with the small beak-like movements of a hungry fledgling. She made no sound,

40

she seemed to recognize no one. She shed her wastes on a bed pan, always within a few minutes of her first stirring. If the moment passed and neither food nor pan was provided, she would return unprotesting to her trance and sleep again until the sinking of the sun the next day triggered some impulse in her brain and spurred her to survive.

Stefano found her stirrings almost more disturbing than her sleep, because she so clearly ignored him then. At least while she was sleeping he could pretend that they were close. For three years he had observed her sleeping so minutely that sleep itself became a constant topic of his thoughts. He tried to fathom what it contained, what its essential elements were. He tried to remember what happened to himself each night when he slept, but he found he could remember nothing. The nearest he came to it was an image of a blanket of fog rising from a dank Lombardy plain and swallowing him up. Everyone seemed to dream and to remember their dreams, but Stefano had no memory at all of what went on in his sleep. What if one night he went to sleep and never woke again? What if he were locked in a trance when his mother finally awoke, what if he missed her through falling prey to the sleeping sickness? Fabrizia said that during the ravages of *la nonna*, whole families had been struck down. Children younger than himself were gripped by the sleeping sickness and never released; they died in their comas.

He was afraid of sleep, afraid of its nothingness. He was afraid of the dark and he was afraid for his mother. He constructed a life for himself built around the obliteration of his fears. There were things that he hid from his father, and things that he hid from himself. In all, there came to be so many things hidden inside him that he became afraid of himself. A numbness grew around him and inside him while his father monitored his outward growth and development with a clinical eye. If anyone had dared to tell him that he was crushing his son, he would have denied it or ignored them. The Giudice Altini prided himself on being a judge not only of the law courts, but also of character. He had decreed that Stefano would be like himself: two drops of water, he told everyone. The boy had none of his mother's inadequacies, none of her ridiculous fancies.

41

The Giudice would often pull Stefano towards him in public and say,

'You want to be like your father, don't you? A lawyer and then a judge and we'll sit on the Bench together.'

All eyes would be trained on him; would he dare rebel, humiliate his father in front of friends? Stefano needed his father's approval, he strove for it, so he would always reply,

'Yes, Father.'

'What are you going to be?' the Judge would demand of him.

'A lawyer.'

'Just a lawyer?'

'A judge, Father,' he would say hastily, and his father would look away with a hint of disappointment crossing his face. No matter how many times in an evening the question was asked, it had to be answered at just the right pitch of enthusiasm and with just enough fervour to convince the unconvincible Giudice.

'I almost thought you didn't sound very keen when I asked you what you wanted to be at the Bar, Stefano. I could have sworn you hesitated a little.'

'No, Father.'

'You must do exactly what you want, you know, you're completely free to make your own choices. If you are not interested in what your father does, that's entirely up to you.'

Everything was a battle, every word and even every dish at dinner.

'I'm going to have some more peas, Stefano, would you like some?' Even a straightforward question could pose dangers. There was always a right answer. Stefano was quick to learn his father's games, quicker than his mother had been. He began to humour his father, treating his every suggestion as a brilliant idea. Stefano became a human chameleon, changing his colour to suit all his father's caprices, filling up the seemingly insatiable well of the Judge's need for reassurance. Every day was a carousel of petty tyrannies that Stefano and Fabrizia survived.

The marks of age passed his mother by; the years in Lombardy had left her as youthful as a child. No lines furrowed her face and her skin retained its softness. It intrigued Stefano to imagine some future time when he would have grown old while his mother remained locked in her adolescence. Fabrizia, meanwhile, seemed to be ageing for both of them; she seemed to be ageing for the entire human race. Every time she struggled through the market square, a conclave of gossips would gather behind her and agree that Fabrizia's heart was breaking, pining for Mara.

One summer, a swarm of wasps built their nest in a small hole in the stone in the wall outside Stefano's bedroom. All afternoon, after school, he could see them carrying grey mud to their task. Cell after cell was added until the nest began to protrude in a welt on the side of the house. One day the Judge saw it and, balancing on Stefano's windowledge, he knocked it down. Part of the nest was still inside the hole.

'This will settle them,' he told his son as he packed the entrance with quick-drying cement.

All that night Stefano heard the buzzing and the beating of trapped wasps trying frantically to escape from the cavity. In the dark, he tried to chip the wall open with his penknife. He dug into the cement and stone with a pair of scissors but he could not release the dying insects. He felt more anger towards his father than he had ever felt before.

The next time he went to the convent hospice in Lombardy, having left the last vestiges of his hope on the gnarled stumps of the pollarded avenue of trees, he found his mother's body taken over by dying wasps. After years of silence, her chest and head were imploding in a frenzy of wings. A bitter taste rose in his mouth with his bitterness towards his father, who was pursuing the dormant Mara even here, harassing her in her sleep, tormenting her dreams. Her chest rattled with every breath. This wheezing would remain until her death, years later when he was seventeen. It was the legacy of a chest infection, but for Stefano it would always be a sign of his father's malice, as though he had somehow managed to control Mara's thoughts beyond the pale of consciousness. It was the buzzing of her punished thoughts, caught at last by her unforgiving husband.

*

43

Stefano lived in a state of numbness. He moved across the surface of his life, skating with the agility of a water boatman over the pond of the medieval town of Castello. The older he grew, the further his emotions retreated; unlike the wasps, they were too well hidden for even the Judge to find them. Stefano's life was mapped out for him like a military chart issued by the government. The Judge was only ever uneasy on two counts where his son was concerned: his popularity and his drinking. The fact that Stefano had so many friends, he felt, must testify to clandestine behaviour. Although he didn't know that his son drank himself into oblivion most evenings, he had detected the smell of alcohol on his breath and he had seen him hanging around the Bar Italia when there was no other reason for him to be there.

If the Judge had a weakness it was his love of fine wines. The cellar under his house was stocked with the best that Tuscany had to offer. He had wines from the Veneto from vineyards that rarely sold to the public; he had wines from years so good that many a colleague dined at the Judge's table despite the constriction of his company. Anyone wanting to please or appease the Giudice Altini knew to make an offering of good wine. He had racks and racks of French wines and a deposit of champagne. He had taught his son to drink. He had made him distinguish the bouquets of this and that year, this and that grape. So sometimes, when he looked out of the window of the Circolo across the main square under the permanent shadow of its surrounding palaces, he would smile at a glimpse of his son leaning on the polished counter of the Bar Italia. They were like two drops of water: father and son. If there were any lawyers present in the Circolo on these occasions, they would grow nervous, misinterpreting the Judge's attempt at a smile as a sinister omen. They would crane their necks to see who was in the square, who was talking to whom below them who might be about to fall prey to the Judge's sense of justice.

So much of Stefano's home life had been spent inventing excuses either for himself or for Fabrizia, covering the tracks of their secret visits first to the bedroom and then to the hospice, that he became adept at getting out of scrapes. Where other children had their

44

family life to occupy their time, Stefano had few commitments beyond the ritual dinner, prepared with increasing difficulty by the ailing Fabrizia and eaten between the daily interrogations that his father composed during his long hours in court. Unable to form any really close friendships because of the distance he always felt between himself and the world, Stefano put himself out to be useful. His manner was easy; whatever grief he felt he hid so well that no one saw the wound. Whatever problems his friends had, nine times out of ten it was Stefano who resolved them. He had the time and the endless energy to procure missing slips of paper from the labyrinth of the town hall. He was a social Samaritan, patching up all rifts and breaches and replacing the minor losses. He obtained sick notes and medical certificates, he found spare parts for cars and motorbikes and bicycles. He found privacy for lovers and alibis for domestic miscreants. He ran errands and played escort, chaperon and shoulder to cry on. Sometimes he saw himself buying friendship with favours and it made him feel ashamed; mostly, though, he performed his self-imposed tasks like a sleepwalker.

At twenty-four he still played regularly, but indifferently, the sports at which he had once excelled. He played from habit, drifting through many unmemorable games of football, basketball and tennis. He drank too much wine and missed too many training sessions to stay on form, but he was popular and too useful to drop. He was studying in his fifth year of a law degree that was threatening to take up his entire life. He felt too numb to oppose his father's will openly. The Judge insisted that his son study the law, so Stefano studied in the ancient faculty of Perugia. He studied for exams he would never take, for a Bar he was determined never to be called to. Whatever other weaknesses he might have in his character, on one point he was certain: he would never have it in his gift to lock anyone away for ever. It was not in his nature to lock away either wasps or women. Perhaps because he was unable to dream at night, he had taken to dreaming by day, turning himself into a fantasist who made only the most cursory contact with the real world.

His uncle Andrea worried about Stefano. He had seen him grow through all the different stages of his boyhood and he had done his best to redress the balance of his brother's heartlessness and pride, providing holidays, kindness and advice at irregular intervals. He had watched Stefano, from his first attempt to ski, turn into an athlete. The local newspaper would write about him, the boy from Castello who had won so many cups and trophies. He won all the laurels of their small town, taking them to the Judge like a stick to his master. He kept trying to please his father in those days, little realizing that after the stick came the branch and after the branch, the tree and then the wood. The forest itself would never have been enough.

Andrea Altini knew what it must be like to live with his brother. He himself had grown up with Edoardo's monstrous egotism. Being the elder of the two, Andrea had survived it; had he been younger, he shuddered to think what the consequences might have been. He saw his nephew growing up alone with only the ancient Fabrizia to buffer the Judge's coldness, and he felt for him. He had tried to get him away when Mara was finally hospitalized, but the Judge would have none of it. Edoardo resented any interference at all where Stefano was concerned. However, Andrea had vowed to help the boy, and help him he did, whenever he could. For six years he had kept his name off the lists at the Draft Board. The poor boy had lived all his life under a strict regime, the least Andrea could do was to keep him from having to do his military service. It was a game he played with his brother. Edoardo wanted to see his son in uniform and get to go to an investiture and toy with soldiers as he had done as a boy, while Andrea strove to keep Stefano within the safety of their city wall. And he worried about him. Ever since Mara had died so mysteriously with not so much as a coffin or a grave, Stefano had seemed to withdraw. His happy-go-lucky manner was an act. Andrea was convinced it had been yet one more mistake in a long line of errors to have had Mara cremated and sent back so suddenly. Seventeen was an impressionable age; the shock had changed Stefano. He didn't seem to care about anything any more.

Something had died inside Stefano when his mother died. Before, he had always hoped that one day she would wake up and either

46

stand up to the Judge or allow himself, her son, to stand up for her. He had hoped that his father would be proved wrong, just for once. He had tried to believe in the power of love and that the strength of his own feeling for his sleeping mother would eventually be sufficient to awaken her. Her return in a small urn cemented on to a shelf in the vault of the Altini family tomb seemed like divine vindication of the Judge's will. Let all things be cemented to their death, sealed and bound to obey him. It was at about that time that he stopped training and took up drinking, injecting some of his old fervour into his new hobby. As with his sport, his heart might not have been entirely in it, but the hours were there, his body was made available. Drinking, he found he was able to play the clown for his friends and also to get through the long hours from one day to the next. Starting each night at six o'clock in the Bar Italia, he paddled down a river of distilled grape and grain that led him along the course of oblivion. Most of his friends were either doing the jobs or studying the courses that they wanted, or were resigned to working in order to earn and stay within the high stone walls of Castello. They formed a tight social group that pretended to live exclusively for pleasure. Stefano was its most fervent member; unlike the others, he had no life beyond it. By day he was numb and by night he played the fool.

Five days a week he drove to Perugia to attend the university. Perugia was a foreign country: a civilization as distant as the Etruscans who had built it. He learnt to live high up on its hill, but only for short periods, and only ever like a plains Indian abandoned in the mountains. He breathed the air as though it were rarefied and strange to his lungs. He moved cautiously through the alien alleyways of the ancient city, waiting only for the moment when he could go home. His heart was at Castello. His mother had left him there. If she wasn't dead, if it wasn't her inside the alabaster urn in the *camposanto*, then she would come back to Castello to find him and he would find himself there, or so he imagined. Sometimes, during lectures, his attention would wander and he would see himself being taken away from his home town and left to die like a fish out of water, straining his gills, flopping about on unfamiliar

47

ground. And sometimes, again during lectures, he imagined himself limbless on the causeway to the hospice, with only newly healed stumps where his arms and legs had been. A platoon of soldiers would be beating the wet grass round the roots of each mutilated tree, flushing out the hiding amputees. Then his father would appear and a soldier would pass him a black cap which he would wear while smiling grimly, then he would nod towards Stefano and his stumps would be cut back. The idea of his father let loose outside the confines of Castello was more frightening even than that of being stranded abroad himself.

Stefano didn't want to do his year of military service – none of his friends did. Not even the thought of spending a year away from his father enticed him, since it would mean spending a year away from Castello. Ever since boyhood, Stefano had known that his call-up would be a battleground. His father was determined that he should serve in the army, while his uncle Andrea was determined to thwart the Judge. His uncle Andrea was a power in the Regional Council and was thus bound to win. He had twenty-two more months to get through before he became too old for call-up. Once a week, Stefano made his way to his uncle's office on the third floor of the great ochre palace that dominated the main square. Here he drank a glass of whisky with his uncle and listened to his gossip, which was mostly retrospective and had to do with the hardships and betrayals of his youth at the hands of his younger brother and a sadistic sergeant major during the days of his own military service during the war.

One of Andrea's favourite sayings was: 'Leaving aside the realm of income tax, which is a law unto itself, I don't believe in breaking the law. But I don't believe in breaking boys, either. It's hard enough to live nowadays without having what little spirit is left us wiped out.'

Stefano had heard it dozens of times. All of Andrea's stories were repeats. 'Your father missed the war and he's never forgiven society for it. He was too young to be a soldier. The nearest he ever got to the army was polishing my boots. At the end, when so many men were going home, absent without leave but safe, I had

48

to stay on. I knew he would have turned me over to the authorities for desertion if I'd showed my face at home without a pass for him to inspect. He was always sure of what was right and what was wrong. He was too young to know what it was like sitting huddled in a ditch waiting to die. Edoardo was always so clear in his politics. He never reckoned with the politics of fear. Some people are born to be either judges or criminals, they impose their will on others. Edoardo was always right, he felt he knew instinctively how things should be and he was ruthless enough to get his way. He never allowed for human weaknesses, even though he learnt to know the nuances of them through his work. He never accepted any behaviour that varied from his own. He doesn't mean to be cruel, he just *is* cruel. But then you know that, you live with him. He'll crush you if he can.'

Every Thursday afternoon Stefano sat across the wide chestnut desk in his uncle's office, tipping the golden whisky around his glass in search of stray rays of sun. After so many years of the same routine it had become comforting to sit and listen to the world according to Andrea Altini. Dodging the Draft together had made them closer friends than all their holidays had done. There were countries in Uncle Andrea's world inhabited entirely by horror stories about the army.

'Say what you will, Stefano, I can't see that it did me any good. I had to go because there was a war on. Who remembers that war now? Yet I can still remember the humiliation of my army days. Thank God there's no war now, so there's no question of duty or cowardice.

'When you were born, Mara asked me a favour the day she came out of the hospital with you. It wasn't usual for a mother to have visitors so soon after her lying in; but she called me and she said, "Help me to protect him, Andrea, I don't know if I can manage on my own." I never paid much heed at the time, I didn't realize what she meant. I haven't done a lot to protect you either, and I didn't do as much as I might have to protect her . . . I hope you know I'm doing what I can over this.'

Over the years, Andrea had grown lachrymose. He had always

49

been an emotional man, but as he grew older he softened in certain places and over certain memories to such a degree that he was a prey to his own triggers. He felt that whatever there was inside his nephew, whatever had survived, would surely die if subjected to the petty tyrannies of the barracks. The more whisky his uncle drank, the more he remembered of his own military days. His memory was never clear, though, or his stories consistent. Sometimes he described campaigns that not only he, but no Italian soldier had taken part in. At other times, he talked of the fifty thousand prisoners lost on the Russian Front as though he had been one of them who had miraculously crept away. The result of all his ramblings was to project his phobia so clearly that Stefano shrank from the idea of a barracks almost as much as his uncle did. It did not disturb him that Andrea's memories were confused, his own memories were, and his mind was continually wandering to the municipal clock and back. His mental clock was always set somewhere in the future, his thoughts darting backwards and forwards over appointments and machinations, touching the skin of his life lightly so as not to disturb anything deeper. Once their crystal glasses were drained, Stefano would dash away, retaining only a vague impression of his uncle's monologue. There were specks of dust drifting into the office, floating over the red roofscape. He too was drifting, running without seeing where he was going, living without feeling his life.

On the day when his uncle Andrea broke the news to him that his best plans had failed, the Judge had got his own way again, and Stefano had been called up, Stefano's attention was so far away from the office that he failed to take in the news. His mind was scheming, sorting out a minor problem for someone else. He was due at the road tax office, the traffic was bad on the periphery of the city, he would have to get his moped out and slip away early. His uncle was talking to him, saying something different from usual, but Stefano couldn't hear him. His mind was blocked. The drink in his glass tasted different, it made his tongue feel numb. He had the sensation of swimming underwater and then coming up for breath. He looked blankly at his uncle and smiled, reaching for his glass.

'I said, bad news, Stefano. The Judge has put his spoke in and he's already got the black cap on his head.'

His nephew continued to stare at him.

'You've been sentenced; you're up against the wall. They're calling you up a week from today. Report to the barracks at Udine.'

Stefano picked up intermittent words. He heard 'black cap' and he saw himself on the causeway. Men were slicing the new growth from the trees, lopping off the red limbs and leaving them in piles.

'At Udine,' his uncle insisted, gently.

'Udine?' Stefano repeated in a daze. 'Why there?' It sounded like the end of the world, that place so near to the end of the alphabet. They would put him in a cell there and seal it with quick-drying cement.

'Stefano, have another whisky, you've had a nasty shock.' He began to divide the remains of the bottle between their two tumblers. When they were ready, he pushed one carefully across to his still-standing nephew and gulped at the other one himself. He drank nearly half of it and then grimaced.

'Sit down, sit down, you don't have to stand to attention yet.' He felt his intended joke fall heavily into the silence between them and he wanted to take it back. He cleared his throat and tapped his glass. They were both in shock. He felt quite tearful and he didn't know if it was with grief or frustration. After ten years of pulling strings and adjusting accounts, it was extremely annoying to have his careful plans turned upside down in this way. It hit the boy worst, of course, but it also made a fool of him. What was influence for if you couldn't use it for your own family?

Andrea had spent the whole day unravelling the affair. There had been a Rotary Club dinner at the Circolo. The Judge had found himself sitting next to Alberto Zannetti of the Selection Committee. Over the *mascarpone* and coffee, Edoardo had leant over and said, 'You know, my son Stefano is really keen to be called up this year.'

'Is he?' Zannetti had asked in some surprise, halting the passage

51

of a piece of savoyard biscuit in his mouth to savour this unlikely event.

'Yes,' the Judge had insisted. 'I get the impression he'd like to get it over with.'

Zannetti had continued to suck his pudding through his new set of teeth. Then he had helped himself to some more. He sensed something strange and made a mental note to check it out with his old friend Andrea.

'I get the impression,' the Judge had explained, feeling the need for an explanation but not understanding why, 'that he'd like a bit of breathing space from the university. I don't expect he'd like the whole world to know it, but I get the feeling he'd quite like to ease the pressure there; get away for a few months.'

The engineer Zannetti was a religious man despite his early scientific training and his later military involvement. He was a man who believed in miracles. He was a devotee of Our Lady of Canoscio and a regular visitor to the grotto and the casket of bones in her sanctuary. He knew that it would take little short of a miracle for the Giudice Altini ever to truly understand his son, or anyone else for that matter, but he had refused to throttle his innate optimism. So he had given silent thanks to Our Lady and put Stefano Altini's name down for Udine. He had done his own military service there, near Trieste. The girls were pretty and the wine was good. He had some fond memories of nights spent carousing when he was a lad. The engineer Zannetti ran his tongue over his teeth and felt suddenly like a young man again. Then he had turned a slightly bleary eye to his neighbour and wondered if the Judge was really as heartless as he was said to be. He was a man with a tragic past. Who knew how the mysterious loss of a beautiful wife might not affect a man? He tried to imagine how he might have been if his own Graziella had been struck down by a sleeping sickness. He felt so protective of his own three sons that he had to restrain the urge to get up and find them to hold in his freckled hands. He wondered if that was how the Judge felt about his son. Meanwhile, the Judge was looking at him strangely, disturbed perhaps by the rush of emotion that was sitting on his face like a fit of apoplexy.

52

'Sons,' Zannetti had sighed. 'It is a love that kills.'

The Judge had nodded and held his peace. A tray of liqueurs had come between them.

By the time Andrea discovered what had happened, it was too late. Certain things could be arranged and certain things could not. Castello was not the South. Once a stamp was stamped or a document signed, there was little to be done about it. The leeway was all before such stamps or signatures occurred. Andrea felt personally responsible for what had happened. And the boy wasn't even posted somewhere within reach like Arezzo or Foligno. He was despatched to a spelling aid, U for Udine.

It was Andrea who took his nephew to the barber to have his dark curls cropped into the regulation crew cut. He even helped to pack his belongings into the long regulation kitbag. The boy was in a daze. All he seemed to know was that since he had to go to U for Udine, he would go there by himself. He refused his father's offer of a lift, and he refused his uncle's. A group of his friends offered to take him there, but he turned them down too. What was the point of sharing his shame? There might not be a war on, as his uncle Andrea insisted on pointing out every few hours, but it was still a long way from home. It was outside his world, beyond even the causeway. He felt a sailor's dread at being asked to sail beyond his chart. There was little difference in Stefano's mind between the end of the alphabet and the end of the world.

Andrea dreamt homicidal dreams about his brother. He dreamt that the Judge was a gloating vulture whose neck he was struggling to wring. Hand over fist and hand over fist he pulled at the scraggy black neck until it stretched to a length of rope which knotted itself into a noose.

Andrea mustered all the help and influence he could to have his nephew's sentence commuted. There was no hope, he knew, of having it quashed: that was only possible on health grounds, and Stefano was as strong as an ox and had dozens of tin cups to testify to it. Most of the boys from Castello got off with the help of a health certificate of some kind. Even a slightly falling arch could be

53

flattened out into a suitable excuse. A wheeze, a squint, any old defect could work in the hands of a friendly doctor. Stefano, however, was undeniably healthy.

A friend of Andrea's at the Military Hospital in Perugia found a way round the problem. After a month of basic training at the barracks, Stefano could report back to the Military Hospital and put himself under their direct command. He would be posted as a 'military companion' to a local war veteran. He would be sent on a daily basis to assist one of the four mutilated victims who qualified for this service in the area. He would have to report for duty at the veteran's private residence, five days a week, Monday to Friday, at eight a.m. By six o'clock, if he put his foot down on the drive back, Stefano could be in the main square in his usual place at the Bar Italia. The Judge knew nothing about the arrangement. They would tell him nothing until it was a *fait accompli*.

The Judge was disappointed not to be driving Stefano to Udine. His disappointment had taken its habitual form of silence. If there was one thing he abhorred above all others, it was insubordination. He consoled himself with the thought that twelve months of discipline would wake the boy up and teach him the error of his ways.

Some of his friends gave Stefano a farewell party the night before he was due to leave. The party, which ended some forty minutes before the arrival of his train, had almost destroyed him. They drove him to the railway station along a road hacked out of a mountainside and made up of an endless succession of curves and hairpin bends. Sickness overtook him. There was a chill in the air and a mist was shrouding the oak and pine woods, a fragile rising mist framed by the first pale light.

In his inebriated state, it seemed that his friends had taken him on a carousel; lurching from side to side in the back seat of the car, he didn't like it. The car was full of noise, it was pounding out some music that he had once liked but now found himself unable to separate either from the shrieking and giggling of his companions or the thumping in his own head. Later, on the train, he wondered why they had taken him along that back road: was it to say farewell to all their childhood haunts – the bends in the river where they had fished, the clearings in the woods where they had had their first kisses, and the circles of stone where they had lit illicit fires?

The car was full of his happily crooning friends, four of them, all oblivious to Stefano's distress. They ignored him when he staggered out on to the grass verge to be sick. They decided that had he been well enough to choose, he would have wanted his party to go on, so go on it did despite him. Half-hanging out of the window, Stefano was aware of a jumble of laughter and music fading in and out of his consciousness, accompanying him like a broken hurdy-gurdy on his ride. Mario, who had been his best friend since nursery school, was helping him in and out of the car. Despite their long friendship, Mario had never seen Stefano so serious and it disturbed him.

'This is supposed to be a ride to the station, not the stations of the cross. That's the fifth time you've dropped to your knees. You'll miss the train if you're planning to do the entire *via crocis*.'

Stefano smiled, the wide vacuous smile that all his friends loved. It transmitted a sense of wellbeing that was contagious. It spread over his face slowly like the rising sun on a summer morning, and then it stayed, growing, stretching to a width that offered to crack his whole face apart. Even when drunkenness crept over him, the smile stayed. It remained on his face long after comprehension had been lost behind it; it was dear to them. He smiled now, drained of all his resources but this mask, exhausted by retching, sweating and shivering on his way to another world.

Once on the train, he sat in a corner seat, leaning heavily against the glass, hoping that it would continue to support him, adrift on the unknown. His cramps travelled with him all the way to Milan. The flat grey landscape was one he knew well, he had travelled through it many times with Fabrizia on their way to the desolate hospice. He thought of his mother bottled up in an urn, and he thought of Fabrizia sealed into her drawer in the *camposanto*, then his memories sank and were lost in his general distemper. He had little recollection of what he had eaten and drunk. He vaguely

55

remembered fish and several jeroboams of champagne that Mario had successfully filched from the Judge's cellar. His friends had given him a party. 'What a party!' he thought, smiling until a sudden cramp changed the shape of his face. He wondered if he had swallowed a fish hook with the fish and whether it was even now tearing through his gut. Thinking about it, it was more likely that he had swallowed an ashtray or eaten one of his friend's mother's pot plants. Whatever it was, it was mangling him and the inside of his body was trying to get out.

The train sliced through empty paddy fields staked out by mutilated poplars. Stefano saw the train nearing the places of no hope and he knew that he had to pull himself together before he reported to the barracks. He had been trying on the train, he had occupied the minuscule bathroom at least half a dozen times. He had sponged himself down a bit, had a wash and cleaned his shoes with tap water, but the bending had made him sick again. What he really needed, he decided, was a bucket of ice-cold Coca-cola. He settled for five cans from the steward's trolley and the train continued to drag him away from his home town. He was to be away for a month. He didn't know how he was going to bear it. He would be brave, but would that be enough? His routine was all that kept him alive. He and Mario had been on holiday for two weeks at a stretch before. He would have to manage.

He ran his hand through what used to be his hair. There was nothing there but air. He looked around, wanting to draw attention to his loss. He was surrounded by strangers. Everyone around him was busy doing their own things. Even the uniformed railway workers in grey and blue were busy, absorbed in each other and in their work, while he was hours away from his group: a lost soul. It wasn't the comfort he would miss, it was the company. The group made a whole, without it he was no more than a stray piece of a puzzle. He looked around, hoping to see a friendly face, a familiar puzzle into which he could slot. The train was emptying, it had stopped he didn't know how long ago, the grey light of Milan was sucking out the passengers, swallowing them up in eddies down the long grey platform. The people on the station were all shadows

56

of people; he was neither a person nor a shadow, he was a fragment. Whatever it was that had lodged in his stomach was struggling to get out again. He heaved into a small wastepaper bin hanging on a column on the platform, but nothing came up: he was empty. He had a long way to go. He had to report to a place not far from the Yugoslav frontier. People fished for grayling there. Not the scavenging, muddy grayling of northern Europe, but the fine trout-like grayling of the Adriatic. That was what Mario had told him.

'When you finish your month, I'll come and pick you up in purgatory, and we'll go fishing . . . have a few drinks . . . have a nice time . . . and then your memories of Udine will always be tinged with grayling.'

Stefano made his way along the crowded platform, lugging his kit and stumbling towards his next train. He was already in the north, in the land of the poplars, he had to continue his journey no matter what. He would be court-martialled if he failed to appear, so he had no choice but to go on into the inhospitable mists. It was the landscape of loss to him, and his memories tinged it with fear.

III

THE VILLAGE

—— IV ——

Mezzanotte's village had swollen and shrivelled and grown big again, like an accordion squeezed by skilful hands. After the war, after the dead had been cemented into their places at the *camposanto* and their names had begun to fade from the conversations over games of cards, the village took stock of its resources. There was no work. For hundreds of years, the poor of the village had worked as woodcutters and haulers, labouring in bestial conditions for a pittance. The woodmen were forced to live away from home, sawing and loading or burning charcoal far away in the surrounding forests. Woodmen earned enough to eat, as long as their diet was frugal, but scarcely any more. Their life was not only miserable, it was lonely. Their children grew up without them, their wives became strangers. Week after week, the woodmen toiled, sleeping under the stars or on the bare floors of animal sheds. Umbrian men cut trees. It didn't say that in the Bible, but it might as well have done, for that was what Umbrian men did. They had done it for the Etruscans and for the Romans, for the Popes and for the Republic. After the war, though, they didn't want to do it any more.

At the same time, new things arrived with the liberating Allied troops. They made roads where there had only been tracks. They brought new inventions with them like power saws, lorries, trailers and chewing gum. All over the country, the war damage had to be repaired. Railway lines that once crisscrossed the entire country had been severely bombed. The British, in particular, had worked with demonic precision at the destruction of the state railway system. Hundreds of kilometres of track had been blown up by their bombs. All the railway sleepers of Italy came out of the woods around Mezzanotte's village. It seemed that the further afield they laid the

61

tracks, the further afield the villagers strayed. Before the war, emigrants and voyagers were those who braved the foreign stares of Castello or Castiglione. For a girl to marry and settle in neighbouring San Severino was tantamount to opting for a life of exile.

People had said that Mezzanotte was possessed by a devil when he had started to comb the railway network in pursuit of Valentina Rossi and her father's fair. How could anyone choose to leave their village? The woodmen left, but everyone knew they would rather have stayed at home than seek the dank forest with its dark entangled paths. The woodmen kept company with snakes and toads, birds shrieked over their heads at night and wild animals stalked their footsteps. The woodmen were *disgraziati*. People were kind to their women and children, knowing that they had little to eat and fractured homes. Then when the army came and stole their men away, the devil was replaced by the Draft Board. There had been military service for as long as anyone could remember, and the burden had always fallen on the poor. But a boy used to be able to run away and hide, or he could chop off a finger and get his papers stamped that way.

At worst, a country boy dragged his heels to Castello and was freighted away to what must have seemed like an incomprehensible concentration camp for a year, and then, if his trapped spirit survived it, he was shunted back home. To most of the villagers who had been forced to go away and march and polish, the outside world was a terrifying place. A year of military service was a year of being screamed at in a language they barely understood. Officers spoke in Italian, they did not. The wearing of boots was a torment. Boots were for Sundays, weddings and funerals. Were other prisoners asked to polish their shackles? Were they forced to keep their manacles gleaming and punished when they tarnished as all things do? The world of the fair was strange to them, but stranger still was the world of the barracks. By word of mouth, from father to son, the dread was passed on and the myths created.

When Alessandro Mezzanotte started travelling for love, the village elders called him a lunatic.

'Fancy anyone in his right mind doing that,' they said, as they

62

gathered around a kitchen table to play cards. 'Fancy a boy taking off like that, and not just to San Severino, or even Castello. He goes out of the Region. The lad crosses frontiers!'

The women of the house were huddled over the dying fire, mending or fine sewing. At the mention of frontiers, they crossed themselves, muttering to each other to ward off evil. They too were worried by Alessandro's wanderings. There were plenty of girls in the village, more than enough to pick a bride. There were more girls than men, there always had been and there always would be. The women made up the largest army, the largest workforce, the most voices. They were the muttering majority. It was wrong for a boy to stray when there were so many girls to settle with in the village. They all had daughters and there were not enough husbands to go round. Why was Alessandro wandering off? It wasn't right. God knew what trouble it might bring, this breaking of the pattern. They crossed themselves again. Crossing was more for familiarity than through any religious observance. To touch their own flesh was to be reassured that they were still there, safe and whole: forehead and breasts. Cunning, motherhood and sex, that was the female trinity, the points of their cross, touching there, safe in the knowledge that they must make the world move forward day by day, turning the great wheel of life, interrupting their toil for the biennial travail of birth, and then getting up again to push and drudge and chivvy life on its circular course.

'Eh, *si*, eh,' the women would sigh. It was a phrase that summed up everything; it contained judgement, acceptance, resignation, hope and despair. Whatever life had to offer, the women had their response.

The men would hunch over their hands of cards. Four players and a chorus of umpires.

'*Dio buono*,' the umpire would shout, regardless of the wisdom of the player's age. '*Dio buono*, what did you play that for! That is a stupid move, it will lose you the game. You're throwing away *briscola* . . . well!' and hands would be thrown up in despair. Each card that was played was accompanied by an argument. Impassioned discussions followed every trick. There was never any agreement

63

about their play, whereas they were in almost total accord on bigger and much more potentially dissentious matters.

The villagers stood or fell together. They were bound by ties of friendship, blood or loyalty. When all else failed, they were bound by habit. Hardship and circumstance ground them together, the element of choice lay in the fair distribution of their yoke. There was want in their parish, and sometimes there were shortages, but, as they often told each other, nobody starved. Marcello Pascolino, the drover, was the biggest man in the village. He had a wide red face that made no allowances in girth for his neck. His head and neck were hewn out of a single piece of stone, a primitive carving that had gouged-out eyes and mouth and nose and then slid from his pendulous ears straight into the top of his coarse shirt. Local children stood and marvelled at Marcello's neck. If anything, it widened from the ear lobes down. He was like a human ox.

'Not an ox,' Marcello would correct the village, 'a bull.' He would pull his testicles, yanking into his trousers with a massive hand to illustrate his words. He was famous for his sexual prowess. His friends said that if there was one thing he must love more than sex, it had to be the sound of his own voice. Marcello would sit and regale them for hours with his lovemaking exploits. Occasionally he would drag his tall wiry wife into the conversation to be his witness.

'You can all see how thin she is. Well . . . I don't give her time to put on weight. You can't get fat when you're married to a repeating rifle.' Then he would pause and tug his wife nearer to him, pulling on her fragile poultry arms. 'You tell them, Estelina, tell them . . . go on . . . what is your husband? An ox or a bull? Go on, go on . . .'

Estelina would smile wanly and nod. 'Eh, *si*, eh,' she would say, watching for the moment when he might release his bone-crushing grip on her arms.

Behind his back there was much speculation as to what would happen if the brittle Estelina contradicted him. Yet they knew themselves what a painful business it could be contradicting a giant. They had to organize coups and mutinies just to get a word in edgeways some evenings, so how was the poor woman to attempt it all by herself? On the other hand, in the days before the Dictatorship, when their ways in the village had been freer and easier and there had been less suspicion and more deceit, several of the local men had made love to Estelina behind the shed, behind her father's house at Nuvole. She had been a little plumper then but her eyes had had the same half-dead, half-scared look of a wounded bird. Behind her inert mask she hid a surprising sensuality. Had she not been so widely admired, many a one of them would have wed her. As it was, they shared the unspoken knowledge of her and her appetites. If Marcello boasted about himself, maybe he was right. He was always bragging about other indiscretions too. The world according to Marcello was made up of a tableau vivant of coupling. The riverbanks were drenched with his seed. No one had ever seen him either give more than a pinch or get more than a slapped chin for his pains, but who knew . . .

Marcello was the speaker because he was too loud and too strong to shout down. He fancied himself as a wise man as well as a lover. He had never been proved wrong, so, although he was a bit more long-winded than some of them had patience for, the villagers respected his opinions. Unlike some of them who were too tired or lazy to make up their minds, Marcello had an opinion on everything. When Alessandro Mezzanotte started wandering around the country, Marcello explained to his friends exactly what he thought about it. Marcello had never spent enough time in school to have qualified for any kind of teaching role, but he saw himself as a vocational teacher. His views were often delivered as classes. He never actually hit his friends' hands with a ruler as his own teacher had done, but something in his wide, lowering face made it clear that he would do, and indeed might do, if there were any interruptions.

He applied his usual question and response method on the subject of the lovelorn Alessandro.

'What do we live under?' he would ask by way of introduction. 'We live under a dictatorship. We keep ourselves out of trouble, away from the coshes and guns of the authorities. And what do we get in return?' He would pause, expectantly, giving someone the opportunity to show off what they had learnt in his last lesson. 'We get benefits. Every time another child is born, the Fascists give us a benefit. True or not true?'

Gelsomino, the blacksmith, who was considerably older than Marcello, was the least amenable of all the village to his tutelage. Sometimes he referred to him as the professor of the bleeding obvious or the government inspector into the wetness of water. Gelsomino drank more than the others. He had a good memory and a sharp wit; even when he was drunk he liked to stir up their evenings with his interventions.

'Eh, Professore, so what do we get every time another child is born? Did you say the benefit of the doubt? Does that apply to the woodmen who have to go off for months on end in the forests?'

Marcello ignored the interruption, he had an invisible theory built like a surrounding wall around his village. If they all stayed inside it, they were safe. To stray was to invite certain ruin and possibly to endanger those within.

'The world beyond is a great cauldron, a stew bubbling on the hob. The King is an Emperor now, the country has grown and given birth to other countries, Abyssinia, Albania, the rest of the alphabet is waiting to be conquered, but what has that to do with us?'

'Nothing,' piped up Ignazio del Gallo, Marcello's deputy speaker. 'Nothing at all.'

'Exactly, we are just snails clinging on to the side of that cauldron. We live in our own colony, our snail colony. Those who are the nearest to the hot sides of the pan suffer the most. The rest of us ride on their backs. We have to stay close and keep down while the world boils inside its pan.

'That boy of yours, Secondo, is going to end up badly. It is not our way to wander. Where does he get the energy from, anyway, to walk and ride like that? That's what I'd like to know.'

'He is in love, Marcello; blighted and possessed. He says he will hang himself from the alder tree by the river like his cousin Albertino if he cannot follow this fairground creature.

'I have told him that she cannot come here, I don't want to lean over any of my grandchildren in their cradle and find they have spider's legs. But he says he is in love, Marcello. What can I do? The Dictatorship is all outside, you know, there is anarchy at home. Sons do what they want to now. My father would have killed him, but who am I to say what the boy can or cannot do? I, who miscalculated my crops and have only my debts to contemplate of an evening.'

The advent of war destroyed many things, among them, Marcello's theory of survival. His cauldron overflowed and spilt scalding stew on all the snail colonies around the pot. Marcello retreated into his shell, bewildered and disillusioned. During the early years of the war, while the village divided into those who were actively Partisans and those who were passively so, there was a great deal of dissension. They missed their spokesman. They urged Marcello to pronounce on events, but he would say wryly, 'How can I, when I don't speak German?'

Some of the villagers were too tired or absorbed in their own problems to become actively or passively engaged in anything. They ignored the war, losing their sons to it with the same resignation with which they sent them to the threshing grounds every year, hoping they would all return but knowing that some of them might not. There were more Socialists than Fascists in the village because the Partisans had arrived first, and since so many of the inhabitants were related, they tended to sway together whichever way they went. Those who were against the Partisans kept quiet about it, to the authorities at least. Since it was the Draft Board that was stealing most of their boys, their sympathies turned to the party led by the people they knew, who spoke to them in a way they understood. There was never much time to spend playing cards or arguing, and the last thing they wanted was to fall out. It had been soothing, they realized, to have Marcello act as interpreter between them and the outside.

When Gelsomino's son returned from the army without his right foot, the boy's loss seemed to add to his father's stature. His friends began to defer to him, so much so that gradually he too began to pronounce, replacing Marcello as the village's social analyst.

'In my opinion,' he explained, 'there are two kinds of trouble: big trouble and little trouble. One is a luxury, the other is a curse. We've often been out and caught skylarks in our nets. Well now, *Dio buono*, and don't ask me how or why, we have become those helpless birds. Eh, tell yourself the time has come, prepare yourself for a broken neck, but it is lower and worse than that. We are in big trouble. We can tell ourselves it will all be over in the spring, like we did last year, but soldiers keep trampling over our fields and pillaging our houses. We do what we can, we keep our children obedient as best we can, we beat the little bastards, we make them behave. We lock our daughters up and you know as well as I do we would keep a padlock on their knickers if we could. But what happens? They grow away from us. Reason and sanity have grown away from the world . . .

'Well,' he said pointing to himself defiantly with both hands, 'eh?'

Alessandro's uncle Massimo was half-rising from his chair. 'Talk, talk. What about some more wine? I say we drink up, the Fascists will take it all away if they find it, so we might as well drink it up before they do. And what has the war got to do with my nephew?'

'You know where the wine is, Massimo, help yourself. You don't usually stand on ceremony so why the formality tonight? Giuseppina!' he shouted, although his wife was only a few feet away from him. 'Get us wine. Go with Massimo to where it is hidden.'

'I'll go on my own,' his wife said, wiping her hands on her thick apron and depositing a sleeping baby on Massimo's lap.

The kitchen door swung open in the wind where Giuseppina had unbolted it, a gust of evening air ushered a chill into the room. There was a sudden silence into which Gelsomino said:

'My boy won't be walking to any stations. I wish he could.'

His one-footed son would be down by the well in the shed full of hay where all the boys gathered in the evenings. If they had managed to get hold of enough wine, they would be drunk. It was Saturday night. Later they would comb the hills, defying the curfew, looking for a dance. If they didn't find one anywhere, Il Gallo would strike up Elio Mezzanotte's squeezebox and play them tunes to dance to with the girls. His son would not be dancing.

68

Gelsomino knew that some of the young people in the village admired Alessandro for his daring; he had ventured beyond the boundary and learnt to navigate the world beyond. They pretended to tease him, but secretly they were envious of his having tasted the stew in the pot. Before the war he had travelled all over the central states following the funfair, and now, in defiance of world history, he followed it too. Less frequently, it was true, and in uniform, but still following.

The girls had wanted to know him better, this exotic daring explorer, but he was either absent on his travels or absent in his mind. He had ignored them, snubbing even their most open advances. Meanwhile, he had grown away from the boys he had been friends with. His mind was forever on Valentina: an unknown outsider whom none of them could share. Every time there was a holiday, Alessandro had taken off in a way that both scorned them and diminished them. They had admired him and been envious not only of his travels but of his passion. Those who were romantic thought of his love; those who were not thought of all the sex he was getting. One way or another, they had seen him as a hero.

There was a lottery in the village from 1939 until well after the war to decide who would go to Volterra to bring back salt. Three boys at a time would cycle there, hours and hours of dirt roads, with a picnic on the way out and small sewn sacks of salt rocks on the way back. Thus they had seen the world outside, the world beyond the edge, the void into which you fell if you ventured outside the village. They had seen the fear and the excitement, the temptation and the madness. All in all, Alessandro Mezzanotte was a lucky bastard who had lived like a rare bird in their midst.

When he left for the army, he was perhaps less missed than other boys. He was so often absent anyway. He didn't have a best friend any more, and his brothers had both gone into the hills before his departure. His mother missed him. She who had always loved Elio best turned her affection to her youngest son, planting her hopes in him as though he were a new and miraculous tree that would bear a fruit to sweeten her latter years. She missed his dreamy shape hunched around their cramped house, and she missed the contention

69

he had caused. Secondo no longer complained about him, so she could no longer defend him, albeit silently. Secondo had grown as still and as quiet at home as a hibernating animal. Regardless of the season, he sat slumped by the fire, sucking on his pipe, bleary-eyed.

Unbeknown to his wife, Secondo also missed his youngest son. Alessandro's rebellious excursions had given him an interest in life. It had been, on the whole, a negative one, but it had been there, a flicker of interest in the evenings, where now there was none. The youngest child of the house was Elena; five years Alessandro's junior, she worshipped him. Because his life had been absorbed in love since he was fifteen himself, he had never really noticed this small, ever helpful girl trailing around behind him. Sometimes he had chased her away, and occasionally he had given her errands to run, but mostly, he had been unaware of her existence. They shared the same room, but Elena slept behind a hessian screen pinned to the rafters. Elena, with her light-brown braids and her dark-brown eyes and her garlicky fingers, missed him too.

Long before Alessandro came home from the war, a letter arrived for his father telling him that his son had been wounded in action. Agostina wanted to go north to find him. She wanted to comfort him in his hospital bed and tell him how much she missed him, how much she wanted him home; how different their lives would be. She wanted to tell him how she would scoop the emptiness out of their lives and fill the void, as her mother had, with love and care. She had decided to help him to marry this Valentina from the fair. She would stand up against Secondo and authorize the wedding. She would browbeat her husband into consent and welcome her new daughter-in-law into the house. She would stand up against the gossip of her neighbours, and, if need be, if a child was born of the union with unnaturally hairy arms and legs or a surfeit of limbs, she would help to hide it. She longed to give Alessandro this promise, and to be, like so many other mothers in the village, at one with her son.

Agostina wanted to go to Alessandro, but the world was a labyrinth she could not find her way through. Even if she had the money and plucked up her courage and caught the daily bus to

70

Castello, and was lucky and found the ferryman to row her across the River Tiber to the city side, would she know what to do from there? The town he was in had a strange name that she could not even remember. It distressed her to think of it, let alone try to get there. It meant changing trains over and over again, it meant sums of money they didn't have. The older boys were in the hills, the *cantina* was bare. The Fascists had taken what little they had to sell in the way of honey and eggs, and Secondo had lost his soul somewhere between Zeno Poggio and their own stone cottage and was looking for it in the fire. He'd been looking for it for so long that he'd nearly lost his voice. He reminded her of his sister, Esmerelda, living dumb and desolate on the hill across the valley. Elena tried to comfort her mother, but it was Alessandro that the older woman wanted to hold.

They said, in the village, that Agostina never recovered from the shock of seeing her son at the Military Hospital at Perugia. They moved him there quite soon after the 'accident'. It was Elena who first queried the word that came to be used so frequently in their household.

'Is war an accident, then, *mamma*? Is it an accident when the bombs fall out of the aeroplanes?'

But there were things that you knew and things that you said, so they all called what happened an 'accident'. Agostina had never been so far as Perugia. She had never been further than Castello. There was a time when she longed to escape from the confines of their valley, yet now that she was out in the world beyond, she felt guilty; guilty for having wanted something born of disaster. She knew that her son was wounded, she knew that he had undergone a series of operations. She prayed that he would be glad to see her, and that he would forgive the silly silences of the past. She prayed that there would be a chance to make amends over his girl. Agostina bore all the confusion and the anxiety of negotiating her way to and through Perugia with an almost girlish humour. She was even prepared to forgive Secondo for his continued gloom. She decided that after the visit she would go home and drag her husband out of the smoke and back into the land of the living.

71

When she finally reached the ward called 'Men's Surgical', she was so agitated she could hardly walk. Elena was with her. It was Elena who had got them this far. It was Elena who steered her past the lines of beds with their rows of wounded soldiers. There was a smell of ether and stale blood. There wasn't enough air in the ward, so there was a smell of effluent disguised by soap. Some of the men were too hurt for her to look at them easily, but because she was looking for her son, and he too was wounded, she strained to look into all the faces that she passed to make sure that she would not walk past her baby without knowing him. Each time she saw a bad case she felt her heart skip in fear and relief. She and Elena had been given a number. All the beds were numbered. Alessandro was twenty-two. When the nurse first gave them the number, she had wanted to contradict her and say, 'No, he isn't, he's twenty, just twenty, he was born in 1922.' She didn't say anything, though, because the nurse had a formidable moustache and a large fob watch which she kept consulting as though to say, 'You are all wasting my time.'

When they finally reached bed number twenty-two, Agostina turned away after a cursory glance.

'I knew it,' she said, almost triumphantly, 'that hairy nurse was wrong. I had a feeling. Now where is Alessandro? How will we find him with all these men?'

Elena didn't answer her mother. She was moving towards the bed. While Agostina had been looking at faces, Elena had been looking at hands. She stretched out to touch her brother's where it lay clawing the hospital counterpane. On the other side of his body, where his right arm should have been, there was only a bandage wrapped tightly around a stump. Her mother stood staring sadly around the high vaulted room. There was nothing on the bandaged head and face pressed into a pillow on the bed to show her that this was what was left of her son. Elena touched his living hand, but it shrank back, immune to comfort.

Strange noises began to escape from his mummified face. They were the noises of the killing shed, the animal moans that followed a slipped knife. Elena felt herself drowning in her helplessness. She began to cry. There was blood on the bandages where Alessandro's face should have been.

'Help him, please, won't somebody help him, he's my brother,' she pleaded.

Agostina didn't hear her daughter, she was deaf to her tears and her appeal. What she heard were the noises that her son was making and she recognized them as the strangled cries of a dying baby. God had taken four of her babies so many years ago and here was Alvaro, the first of them, with swaddling bands around his head and he was choking again, gurgling on his diphtheria through the maimed throat.

God had taken her youngest son away and turned him into the writhing larva of a monstrous insect. She forced herself to look down on the covered mound on the bed. A savage feeling rose up in her when she saw that he was missing his arm. She wanted it back. She wanted to pick it up and lay it down beside him, where it belonged. She wanted to find the hairy nurse and tell her to, rather make her, give it back. She would shake her. How dare they cut it off, how dare they mutilate her son? She didn't know then that both his eyes were also gone, or she would have wanted to put them back too, to lie on the stained gauze over the scooped-out sockets where they belonged.

It was not until six months later that they finally brought him back to her. He arrived in an ambulance. It was 1943. The ambulance was a white bus so wide that it couldn't get through the narrow village streets. It stopped beside the ruined pediment of the stone arch that had once linked the two sides of the village. They had been told in advance that he would be coming home on that day. His friends and Elena had put the church bunting out to welcome him, forgetting that he was blind. The coloured flags were rigid with frost. During the early days of his return, even the early years, it was hard to remember how consistently the blind cannot see.

Between her first visit to the Military Hospital and his homecoming, Agostina had grown old. Her hair had turned a yellow white and the muscles in her face had all let go, giving her the appearance of one permanently about to cry.

73

Elena and her uncle Massimo guided Alessandro through the village to the steps of his father's cottage. The arm that Elena was propelling was made of plastic. It had chilled on the ride from Perugia, presumably it had been pressed against the glass. It was cold and hard and horrible. She looked up at her brother guiltily to see if he had noticed her state. He had two sewn sockets, stitched in a style between her mother's fine sewing and her own rougher cobbling. He had two darned holes where his eyes should have been and the rest of his face was worse than one of his grandmother's darned socks. It was traced and veined and ridged with scars, dozens and dozens of scars distorting his once handsome features. She shuddered.

'*Dio buono*, come on in.' He grunted something that she could not understand.

She squeezed his hand and then remembered that it was not his, it was government issue. He had been lucky to get it, they had told her in Castello, most veterans had to do without. The other children had always said he was a lucky bastard. She led him into the cool dark kitchen of their house. Although he stumbled a little over the steps, she led him in more easily than he was later able to lead her into his own mysterious world of darkness.

V

None of the villagers could agree on exactly when Mezzanotte began to roam their streets, hugging the stone walls, picking up gossip. Occasionally it became a matter for debate for the men who had gone away and come home again and who were also threading all the beads of their social history together, reconstructing the years of their exile. They had left in the years after the war when work was scarce and food was short. The exodus of railway sleepers had awakened them and they had left their village in the wake of the forestry trailers laden with local oak. They went to Milan to work in the building trade, reconstructing the city out of hills of rubble. Many of them went to Switzerland, where there was work to be found and good money to be made. It was Mezzanotte's generation who left, and the boys who came after them, handing their pride over with their passports to the customs guards high up on the Swiss frontier.

The Swiss Brigades lived a life of degradation. Despised by their hosts, they were treated worse than cattle. As they pointed out, 'You paid good money for cattle, you owned them, but we immigrants came and went.' With their fine skills – for many of them were artisans: carpenters, blacksmiths and masons – they were taken mostly to work on churches. Beside the lakes they laboured with thick chilblained fingers to restore the austere stone churches built for the cold God of the Alps. There were no statues to the Madonna there, no candles and few paintings, so even the churches had a desolate, unfriendly face. They thought of their own church of Santa Maria wherever they worked. They remembered the heavily embroidered altar cloths, the pride of their mothers, and the thin smelly candles, the smoke stains on the vaulted ceiling, the flowers, the ornate stencilling behind the choir, and the statue of Our Lady.

They had never appreciated how much their little church mattered to them. It had been women's business. When they returned, they would make a point of joining the Sunday mass. They would take their future children there and teach them the importance of warmth and kindness. Their children would never know this scorn. Their children would not be outcasts in a foreign country. They would be proud of their Umbrian blood, not with the mad pride of the Dictator, but with something more lasting and better; the wholesome pride of their village.

The exiled workers went home to choose their wives, commuting between the scorching summers of Castello and the regimented chill of Switzerland. The Swiss lived well, they lived surrounded by luxuries that seemed like science fiction to the incoming labourers. Hostility to them was widespread, but sometimes there were chinks in the northern armour. There was the odd Swiss family who tried to make up for the injustices and often brutality of their neighbours. Yet none of the Umbrians stayed on in the Alps. They all returned, as they had said they would, to resettle in the village that poverty had driven them from. And they returned with enough money to marry and live as something more than beasts of burden. The war had changed everything.

When they finally went home, the Swiss Brigades were jealous of their missing years. They wanted to know, in the most minute detail, everything that had happened in their absence. Thus they wanted to know exactly when Mezzanotte left his dark cottage to take his world of darkness on to the streets. Did he attend his father's funeral? Was he in or out of the kitchen when Secondo died by the fire? Afterwards, did his widowed mother take him out? Or was it Elenita, his sister? The card games became crucial. Information was sifted and swapped over them. The register of events was decided and approved by the players and the watchers who swilled back the abundant local wine and drank in their past as a way into their future.

So it became established that Elenita died of the Chinese flu in 1946 and Secondo, her father, was weakened by it and fell into the dying fire, but was neither burnt by the ashes nor carried away by

76

the virus. He died in the corn fields of the *padrone* where he had worked all his life. A massive heart attack shook him like one of the new electric wires. Before he fell into the growing corn he cried out, raising a flock of skylarks into the air to hover over his last breath. Alessandro, they finally agreed, did attend his father's funeral, and also his sister's. In fact, although not everyone was aware of him there, he stood outside the *camposanto* every time one of his friends or family died. So he stood there often. He must have stood there when Marco's young wife was buried. She had died in childbirth. Immediately after the funeral, Marco went away to Milan and he never wrote to his mother or his blind brother. They hoped he would return for Easter or Capodanno, but he never did. His mother hoped he would return for his father's funeral but he didn't show up, which was how they all knew that the world must have swallowed him up.

'When you think about it,' Estelio used to tell his drinking companions at the new bar, 'these Mezzanotti are a terrible family. They just died out. Four children, uncles, aunts, there should have been cousins, grandchildren . . . Secondo knew what he was moping about in front of that kitchen fire of his. We all used to say, "Cheer up, Secondo, it's not that bad." '

'Eh, *si*, eh,' Gelsomino interrupted. Gelsomino still had the word at these informal meetings, he was to keep it into his dotage.

'Eh, it's true, the poor man was staring into the future, seeing his entire family eliminated. The good Lord takes his reprisals too, an entire family dead, wiped out.'

'Mezzanotte is the only person in this village who has no relations,' Estelio pointed out.

'He has friends. He has us.'

'True, but we are here, drinking this good wine, while he is who knows where, feeling his way around the ramparts.'

It was hard to get truly close to Mezzanotte. Mostly out of pity, some of his old classmates had tried to, but with only marginal success. They drank together and they exchanged pleasantries, but Mezzanotte made them feel uneasy, like a false note in their choir.

By the mid-1950s, tobacco had been introduced to their valley, bringing with it not only full employment, but a staggering and unprecedented prosperity. The days of serfdom came to an end. The potato, barley and flax of old disappeared, together with the daily drudgery for token wages. The combination of Milanese and Swiss earnings and the ready tobacco money made the village rich. The bad times were over. Scratching the surface, everyone had a war story to tell, but a thin skin had grown over them, a protective layer no thicker than a dried tobacco leaf covered all their wounds. Those who had died had died, and those who had returned had returned. The civilian survivors folded their memories away like so many uniforms. The Partisans' guns were unburied and handed in. The grief and the loss, the bombing and the fear, had all been set aside, covered over, dug into the ground and reborn as wide-leaved plants. It was suggested that Secondo – who was gradually and posthumously acquiring the status of seer – had foreseen the tobacco boom in the smoke he studied, and seen himself as a burnt-out dog-end trampled by destiny, remote from such success.

By the time Gelsomino's maimed son died in the mid-'60s, the war had come to seem as distant as a fairy-tale. There were a number of villagers with missing fingers or hands, but these had all been caused by industrial accidents. There were sawmills in the neighbouring towns, trees were reduced to geometrical shapes and used as parquet flooring. For those who were unable to forget their memories of hard usage on the land, these factories offered profitable employment. Ubaldo Bernacchi had lost his hand to just such a saw. He wore a bandage over the stump, declining the state assistance of a plastic hand. It always looked as though the accident had just happened and was still healing under the pristine gauze.

'*Oddio!*' Ubaldo used to say to Estelio and his friends. 'We work in the factories, but we're peasants at heart. A passing hawk, a rustle in a ditch, a messenger on his way up the hill, it's in our nature to stop and look. Anything new, we stop and look. I tell you,' he'd say, flapping his thin stump of a wrist, 'you need concentration in a sawmill, and that's the one thing we haven't got. Eh, we work hard, we're grafters and everything else you like, but the minute someone comes into the workshop, or a wasp gets caught in the fan, we look up and . . . *trac* . . . another hand.'

'*Dio buono*,' Estelio sighed with a fond smile both for Ubaldo, whom he particularly liked, and for God himself who he believed was, finally, really being good, if you didn't count Ubaldo's hand.

Old age and industry accounted for the maimed and the mutilated. The rest had surged forward with their wealth and their dreams. The past travelled with them like a sacred relic. They had made a big bundle of all that they wanted to salvage from their most recent past and they honoured and celebrated its rites. They danced under the trees on feast days, crooning to the same tunes that their fathers and grandfathers loved. Women rose at four in the morning to prepare the special breads and cakes that had always been a part of these traditional *festas*. Their diets remained strictly within the bounds of their regional cuisine. Their lives revolved almost entirely around the tiny spiral of their village. They moved freely, backwards and forwards in their expensive cars, to Castello and even Perugia, but rarely further, home was home in this green valley between the woods on Zeno Poggio and Sant Agnese.

Because their beginnings had been hard, and because they were born of generations of silent suffering, and because they saw a chance to live their lives as a fulfilled dream, they had left out most of their bad memories from their bundle. The past became tradition. It became myth. Mezzanotte was a disturbing plumb line into a shared nightmare. Even the cemetery had filled with new faces. The oval photographs at the foot of each immured coffin were no longer of soldiers. Just as the new weedkillers eradicated all the grasses and wild flowers that sprang up in the tobacco fields, a new culture, and the passing of time, wiped out the surprised black and white faces of fallen conscripts in the cemetery. The flowers continued to be left to rot in their small perforated vases, but the collective memory had moved on and the evidence was slowly eroding. Of all the war dead, the most remembered was Mezzanotte who was still alive. Everyone in his family was now dead, brothers, sisters, parents, uncles, aunts. Yet, despite all his injuries, his missing limb, his missing eyes, his patchwork face, his blasted lungs, his burnt throat, his broken gut, Mezzanotte refused to die.

He had taken it upon himself to patrol the village. He walked around it continually like a mule at an olive press. He dragged the burden of his injured body up and down the steep hills that led from the bar on the road to the bar by the church. There were parts of the village that were unchanged, not only since he was a boy, but unchanged for centuries. The squat grey church of Santa Maria with its small noisy bell tolling uncontrollably was the same, as was the priest's house beside it. The incumbents changed, but they all used the same incense and carried the trace of the same sweet thick *vin santo* on their breath. The schoolhouse across from the church was the same, although there were hardly enough children to keep it open. It seemed the more money and food everyone had, the fewer people there were to share it. The Pascolinis' bread oven still jutted out into the narrow road that skirted the top of the village.

Rosina Pascolini still made bread there early on summer mornings before the heat became unbearable. Mezzanotte often listened out for her limping gait as she lit the furnace inside the brick oven and scraped the stone griddles across the hot ashes inside it, tending her bread. Rosina had been a friend of his mother's. His mother would be over ninety now if she were alive, as Rosina must be too. He remembered her as she used to be, a pretty, chattering woman with amazingly white thighs that she used to show when she came to their kitchen, lifting her skirt up and flapping it to ease the heat. It was his brother Marco who advised him to look up Rosina's skirt. Mezzanotte had just turned eleven at the time and had developed an overriding interest in sex. He had spent his first summer working in the fields and seen his first harvest. Together with the other boys, all unpaid helpers like himself, he had seen enough secret erotica behind bushes and bales to keep him awake and aching for the rest of his boyhood. After the licence of the harvest, though, bodies were covered again and the sexual rampage subsided, but his desire to see naked flesh did not.

As a boy, the difference in age between him and Rosina seemed huge. No one married an older woman, it was not done, and yet he had always felt a tenderness for Rosina. He often wished he could have carried her away from her unloved servitude. He still

80

remembered seeing up her skirt for the first time; looking so that he could creep away and masturbate with his brothers. He had seen the colourless flesh of one thigh and been gripped simultaneously in his groin and throat by a desire that made him blush. Seconds later, he saw the other thigh with its equally transparent skin disfigured by a jutting bone and a livid welt of scar. His desire fled but his flush remained, fixed by the shame he felt that a man, her father, had beaten that leg and kicked it out of shape, punishing her for succumbing to another man's desires. Rosina of the limp who knew nothing of dictatorships beyond the tyranny of her father and brothers. Rosina who ran away to laugh in his mother's kitchen, secretly enjoying her life still until they recalled her with their menacing shouts, forcing her to hobble back.

She must be old now, as old and ugly as the Befana, but she would always be young and pretty for him.

'O Mezzanotte,' she would call to him as he passed, 'stay and eat warm bread with me. We old folks must stick together.'

She said this, in truth, for his mother who had been her friend, because she was older than Mezzanotte by a long chalk and she had little in common with him. She was still running a house full of men and children while he had been creeping around in his darkness for decades. She pitied his uselessness, his loneliness and his lack of occupation.

Mezzanotte would sit on the cool sculpted ledge beside the oven, blocking even more of the road. He would have liked to have spoken to Rosina more over the last fifty years, but he remembered her as a Madonna of laughter, a Madonna robbed of her child who struggled to keep her gaiety, balancing on the fine line between happiness and hysteria. Her family had been decimated during the war. There had been a reprisal and she had been witness to a summary shooting outside their hayshed, it was said. To talk about his own wounds would be to reopen hers. So he kept silent with one of the few people to whom he might have spoken. Even on the subject of his worst wound, his broken heart, he kept his peace. It was not age, it was love and loss that bound them, that and the early mornings and the warm bread.

81

Every day, Mezzanotte patrolled the village, edging past the walls of gardens, smudging the heart's-ease back into its cracks, knocking snails off the blocks of stone as he continued snail-like on his way. There were houses that smelt of geraniums and houses that smelt of caged birds, coffee, singed feathers, talcum powder, washing and woodsmoke. After fifty years, he knew the contours of the village but not its contents. When it came to the muddle of homes he had known as a child, he could see them still, in his mind's eye. He knew that bombs had scarred the face both at the top and the bottom of the parish, but the middle lay sandwiched just as it had always been. Everyone said so. There was a shop now where there had once been stables and the new bar had opened a terrace in what used to be Ferini's croft. People said there were Canadian vines growing all over a pergola on the site.

Mezzanotte had never seen a Canadian vine, but Estelio had described it as just like a proper vine without any grapes and with all the shades of red wine stained into the leaves. The idea of this flaming pergola was almost as disturbing as the new houses built on the slope under the once ruined church of San Crescentino. The building site had routed a vineyard. He remembered the vineyard well, but the new houses were hard to grasp. Every day he forced himself to turn left where the road forked to the *camposanto* or the new sports ground and make his way through the small housing estate where half a dozen dream houses had been built by the new tobacco barons. At the end of its bewilderingly clean and scentless street, an old acacia welcomed him. Beyond it was a dirt track, a slip street back to the tobacconist and bar at the top. The Giulianis' geese were those foraging in the weeds.

Mezzanotte never took this shortcut. He was a man of habit. He knew that it was the precision of his habits that rendered him harmless to the rest of the community. Everyone had become so used to the blind man with the black glasses and the plastic hand shuffling past their houses that they scarcely noticed him any more. To some he had become virtually invisible. To others his presence was comforting, he passed as regularly as the chiming of their clocks. If anyone wanted to know the whereabouts of anyone else

82

within a radius of half a mile, Mezzanotte could be depended on to know.

All along his route, people called out to him, '*Salve*, Mezzanotte!' and he would call back '*Buon dí* . . .' and then the person's name. He knew everybody's name. Like an infallible circus trick, he picked up their names from their voices. The greeting was always the easiest part of the conversation. After that, very few of the villagers could think of what to say to this man who had survived the past, dragging it into the present in this unrecognizable form. There were things underneath his scars that would be too painful to recall. No one wanted to go back to the dark times his disfigured face threatened to unfold. It was a blessing that he had paid companions, or they would have had to send someone to sit with him, a sacrificial victim to listen to whatever he needed to say.

As it was, his communion with the village was always superficial. They skimmed the surface with their talk, filling in gaps in the daily gossip. Gradually, he became an oracle of trivia. He could be relied on completely to know to the day when a child was due to be born or a batch of eggs to hatch. He knew where children would be playing when they were late home for meals. He knew where borrowed tools had been left and when birthdays and saints' days were due. He knew when the parish priest was in or out, when the erratic petrol pump was open or closed, whether the thrice-daily bus had passed; and he also knew, from his numerous scars, when it was going to rain.

Twice in the morning, and twice in the afternoon, he stopped at the upper bar for a drink. He only ever drank *cynar* on these occasions, a thick black bitter liquid made from artichokes. He drank *cynar* not, as some people claimed, because its black sickly bitterness suited his condition, but because his wartime friend, Massimo Gavarini, had called it a serious drink and the only one worth drinking. Some people in the village, like Marcello Pascolini for instance, drank to forget, but Mezzanotte drank to remember. On entering this bar, having manoeuvred his way up the three steps to its doorway, he would walk slowly towards the counter and then lean on it, secure in the knowledge that there would always be a space for him there.

83

'*Salve*, Mezzanotte,' the bar lady would say, hurrying from the shop half of the room to the bar.

'*Buon dí*, Concetta,' he would reply and then wait while she bustled nearer the counter.

She always smelt of the cheese, pepper and vegetables that she served, with a hint of wax from the paper she used to wrap up her wares. She had secrets that she would have liked to tell Mezzanotte, but she didn't dare. Her husband never listened to her. She had bad dreams and endless anxieties. She needed to ask someone about them, or rather to tell them, she sensed that Mezzanotte would be discreet. She always smiled at him, fluttering her pale blue eyes in her most coquettish manner, hoping that this would induce him to linger and chat with her. She had heard from some of the women down the street and in the new houses that he had a kind ear and a gentle manner that invited disclosures, and she hoped that despite his blindness he would perceive her need. Every time he picked up his glass to drain its thick liquoricey contents, he sensed her fluttering tension and recognized it as fear. It was not, however, the fear he imagined, caused by his own mutilation; it was the fear that he would go away yet again without hearing her out. She envied the conscripts who came to their village to keep Mezzanotte company. They must get the benefit of all his talk, while her own twin sons spoke only to each other and to their father, leaving Concetta to talk to her customers or, more often, to herself.

By the time Stefano Altini arrived in the village to be his military companion, Mezzanotte's life had become enmeshed in a web of misapprehension. From the depths of his loneliness he had dredged up an acceptable veneer. After the last of his family had died, he had moved into the Giuliani's household, renting a large room and a bathroom and a larder in the basement. For this he paid a handsome rent, far more than they had wanted to accept at first, but he explained that he wished to pay them as he saw fit because he had a war pension of millions of lire a month that he could never spend, and he hoped that when his time came they would perform the rites that his own people would have done had they lived. The Giuliani family were fond of Mezzanotte; he had been to school with Assunta, the wife, and they would have gladly stood by him at his end, whenever that should be, without the bribe. They told him so.

'I don't indulge myself much, as you see. Why not let me have my way in this. Let me share my money with you, it would mean a lot to me.' So he lived downstairs in the room next to the *cantina* and the barrels of wine; coming and going as he pleased. His midday meal would be prepared for him by whichever conscript he was with at the time. He would then sit chewing slowly and painfully, as he always must, on a piece of unsalted bread and a couple of slices of ham or salami. In the evening he chose to eat alone. His unvarying supper was of tepid pasta with tomato. This gave rise to rumours of neglect. Even in the hard times before the tobacco a man ate properly prepared food. It might just have been polenta with a scattering of sauce, or even chestnut bread with a rind of cheese, but it was hot and freshly cooked. On this point, though, Mezzanotte was obdurate. He insisted on eating alone.

On weekdays, it was always the conscript who went to buy his bread. Concetta, who often felt sick with curiosity, would wrap it up slowly.

'I've always wondered,' she'd say with a nonchalant smile, 'what he talks about.'

Often as not, the conscript would shrug. He'd be a stranger in the village; even after eleven months of military service there, he'd rarely get to go out and meet people. Mezzanotte didn't like any company on his walks around the streets and he spent most of his day wandering. It was an odd way to defend one's country, buying bread and salami for an absentee blind man. On the other hand, it was a doddle, and no rash comments were going to land him back in the barracks.

'So what does he say?' Concetta would insist.

'Nothing much,' the reluctant soldier would tell her, beating his retreat as fast as he could.

The mystery grew with the denial. No one believed that Mezzanotte kept these soldiers in his house day after day from eight in the morning until half-past five just to shop and clean for him. It was generally believed that these lads were like a surrogate family.

Nobody knew that he was as much an enigma to his so-called companions as he was to all the village, and almost as much of a stranger. He kept his loneliness close to his chest and he kept quiet, living his life alone inside his head with only the cursory greetings of acquaintances to save him from half a century of total silence.

During the months of Stefano's service, Mezzanotte often wondered if he would have continued in this manner had it not been for the return of the fair.

—— VI ——

Where once the arrival of the funfair at San Severino had been the most exciting event of the year, by the end of the war the pattern had broken. The miraculous shards of that moving kaleidoscope had been seen for what they were: no more than a handful of glass. In a world of cars and access to municipal zoos, there was no longer any enchantment in a mangy camel. The human freaks lost their value and were sent to dreary seclusion in institutions. Since boys no longer had to help to unload an entire lorryful of fizzy drinks to get a free sip from one of the bottles, the tin cups of drink lost their allure. Boys could buy fizzy drinks by the crate and candyfloss by the pan. Any child who had been into town had ridden on the metal horses provided by the local Council, and even the magic of the carousel shrivelled away. The travelling fairs lost their revenue and their charm. Instead of the dusty trails of eccentric wagons, caravans, carts and blinkered beasts, a couple of lorries and a truck or two would pitch camp on a bare field and set up their whirling swings and a carousel and resign themselves to a sporadic and critical clientele.

The funfair that used to flower annually by the curve of the river at San Severino hadn't returned for over forty years. At first, some people blamed the bombing of the site by the Americans, while others thought it had more to do with the love affair between Mezzanotte and the Maestro Rossi's daughter. In Castello it was explained away by the emigrant workers. With so many men gone and so little money in the villages, it wouldn't be worth while to pitch a fair there any more. By the time the exiled labourers returned, a whole new wave of entertainments had arrived. There were dance halls and radios, record players and cars, television and cinemas, so nobody seemed to miss the ox-drawn convoy or the rationed hysteria of the fairground. Some of the villagers were grateful, for Mezzanotte's sake, that the fair didn't return. Surely he had suffered enough without the added indignity of having to confront his former fiancée and her family and show his disfigurement.

Nobody knew what had happened over the engagement. After the 'accident', all the details blurred. One thing was certain, though; if he had chosen a local girl, she would have stood by him no matter what state he had been reduced to. A local girl would have married even less; fifty per cent of him, as they said at the bar; or maybe less still. Gelsomino maintained that you needed at least fifty per cent of a person to sign the register, otherwise the marriage wouldn't be legal. Mezzanotte could have had a frolic and then had a nurse. There was a lot to be said for abiding by the mores of the village. Over the years, they came to regard much of Mezzanotte's loneliness as self-inflicted. A boy shouldn't go hobbling over the countryside picking up gypsies. You had only to look at the emigrants, at the Swiss Brigades and the Milanese; none of them had broken the taboo, they had all come home to marry. Mezzanotte had cast his hook in foreign waters. Sweet waters, it seemed, but alien and out of bounds. In some ways, he had only himself to blame. If the girl had left him, it was what you'd expect from such a one.

It was in the summer of 1990 that the fair returned, no longer to San Severino, but to Mezzanotte's village itself. There had been a drought since January, and the water table was disturbingly low. The tobacco was in danger. The Region had declared a state of emergency. Water was being rationed in Castello, and those in the countryside who did not have their own wells were allowed to spray their fields for only a limited number of hours each day. Holidays that had been planned were cancelled, it didn't seem safe to leave the crops. If it hadn't rained by the middle of May, there would be widespread disaster. The temperature had leapt into the thirties in April. Each day was sweltering. When May arrived it was like mid-summer. It had finally rained in May, but there had been hailstorms; and hailstorms tore the tobacco leaves and flattened

88

their corn. The long summer holiday was on its way. The schools would be breaking up in June and not returning until the end of September. The village elders were anxious about the restlessness in the village. Everyone was speculating about the weather and worrying about their desiccating crops. It was the elders who brought in the fair. They hoped its novelty would take people's minds off their obsession with the drought. Morale was low; they needed the fair and its music to divert them.

Its arrival came as a surprise, a summer treat. It installed itself almost noiselessly on the building plot beside the last of the new houses under the shadow of San Crescentino. For most of the children, hardened by hundreds of hours of television, the funfair was a disappointment from the day it arrived. Something of the old fair had been handed down through generations. They had heard from their grandparents about the hunchbacked horse, the dozens of huge white oxen dragging equipment along dusty roads. They had heard of the screaming fancy-dress monkeys racing along the caravan roofs. They had heard of the bands of gypsies who manned the stalls, wild colourful men and women who ate raw meat and smoked clay pipes, played violins and danced like frenzied dervishes under the aspen trees.

By unanimous decision, everyone over the age of five decided that the half-breed Irish wolfhound, the morose parrot, the apparently half-witted monkey and the solitary llama tethered to the tow rail of a dilapidated motor home did not live up to the myth. They took their grandparents' descriptions to be yet another exaggeration of the good old days of serfdom, and were irritated with themselves for having fallen for them.

In the days before depilatory cream, there could, of course, have been bearded ladies. They all had at least one hairy female relation. They felt like fools, though, for having ever seriously believed in a spiderwoman. Most of them had seen other fairs, in Castello or Perugia or even further afield on school trips or holidays, but the old people had said scornfully, 'You should have seen the fair that came to San Severino. That was a fair. A human circus, *Dio buono*!'

89

By the time the swings were up on their long chains, suspended from the red and white and green striped maypole, the children had gone back to their football, kicking and sweating through the parched hours of the day. Later, when the music started up in the evening, and some of the children from the outlying hamlets had been brought down to ride on the undulating carousel and get candyfloss moustaches, a few of the children drifted back. By the end of the week, a regular flock of the younger ones stood guard over the llama, supplying her with buckets of water to encourage her to spray any passers-by.

Stefano Altini reported for his first day of duty with Mezzanotte on the same day that the fair arrived. It was 10th June. He had imagined that the sight of a soldier in the village would arouse some curiosity. The situation seemed so odd to him that he thought it must seem equally curious to others. He didn't know it at the time, but he was Mezzanotte's fortieth companion. All the previous soldiers had, like him, shorn hair, a uniform, their youth and a determination to hang on to their comfortable posting. When he went into the lower bar, the woman behind the counter hardly looked up.

'If you're looking for Mezzanotte, he's at the top of the hill and turn right by the church.'

Stefano had been in the bar before, he and his friends stopped there occasionally for ice-creams or petrol on their way through to Castiglione. He had never noticed that it had a village around and behind it. As he walked up the steep hill to the blind man's house he felt that he was walking into a rabbit's warren. There were lanes and narrow alleyways, bits of tunnels and cavernous stone doorways on either side of him. He hoped that he would be able to find his way out again. It ceased to seem like a small medieval village internally updated to the brink of the twenty-first century. He ceased to see the new houses below; the frilly petticoats that hung below the ancient hemline of the village wall. He failed to see the forlorn maypole of the rising funfair. He seemed to be entering a trap, a sinister maze that would swallow him up and never let him get back to the wide open spaces of Castello. By the time he reached

90

the blind man's house, he was afraid. He had heard from the previous companion that he would be expected to stay in a dark room all day, pretending to be busy. He would be expected to hover in silence in his big bare room. When the old man went out, the companion had to stay back. The conscript had to stay with Mezzanotte or where Mezzanotte said. Dereliction of this duty was a court-martial offence.

'So you go to prison if you leave that house, and God help you if you try to help him when he's stumbling around. He has to do everything for himself. I can't imagine why he has a companion with him every day, year after year, it's obviously the last thing he wants. I thought it was just me, you know, that the old man didn't like me for some reason. I didn't want to lose the job or wind up behind bars or something, so I checked with the soldier before me. He said, "He never speaks. Buy yourself a pile of comics and some earphones and tune into the radio." So I did.'

Stefano had wanted to ask the outgoing soldier a lot more questions. He would have liked to meet up with him after his first day in the village and sort out whatever problems might have arisen. But the ex-companion came from Gubbio, so he had only a marginal sympathy for Stefano. There was no love lost between the two cities. And besides, after a year of that clinging claustrophobia he wanted nothing better than to be shot of everything about Mezzanotte and his underworld.

Nobody had ever asked Mezzanotte himself why he kept a companion only to spurn him. Had they done so, he would have answered quite frankly that the Government gave him a companion, a daily escort; it was his right as one of the district's four severely mutilated veterans from the war. He had been brought up not to be wasteful. Thrift and economy had ruled his childhood. His father had been a disappointed man whose best efforts had failed to keep the clammy hand of ruin from knocking at their door. Mezzanotte paid nothing for the conscript. It was like his drawer full of spare arms. He paid nothing for those either. Every five years he was allowed a new one. A health visitor came to his house and explained: he didn't have to have a new arm, but if he wanted one, he could, it was his right. So he took them and they lay in their wrappers, a macabre collection of pristine limbs. Likewise, it had been explained to him that he was entitled to a military companion. Again, he didn't have to accept this, but it was his right. So the succession of soldiers came and went. They never stayed the night. It would have cost him a deduction from his war pension for the soldiers to stay, and he didn't want that. He didn't actually want them at all, but it seemed wasteful to refuse what was his.

He never knew how hard a boy's family fought to pull the strings that could land a lad by his side. Technically, the choice was his, but he had long ago relinquished any interest in who got the post. So of all the escort jobs in central Italy, his was the easiest, the most sought after. Forty favoured youths had sat by his side. Before their job began, they anticipated their eleven months of service with relish. Here was a sinecure if ever there was one. Mezzanotte: midnight. Didn't the very name conjure up good times, discothèques, illicit sex? On the way to their appointment, it carried all these meanings stroked by a moonlit, sensual, black-velvet darkness. However, on the way back from their posting, a pruned year later, the word Mezzanotte summed up an indefinable fear. It was as though the blindness was contagious. They were afraid of his loneliness, and afraid of the fading junctions of pain that traversed his face. When he smiled, a crooked half-smile that rippled the scars on his left cheek, then they were more afraid because it was a rare event, and one that showed them there was a stranger suffocating under that carapace of scars.

As Stefano approached the door of Mezzanotte's basement room, he felt that all the snippets of information that he had received were sitting in his uniform pockets, weighing him down. He hesitated at the door, fearing to go in. He thought of the barracks at Udine. Contrary to what his friend Mario had said, he did not think of grayling or fishing lines or pools, he thought of the barracks themselves, their high barbed-wire fence, the strange environment, the darkness of the dormitory, the loneliness of his time there made bearable by the sure knowledge of his forthcoming reprieve. Stefano was afraid of darkness. He always had been, ever since he was a

92

child. His mother had been kind about it. She had allowed him a night-light by his bed to lessen the terror of the unknown. When she first went away to the clinic, the Judge had discovered and forbidden the night-light. He had told his seven-year-old son to be a man. Stefano imagined a man to be a hybrid somewhere between his father and his uncle Andrea. He decided that he so disliked the barracks that he would do whatever he had to do, touch the parts of this old man that no longer existed if need be. Twice a week he would readjust the plastic arm as he had been shown how to at the hospital in Perugia. He would hover in the darkness while the wounded soldier made his interminable rounds. He would do anything so long as he didn't have to go back to Udine.

The church bell was chiming for the eight o'clock mass. It had a loud distinctive toll as though some defect in its casting had made it reverberate more than other bells. He realized that if he didn't knock soon, nosy churchgoers would come and do it for him, so he plucked up his courage and banged, more loudly than he had intended, on the rough chestnut door.

Once inside he saw Mezzanotte sitting slumped on the edge of his high iron bed.

'Altini Stefano reporting for duty, sir,' he said, saluting and then adding the name of his battalion and his company rather less briskly. He had got it wrong again, got it all in the wrong order. The only tongue twisters he was good at were the obscene ones they had learnt in the playground at school. These army ones were way beyond him. There was an odd smell in the room. It had a faint undertone of age; old food, old clothes, old air and old flesh. He made a mental note to open the window when the old man went on his daily shuffle. He had been warned that Mezzanotte would take little or no notice of him, and he was quite prepared to amuse himself for the day.

'Who are you?' Mezzanotte asked, scarcely raising his head.

'Altini Stefano reporting for duty, sir, from the Military Hospital in Perugia, sir.'

'It's back. After all these years, it's come back to unpick my stitches.' No one had warned Stefano of the desolation in the old

93

man's voice, or of the power he held, concentrated around him like a bitter bale.

'Do you drink, boy?'

'Yes, sir,' Stefano replied and then regretted it. Perhaps that was the wrong answer.

'Drink some *cynar* with me,' the old man said, flatly.

Stefano relaxed his salute and began to search in the debris of the room for some sign of this *cynar*. On a long shelf beside the bed there were three rows of empty *cynar* bottles, each with its artichoke leaf label facing out to him.

'Who are you?' Mezzanotte repeated.

Stefano made a mental note to put sugar in the soldier from Gubbio's petrol tank if he ever met him again. Why hadn't he mentioned that the old man was gaga? Silent was one thing, senile was another. One corner of the room comprised a kitchen. There was a stainless-steel sink and draining board and a small Primus stove of the kind he and his friends took to the beach with them. Beside the Primus stove, ringed on to the Formica table-top by spilt tomato paste, stood a bottle of *cynar*. He held on to the hangover in his stomach and rinsed out two chipped enamel mugs from the congealing sink.

By the time he and Mezzanotte were stumbling down the cock-legged street below the village school, he felt that he had already served a fruitful apprenticeship in the management of the blind. Little things like serving a drink and getting the cup into the blind man's hand had all been accomplished and learnt for future occasions. As to the *cynar*, he had never drunk it in his life before. Its extraordinary bitterness had wrapped itself around the inside of his head and virtually lifted it off his shoulders. Once he had recovered from the savage undertow of its concentrated laxative taste, he could see why the old man drank it. In fact, as he kept hold of Mezzanotte's elbow, he realized that they were steadying each other. He couldn't wait to get back to Castello and tell his friends that this was not just a doddle, it was a drunken doddle at that. The bells were chiming nine o'clock and Stefano already had a beatific smile on his face.

Walking up through the village on his way to Mezzanotte's house he may have aroused no more than the most cursory attention, but walking down with the old man on his arm, everyone who was out and about in the village stopped and stared. No one who had not seen Mezzanotte in this new embrace could believe it; after almost fifty years of reclusion, why had he suddenly changed his ways? They would tell it that night at the bar, to all those who had been away at work and missed the spectacle: 'There was the new recruit with a huge and gormless grin, and there was Mezzanotte almost cracking the surgery on his face as they made their way down the hill to the vineyard.'

Their pace was funereal though their mood was not. Every time they passed a doorway someone spoke out,

'*Salve*, Mezzanotte.'

'*Buon dí*, Giuliana,' or whoever it happened to be. Since the pattern was broken, it continued to break. The women asked Stefano questions, their curiosity getting the better of them.

'You've finally found a real companion, Mezzanotte,' and then to Stefano, 'You must have known each other before. Are you related to Marco? When did you arrive? Is your father coming? Are you an only son or are there more of you? How many? Will you be staying here?'

After each barrage of questions, Mezzanotte squeezed Stefano's arm. They understood each other, not a word to the women, or indeed to the world. They must reserve their talk for each other, and their secrets. The sun was rising higher, it was thirsty work doing these rounds, they should get back to the bar.

They spent the morning commuting from the top to the lower bar. By eleven o'clock Stefano was in grave doubts whether he would be able to stand the pace. He was relieved when Mezzanotte pulled him back into the veiled stagnation of his room.

'My mouth is rusty,' Mezzanotte said and lay back heavily on his unmade bed. He felt as though a bird were being strangled in his throat. He wanted to talk but his voice was full of feathers and blood. He wanted to ask about the fair. He needed to know. Whose funfair was it, was it the Maestro Rossi's? Could Valentina be there? Might they know where she was? Would they tell him?

95

The war had torn his eyes out, but he still saw in his head; it had cut his arm off, but he still felt it hanging by his side. Even without the thick plastic boomerang they had given him, he still felt the weight of his missing arm and the itching of his absent fingers. And he had lost Valentina. She had been both torn and cut from him, but she was always there. The taste of her sweat and of her mouth remained, even though all other tastes had died from him, dulled and dwindled; but not so she. Valentina was clenched in his good hand, stroked by the missing fingers. She lived inside his lacerated brain. She had always lived there. The village had swelled and emptied and swollen again, but her slight, sharp person had never left. He had a part of her, he had been keeping it ever since his last leave from Desenzano, those few precious hours spent with her in Bologna. One day it would fit exactly into the missing part, the matching part of Valentina Rossi, his *fidanzata*. They were to have married immediately the war was over. They should have married then, in 1945. He had waited for her, waited and waited and never given up hope or grown disillusioned like his father.

'My father was a disappointed man,' he told Stefano, 'he used to sit and stare into the fire. I remember that. I vowed then that I would never get like that. Not that there'd be any point in my staring into a fire, I've had all that, it burnt out my head. What I mean is, grief has found me a moving target. I have not sat and let it envelop me.

'I was fifteen when I fell in love. I used to think that to speak of her was to steal something away from her, to lessen what I had. Now, I know that I must speak of her or her memory will begin to fade. It has not faded in forty-nine years until this morning when I heard the arrival of the fair. Fate is unpicking all my stitches. The world inside my head is beginning to escape.

'Have you ever been in love, boy?' Mezzanotte asked him, bringing his big bovine face nearer to Stefano's as though to read the truth of his answer by some method known only to him.

'Yes, a few times.'

'A few, less than lots and more than two. Were you so unlucky then, that nothing lasted? Were you so unlucky as not to know?'

96

Stefano said nothing. Nobody could say he was really unlucky in his love-life, he had the pick of almost every girl he knew. He had more girlfriends than lovers, really, more confidantes. He hadn't come across his Song of Solomon yet, but then he was only twenty-four and he didn't have enough time to spare for this sort of apocalyptic stuff.

'Mezzanotte, o Mezzanotte,' he called, touching him lightly on the shoulder. The old man had fallen asleep. Stefano didn't know whether to undress him or leave him. He was still feeling queasy from all the *cynar*, so he left him, and set to work tipping out the tepid, heaving contents of the sink. Having once started, he felt obliged to continue, but he found it a great test of his courage. He went backwards and forwards to Concetta's little shop buying bleach and a scrubbing brush, a broom, a dustpan, a dishcloth, two new enamel mugs and some bread and fresh pecorino cheese. He quite forgot that for each of these short excursions he could have been court-martialled. He was not allowed to leave the premises without Mezzanotte's permission. In fact, he had a book like a schoolbook which Mezzanotte had to sign each time he left his sight. He remembered laughing about that at Castello, with Mario and Rosanna:

'Well, I suppose the order gives you an insight into the inherent tact and sensitivity of your superior officers.'

Before he left Mezzanotte for the evening, Stefano had come to feel quite at home in the bare concrete room. He had opened the window and changed the air, cleaned up the minuscule kitchenette, straightened up the rest of the room, stocked the food safe, emptied the rubbish and christened the lavatory by being sick in it twice. By half-past five he was ready to go. Mezzanotte was still comatose on his bed. Stefano curbed the desire to leave him a note. Perhaps his officers weren't as stupid as they sounded; it was difficult to remember that Mezzanotte was blind. He didn't know if he had been a good nurse or a good housewife, but he felt pleased with himself.

As he drove back along the crowded road to Castello, he made a mental note not to mock Mezzanotte with his friends that night. It

97

was always so easy to make people laugh by imitating others. He could have done a perfect Mezzanotte: the lurch, the stiff arm, the biblical boom to his voice. He felt a sudden urge to go back to see if the old man was all right. His car swerved off the road and on to the grass verge. The driver of the car behind him booed and jeered.

'Imbecile! Road hog! Don't you know where you're going?'

Stefano smiled to himself, and steered back into the traffic. He was going to Castello, to the Bar Italia. It was nearly six o'clock and far from yearning for a drink, he felt strangely sentimental.

VII

When Stefano arrived at the village the next morning, he got the impression that Mezzanotte was waiting for him. He arrived without any of the previous morning's dread, armed with a packet of indigestion tablets. He had also taken the precaution of having an extra brioche with his milky coffee so as not to start drinking *cynar* on an empty stomach. Mezzanotte was sitting on the edge of his bed again, but he was neither slumped nor despondent. Stefano took up the greeting of the village which he had heard the day before and combined it with his more official one.

'*Salve*, Mezzanotte. Altini Stefano reporting for duty, sir.'

'Altini,' he said, as though hearing the name for the first time. 'Altini . . . there used to be Altinis in the Petriolo valley. We used to sell partridge eggs there when I was a boy. It was a long way over the hill, too far usually to bother with.

'I was waiting for you. I have an errand. I want you to go down to the funfair and find out what you can. Firstly, how long will it stay? That is crucial. Then find out who owns it. I am looking for a girl called Valentina Rossi. The gypsies are jealous of their women, so be careful who you speak to. She has speckled brown eyes like a sparrow's wing, long, long black hair and skin the colour of baled hay. Her hands are thin and quick-moving with chiselled ends to her fingers. On her neck there is a beauty spot just below her ear, but it is hard to see for the darkness and the thickness of her hair coiling into the nape.

'Go down to the fairground for me and tell me if she is there.'

It didn't take Stefano long to question everyone involved in the fair. There were only five of them, and three small boys who trailed after him, intrigued that anyone should show interest in their entourage by day. The opening night had been disappointing, so

99

much so that although the proprietor had a healthy dislike of the police and the army and tended to steer clear of anyone in a uniform, he was content to ease the tedium of his morning by talking to this curious recruit. The proprietor had been trained in the circus. Some people would say he had been brought up in a fairground but he liked to refer to the splendid, crowded sights of his boyhood as a circus to differentiate them from today's pathetic sideshows huddled around the mechanical high-flying swings. He had been brought up to tend the animals. It was he who had to rise at four or five o'clock every morning and procure fodder for their motley convoy of beasts.

At first he had been assistant forager, under the tutelage of a savage older boy. By the time the job fell to him, he had grown to love the animals. He found solace in their company. He kept them well, or as well as he could; and he was proud to steal the hay and corn from other people's barns. They had a stock of their own food, of course, for when the *carabinieri* should be called round to investigate complaints, but they mostly depended on the unwitting bounty of others. He had risen so early every day that it had become a habit, a reflex, something ingrained in his system. Now that the remnants of the fair were his, he still rose early. There was nothing to do any more. The mornings had died for him. He kept on the llama, the parrot and the dog against all the derision of his family. He felt more in common with the animals than he did with his wife sometimes. Best of all he loved his monkey, Tita, who pretended to ignore the world, keeping all her attention and high spirits for him alone. Tita was like a treasured and loyal mistress, hiding all her charms, incapable of flirting with friends or strangers.

The proprietor rose early and wandered disconsolately around the balding field. When he saw the soldier coming up to speak to him, he felt a sense of relief.

'Hello,' Stefano called. 'Forgive the intrusion, but I've never seen a funfair from close up and I wanted to come and have a look at it. You don't see a llama every day around Castello. It is a llama, isn't it?'

'She is indeed, a Peruvian llama, the last of three. They used to do an act together, jumping through a fiery hoop and then spitting the fire out. The others died years ago . . .'

'My father used to talk about a funfair, the Maestro Rossi's Fair. Have you ever come across it?'

'Come across it?' he laughed. 'I am it, *sono io*!' And he pointed to himself, giving congratulatory pats to his chest.

'Then you are the Maestro Rossi?'

'I don't know, do I look as though I were over a hundred years old and had been dead for the last forty years?'

'Forgive me, I . . .'

'Maestro Rossi's, yes this is his fair. But the Maestro Rossi in person was killed in Calabria just after the war. I was a boy at the time. I don't remember it well. I know he was a brawler, everyone said he was. He'd turn up of an evening and the first person to look sideways at him would be his man. They knifed him down in the South. He was a ladies' man, I've heard say, and that doesn't go down too well there.'

Stefano had grown silent. He was still attentive, but he made no attempt to interrupt. He did not know it but this was the very way to induce the proprietor to speak.

'Eh, and if you're wondering about the children, I'll tell you. The Maestro Rossi had enough bastard sons to make up a private army. He could have organized them and liberated Italy without the help of the Americans. Imagine it, he could have been the new President, but no, he never recognized a single one of them. After he died, they came out of the ground. If they were old enough to grow a moustache, they started training them down and out into the handlebars that the Maestro had himself, as though to emphasize the likeness. Some of them, I tell you, some of them were dead ringers. You didn't need a document or a surname to know that some of those little buggers were Rossi's. But, like I said, he never recognized them in his lifetime, so it was useless them trying to claim a part of his legacy after his death.

'I was ten when he died. Everything went to his nephew, Garibaldi Rossi. The Maestro doted on that boy. He was blind to

101

all his faults. It was Garibaldi who ruined the fair; his only interest in it was as a way of bringing in young boys. His uncle was a ladies' man, but the nephew wasn't. It wasn't queue up for the stalls with him, it was queue up for his own caravan. He wasn't a bad man, just weak. He fell in love with a lad from Le Marche and they lived together for two years like a honeymoon, selling this and that. Selling my animals, the carts and caravans, the big marquee. They managed to get electricity into their caravan using a car battery, and they set up a gramophone. They used to play American music all through the night. Some of the crew said it was to disguise their caterwauling, but I looked through the window and I know that they danced to those love songs, holding each other tight.

'Once the equipment was gone, and the money ran out, his lover disappeared. We searched for him up and down the country. We scoured Le Marche, visiting every village and every hamlet, and that finished off a lot of what had survived in the way of transport. One morning he called out of his caravan for help. He was dead by the afternoon. They say he had seven heart attacks that day. Evil tongues say he probably had seven men in the night.' The proprietor shrugged and began to untwist the llama hair that he had been unthinkingly plaiting.

'There weren't many of us left by then. A few of our crew scarpered before the police were called in to the body. That really left just me and Emiliana Cotechini with any say in the future of the fair. So we married and here we are. But I tell you, you've no idea what the circus I grew up in was like. It wasn't at all like this.

'One day, who knows, if I win the lottery, I'll put the zoo back and the trailers. I'll get a rhinoceros, too.'

'And the daughter,' Stefano asked gently. 'The Maestro Rossi's daughter?'

'Eh,' the proprietor said, shaking his head somewhat irritably as though awoken from a dream, 'didn't I tell you, there were literally hundreds of kids, girls and boys, all claiming to be Rossi's children.'

'Yes, yes, I understand, but my father said, in the times when he

102

knew Rossi, ten or thirteen years before that, there was a daughter, a grown-up daughter who lived with him, a pretty girl with black hair.'

'Yes, you're right, there was that daughter, not that I've ever heard her called pretty, sharp more like. But she didn't live with him. She was brought up by the gypsy Agata. Something happened, though, during the war. She ceased to exist. Not dead, mind, just never mentioned again. Some disgrace or other − you can imagine, on a fairground there was plenty of space for that, and plenty of opportunity.'

'Valentina, Valentina Rossi.'

'That's right . . . a bit less of the Rossi, though, since the old man disinherited her. He was a vengeful old tyrant. I wouldn't put it past him to persecute me from the grave.' At the word grave, the proprietor's right hand shot out to ward off the evil eye.

'Wasn't she engaged to a soldier?' Stefano insisted.

'*Oddio!*' the proprietor shouted petulantly. 'What is this, an interrogation? How would I know, haven't I just told you that she disappeared when I was a tiny child? Has your uniform gone to your head? Get off my site, this is a fairground here, you know. Can't you read the sign? Keep out, go away.'

Stefano beat a retreat, muttering apologies as he went. The women from the house nearest to the fair were leaning out of a window to see what the shouting was about. Looking back from the street above the site he saw that an approximate square of land had been demarcated by a strip of plastic ribbon wrapped about some sticks. One of these sticks had a notice hanging from it, facing the street. It read:

PRIVATE. KEEP OUT.
AUTHORIZED PERSONNEL ONLY.
BEWARE DANGEROUS ANIMALS.

Later, Mezzanotte told him:

'I'm not sorry that she isn't there. I would be sorry if she was. She never had much to do with the real world, she lived on dreams

103

and trinkets. She reinvented her past and then she worshipped it. She had little regard for truth, she reconstructed events to suit her. Her future was something she imagined and then projected on to a screen. The present was of scarcely any interest to her. She had so little upon which to build her past, yet her greatest enjoyment lay there. They say that lovers grow to be like each other, adopting each other's likes and beliefs. I know I have grown to resemble Valentina in that respect at least.

'My past was not built on sand, it was built into the rocks of this valley, it was embedded in and between all the stones of this village. Of the past that she cared for, she had only her trinkets; the pink and green beaded evening bag, the photograph I ruined myself, a chipped tortoiseshell comb and a pair of dancing shoes. From these Valentina created not just a mother, but an entire family and a life to support them.'

Mezzanotte paused, thinking that he had so many touchstones, they could wear his fingers down. 'Her past had been spent out in the open fields, along the open roads, covered by clouds of dust. Everywhere the funfair stopped, bits of that treasured past could be forgotten, left behind, rubbed away. After they had gone, grass and weeds would grow over the place where this fragile past was scattered. If they didn't return again, if they chose a different route to follow with their convoy, nobody would be able to find the lost fragments again. Valentina was vulnerable, she always had been, we both knew it.'

By contrast, he lived in an impregnable beehive. Every cell of his memory remained intact. If he were to forget anything, the village was like a museum. Anyone who blurred on a detail could call a junta down at the bar and ask. Their lives were mutually monitored and their archives communally stored. Even his love for Valentina was known and registered. It was not approved of, but it was accepted with the same resignation with which other unpleasant events had been accepted. Nobody actually liked the earthquake of 1917, yet nobody could deny it had happened or diminish the damage it had caused.

As a boy, he had been almost unaware of his past. Certain relations impinged on his consciousness, his grandparents for instance, whose backs were bowed by their memories. For him, life was the present, infinitely extended into the future like a magical piece of elastic that never broke.

'Valentina saw time differently. For her, the present was merely a doorway into the future. She was able to ignore her immediate surroundings so long as she saw an enjoyable ride ahead. Her past was sacred and her future must always be bright, as gleaming and multifaceted as the gypsy Emiliana's crystal ball.

'Valentina didn't let me down. I let her down. She depended on me. She loved me, I know she did. She wanted me to share in her visions, walking into all these chinks of light.

'She was happiest when we were dancing, even happier, I think now, than when we were making love. "My mother was a dancer," she'd tell me, with all her authority and knowledge invested in that one abandoned pair of dancing shoes. At the time, it puzzled me why no one ever talked about Valentina's mother. She had ceased to exist, not dead − though she might have been − but disgraced somehow in their eyes.

'I have often wondered whether Valentina fell in love with me in the hope that I would carry her off and disgrace her in the eyes of her father, thus making her even more like her mother.

'I walk and my shoes collide, my shoulders scrape against shifted barriers. Distances expand, but the world is a watery labyrinth that I have learnt to navigate. The darkness of the day is as nothing to the darkness of desolation. I have known them both.

'I have never felt able to talk of certain things to my neighbours. So I have missed the chance of taking part in their more serious talks and of sharing their emotions. It was my choice, and they respected me. I have many times wished to break out of the mould, but I know it is dangerous to disrupt rituals. It would be like waking a sleepwalker. I have lain like a splinter of shrapnel in their flesh for so long that it has healed and scarred and the scar has faded. To change would be to reopen that wound.

'Under the surface, all these people have suffered. There is not one of them born before the war who could not dredge up the stuff

105

of nightmares. How long do things get talked about? How long is a period of mourning, how long should grief be permitted to last? Our lives would stop without the social rituals. Speech has to become thought if it is to avoid becoming madness. And now thought has become speech again for me.'

Over the weeks that followed, Mezzanotte spoke to Stefano of his love. It was a love that had begun when he was a boy and had never ended. It was a love so strong with remembered passion that it made Stefano ask himself many times if indeed he had been unlucky not to know one like it. Each day, as he drove to and from Mezzanotte's village, with the top of his Alfa Romeo rolled back and the radio blasting out some momentarily favourite song, he noticed more and more of the clusters of houses that adjoined the road. He found it disconcerting that these hamlets were all unknown territory to him. He knew only how to cut past them; if his car broke down and he had to find his way to their stone centres, he would be lost.

By the autumn, he had taken to spending more and more time with Mezzanotte. He still arrived punctually at eight o'clock, parked his car in front of the lower bar and walked up the slope to the accompaniment of the erratic church bell of Santa Maria and the more regular echo of San Crescentino. Yet when it came to leaving, where before he had stolen glances at his wide-faced watch, he now forgot the time and often found the evening well advanced before he began to make his way.

Mezzanotte himself knew the time whenever he stopped to think about it. He could tell it from the footsteps, voices and general noises of the street. He could tell it by the heaviness of the air and the calls of birds. There were evenings when his monologues carried him away and he would become lost to the passing hours. Even so, he would usually realize, before Stefano, that the afternoon had slipped away and his companion was due to leave. It had taken Mezzanotte several months to call Stefano by his name. To begin with he had been 'boy', then he had tried Altini; it was only since the week when the grapes had been harvested and together they

106

had forayed to all the neighbours' vineyards, sampling now this grape juice and now that, always accompanied by a sip of the last year's wine, that they had become friends enough for Mezzanotte to address him as Stefano. Stefano felt able to carry a bottle of *cynar* in his pocket and pour it into every glass that Mezzanotte sampled and laugh with him over the result until much of the village was laughing; but out of respect, he continued to call him Mezzanotte.

In October the village was deserted in the evenings for the bringing in of the grapes. In November it was deserted for the gathering of the olives. The pockets of hillside containing the squat olive groves were festooned with bright orange nets. All the groves were out of bounds, off Mezzanotte's beat, even the nearest ones at Nuvole were too far away. Stefano offered to drive him up towards Sant Agnese to be close to the harvest, but he declined. It was a bad year, and only a few *quintales* per hectare were being taken down to the press at the Castello end of the village. There was talk of this presaging a bad winter, as bad, some said, as the winter of '84. The olives and the old people had succumbed that winter. People who had survived everything from the earthquake to the Occupation, and who had seen their world become more fantastic by means of technology than any funfair, were carried off by the cold.

'Eh, *si*, eh,' they all agreed that had been a bad year and there was another one coming.

'O Stefano, what are you doing here at this time of night? Be on your way.'

More and more, Stefano would have liked to stay. He had become involved in the story, he was anxious to know what happened to all the different characters, all the strands of the skein that Mezzanotte was winding. He also found his life as a budding gourmet mysteriously suspended. He felt little appetite for the lavish meals he had gorged on for the last ten years. He found himself longing to be invited to stay and share Mezzanotte's nightly dish of *penne al pomodoro*. One day he plucked up the courage to ask him why he always ate the same frugal dish of macaroni with tomato sauce.

'I don't know,' Mezzanotte told him. 'I suppose it was the first thing I learnt to cook by myself and I have grown used to it, it seems like family. Almost every day Assuntina says to go up and eat dinner with her family. She is kindness itself to me, she offers to bring my dinner down here if I want to eat alone. But I like my independence, and then, food has a strange flavour for me. Like everything else I have to decipher what it means, what it tastes like. All the sweet things in my life are inside my head. Smell is a foreign language. I don't always have my dictionary to hand. It can confuse me very easily. Food and drink have the power to destabilize my life.'

At first, it had seemed that it was Mezzanotte who was most keen to talk to Stefano; by the time the last flagons of thick virgin olive oil were ready, Stefano was equally keen to listen. By day he sat on the edge of the bed by the old man; by night he lay in his own room in Castello with its fitted shelves for encyclopaedias and trophies and he dreamed about Valentina and the young Alessandro and the passion that had taken them across the entire peninsula.

He began to see Valentina Rossi as Mezzanotte saw her and not as she must be now: a 67-year-old gypsy woman with a past. She had been nineteen when Mezzanotte last saw her and she would always be locked at that age. So she seemed, by some strange treachery, a girl more fitting for himself than for the old man who loved her. One night he dreamt that he was holding her, burying his face into the nape of her neck, burrowing with his sex between her thighs. There was music in his dream, the rising and falling of a carousel surging with his own body as it drove deeper and deeper inside her. Mezzanotte had said that in winter her skin had the hue of the flesh of a boiled chestnut. He felt his hands kneading that beige transparency and tasting now not only the rubbery taste that Mezzanotte had described with its blend of burnt sugar and rosemary-flower water, but also the thick doughy taste of boiled chestnuts. He came and woke simultaneously, calling out in a moan of pleasure that turned to shame.

That year, the winter arrived without any of its usual preliminaries. It set in overnight, besieging the whole of Castello with frost. The streets were slippery with ice, the fountains froze. Car doors refused to unlock. Entire façades of geraniums in window boxes froze and died. Lemon trees dried in their summer pots and oleanders lost their limbs. Central-heating systems burst, together with thousands of water supply pipes. Statues cracked in the public gardens, pieces of cornice fell off the churches. The whole of central Italy was unprepared for this vicious climatic reprisal. For Stefano, it was the first day that he was late for Mezzanotte. Even on those nights when he had relented and joined his friends and made such exhaustive rounds of the bars and discothèques that none of them got to bed before six, he still crawled into Mezzanotte's village punctually by eight.

For reasons Stefano did not understand and did not want, he was beginning to grow away from his friends. There was always a place for him in their group and he felt that there always would be, but the reins that he had taken such care to hold firmly in his own hands were slipping. He used his military service as an excuse. It was always, 'I can't get round to the basketball practice, I'm tied up with my invalid.' If he was at home, brooding in his room, he would often tell his friends, 'No, I can't play in the match tomorrow, I'm tied up with my invalid.' It was always with his 'invalid', he didn't refer to Mezzanotte's blindness in front of his friends. He didn't like the talk that inevitably followed about the name. It was strange for a blind man to be called midnight, he knew, but he didn't want anyone else to point it out. When his father, who was more intrusive than his friends, came into his room and tried to lure him down for a drink and what he called a chat, Stefano always refused him too, pleading legal case histories to read up. He regretted only that there was nothing to read. All Mezzanotte's background was inside his head.

Sometimes he despaired of ever getting to know his charge. He felt that the months were running out. When he started, eleven months had seemed interminably long; now, half-way through the stint, he feared what he would do when it was over. He knew so much about the missing Valentina that he physically desired her, but he still knew very little of Mezzanotte himself. He knew from the hospital that he had been blown up by a shell. He knew for himself that he had lived inside a shell for half a century.

109

Stefano began to sleep badly, waking in the night and lying staring at the shadows on the ceiling while his mind wandered in and out of unspeakable fears. He thought of his mother, and how nobody, not even Fabrizia, had ever told him, 'She's not coming back,' she just hadn't. At first, because she had been away before and always returned, he was not afraid. She would be back soon, and she'd be awake. His father, who had no difficulty in sending people to prison for the rest of their lives and who always rolled his r's when pronouncing sentence as though he relished it, felt embarrassed to tell his son of his mother's permanent exile. It was after she had left the house for good that Stefano experienced his worst fears. He was afraid to sleep for what that void might bring. The Judge's brusque methods didn't cure his terrors, they just drove them inwards until he could cover them up.

Night after night he trained himself not to think. Not to think about the darkness and the fear it hid; not to think about his mother, her absence, her illness. He taught himself not to deal with anything but surfaces, and he learnt to feel his way along them. School had been a dangerous place which threatened at any moment to disrupt the delicate balance he had achieved with his subconscious. He had excelled at sports and had thus protected himself from the necessity of thinking.

Now, night after night as the frost crept through the town, Stefano lay awake hoping that Mezzanotte would exorcize his childhood fears.

IV

THE ACCIDENT

VIII

The winter brought a wind so sharp it killed Assunta Giuliani's budgerigar. Every chicken in the village stopped laying eggs. A new-born baby died in the parish of San Severino and then the baby's grandfather caught a chill at the funeral and was buried beside him only a fortnight later. One afternoon a cloud of orange dust passed over Mezzanotte's village and settled in a vivid film over everything. They said in the bar that it was sand from the Sahara brought up by a freak sirocco. The cold turned the scars on Mezzanotte's face a blue-grey which contrasted oddly with the baby-doll pink of his plastic hand. The old man's skin looked like a faded railway map with its stitched lines and innumerable junctions prickling him to remember his boyhood wanderings. The branchlines and mainlines of the railways of central Italy were traced indelibly across his face.

Once he had owned a battered timetable with all the times of all the trains, even the most remote ones, even the night trains that crawled down to the farthest parts of Calabria and the mountain lines that veered over precipitous tracks along the Ligurian coast. He had found it in a litter bin on Forlì station, and treasured and memorized it over the next four years. It was thanks to this timetable that he was able to follow the fair; thanks entirely to its deciphering of the intricacies of the thousands of possible connections that had led him week after week to Valentina.

It was the pride of the Leader that all the trains ran on time. If Alessandro's timetable showed him that he had four minutes to change trains at Arezzo, he need only rely on the swiftness of his own feet as he ran under the tunnels to reach the platform – also shown in his railway bible – and rendezvous in Montevarchi or Impruneta, Empoli or Pistoia, Bibbiena or Borgo San Lorenzo would always be possible.

When the fair had first left San Severino and decamped to Umbertide some fifteen miles away, Mezzanotte had risen before dawn and tramped the broken roads to the outskirts of that town to sit on the banks of the Tiber and push his feet into bulrushes carded by finches into sticks of white candyfloss. He felt both afraid and excited to be courting Valentina so far from home. He knew that if he waited for the return of the Maestro Rossi's fair the following year, the girl with the speckled eyes whom he loved so suddenly would scarcely remember him. Instinct told him to follow his prey, to track her down relentlessly and give no quarter in his pursuit of her favours. She was a girl besieged by attentions, surrounded by boys far worthier and more handsome, no doubt, than himself. His only hope was to be like the poor boy of the legends who slayed dragons and travelled to the ends of the earth to bring back the arbitrary prizes set to discourage him. He would follow and follow her, a suitor in search of a pearl. He would prove his love to her, and to her father, and to the gypsy Agata who despised him but still allowed his love to flourish as part of some personal vendetta against Valentina's father. All around the fair there were webs of intrigue like the frail grey bandages of spiders' webs.

When it rained, there was a silt of slime where wheels and hoofs and many feet had pounded the mud into a swallowing bog. When it was hot, the debris of the fair, the detritus of the stalls and the excrement and rotting food of the animals putrefied and stank. Every week the young Mezzanotte made his way through this mess, immune to all political and social nuance, led only by his love, as by a star, to the place where he would find Valentina waiting. Week after week he reached her, forcing himself out of his shell to sit by her and then to hold her hand, and then to touch her cheeks, her olive forehead, her lips, and little by little all of her, except the mystery that she kept hidden in her head and only seemed to unknot and accept him when he held her tightly and turned her round and round to the tune of a polka, a waltz or a mazurka.

Mezzanotte often wondered whether she would have loved him if he hadn't been able to dance, and he thanked God that his

114

brother Elio was the village musician who practised endlessly on his accordion, forcing his brothers and their little sister to dance to his tunes. Sometimes they danced together, in couples, boys and girls, boys and boys, girls and girls, but mostly they danced with partners hacked out of the hills: armfuls of broom twigs that began life as surrogate girls with the soft scent of honey and sex and ended it dried and wizened as bundles of kindling. Alessandro learnt to dance as a tiny boy stumbling beside his brother Marco, tripping over and then twirling his broom twigs. By the time he was fifteen, he was one of the most accomplished dancers in the village; despite his size, he was delicate on his feet and his sense of rhythm was perfect. He had long since surpassed Marco, who was also a good dancer. On summer nights, in the clearing in front of the old *palazzo* on the hill with its ruined towers and its hundreds of flapping shutters and its façade of sculpted terracotta, he had danced with most of the women in the village. Old and young turned out for these dances. With the cypress trees filtering the moonlight, he had perfected routines that would later impress the dance-hungry Valentina.

Valentina had grown up so accustomed to rarities that her sense of wonder was in suspension. The miraculous was not enough for her; she needed more. As a child she had been visually sated, smothered by an excess of curiosities so that her appetites tended to be either dormant or depraved. She either ignored people or she expected them to perform continual tricks for her. However, her boredom with life and her occasional caprice were never enough so much as to take the edge off Alessandro's own sense of wonder. Through Valentina he discovered love, sex and a life outside his village; and as a continual bonus, there was the phenomenon of the fair. It was a mixture of this enthusiasm together with his tenacity which eventually won him his girl. His excitement moved her where the animals and the antics of the fair itself that were eliciting his response had failed to do so. Knowing that the hunchbacked horses were actually camels brought from a Roman zoo did not alter his astonishment every time he came face to face with them. Knowing that camels came from Africa, from the Sahara desert where they

115

walked for weeks on end without drinking any water, picking their way over endless fields of sand, merely made them the more remarkable. He had heard a great deal of talk about these hunchbacked horses, not only in his village, but in his family: his maternal grandmother had conversed regularly with one over by Ghironzo. Alessandro knew that the circus camels were called Leviticus and Sabia. Whenever he went to the fair and found himself waiting for Valentina, he would speak to them gently, calling them by their names, always hoping that one or other of them would answer him, as they had answered the old lady in the woods.

It seemed to Alessandro that the fair was like a troupe of fallen angels: a band of superior beings who made a virtue of, and a living from, being so entirely out of place. If one day Valentina had pulled out a crumpled tissue from her bag and told him it was her birth certificate from a distant star, he would have easily believed her. She herself had a power and a beauty that set her aside from any other girl. Her mother was an enigma. Her father with his huge moustachios and his rhinoceros-hide whip, his striding boots and his eagle eyes, stood out among men. Nando *il Nano* was, without doubt, the smallest dwarf Alessandro had ever seen. And although the spiderwoman didn't really look like a spider, she did have arms so long she could scratch her ankles without bending down, and a terrible thinness. Then, the fat lady was hugely fat and the bearded lady was bearded; and the spangled Cotechini twins could walk their tightropes and turn somersaults in the sawdust with an agility that defied human skills.

There always seemed to be dozens of people attached to the fair, and dozens of children crawling in and out from under the caravans. Alessandro was so full of his love and so surprised at having managed to find her again among all the baffling obstacles that fate and geography had put in his way that he failed to notice the hostility with which his arrival at the fairground was greeted. He knew that the gypsy Agata hated him, but then he knew he was stealing her charge. He was blind to the others' dislike. It never occurred to him that other hands than his had long been reserved to hold the Maestro Rossi's daughter. At first, the affair began because nobody

116

believed that a child as spoilt and as fine as Valentina could possibly fall for a penniless peasant boy too young to grow a beard. Once the love was declared, several crystal balls were consulted and all blurred identically, assuring a bad end to the affair and a short duration. Everyone was confident that the Maestro Rossi himself would come down like the wrath of God on his daughter and protect his honour and whip some sense back into the ungrateful girl. They were sure that the Maestro would not tolerate such goings on. He was a hard man, a libertine, but a hard master. No one would ever be good enough for his daughter: Valentina, the one and only recognized Rossi. The Apennines and their surrounding plains were as full of little Rossis as the wheels of their carts were full of flakes of rust, but the Maestro was a lover and a leaver. Of all his scattered progeny, Valentina alone had been cosseted and groomed to inherit the fair and all its paraphernalia.

It was the gypsy Agata who had kept up a grumbling commentary on the Maestro's doings during the preceding decade, and it was she who would sit on the wooden steps of her caravan and say to anyone and to everyone and to nobody in particular, 'Sometimes the fire-eater burns his throat, and sometimes a twin falls off her rope, sometimes the stalls are empty and the candyfloss goes grey with dust. Sometimes the Maestro goes blue with rage and sometimes he goes blue with lust. In my time I've seen most things and I certainly never expected to be surprised again . . . certainly not that. Now something has flown into the Maestro's head and captured his brain.' Then she would shrug and tut and shake her head for so long that anyone who didn't know her would think that she was seized with St Vitus's dance or some other rare disease.

When she had finally shaken the disgust from her body she would return grimly to her jars and phials of bitter herbs and grasses. Her dark caravan was full of twists of paper with dried leaves and sprigs of herbs hung out around the black stovepipe. The gypsy Agata had a cure for most ailments, both physical and spiritual. Although she had no particular friends in the troupe, she commanded respect, she was their doctor, the ironer of their creased

117

limbs, the soother of their minds. She was not only the keeper of the Maestro's daughter; she alone knew all the byways of even the most misshapen of their bodies. She knew the aches and pains concomitant with monstrous obesity and both atrophied and extended arms. When she sat mumbling and grumbling on the weatherbeaten steps of her caravan, the others assumed that her bile – made manifest by the frequency of her spitting – was the aftermath of her medical inquiries.

When Annibale D'Agnano, who swallowed fire and was obsessed by cleanliness, made his way down to the river that was to service their camp for yet another bath and scrub of his unnaturally white skin, he whistled and called to her.

'O Agata!'

'*Buon dì*, Annibale.'

'I'm off to bathe,' he croaked through his damaged vocal cords.

'Too much water will wash away your person. Purify yourself from within. I've got a little potion for you, come up and I'll give it to you.'

Annibale D'Agnano smiled wryly and went on his way. He was afraid of the gypsy Agata and her potions, more afraid almost than he was of being dirty. He never went voluntarily to her cabinet. Sometimes when things went wrong and he burnt his throat, the others dragged him there and she had ways of dousing the fire in his head. But there was something dark and sinister about her ways. He preferred to throw himself into a cold stream and finger the weeds underwater and watch the small fish darting past his naked flesh. He preferred to crouch in deep pools as motionless as a stone. He had seen herons make their nests, he had seen otters mating, he had seen Valentina bathing in her cotton shift and he had seen the peasant boy making love to her.

Some of the men on the fairground, ranging from Nando *il Nano* to the Cotechini twins' decrepit father, were in love with Valentina Rossi. Annibale himself had lusted after her, and still would from time to time for years to come. But he didn't love her or fantasize about running away with her, as the others did. She was half-Rossi and Rossi was half-devil. He didn't like the Maestro and he didn't

118

want to tie his blood to any of his kind, no matter how great the dowry. The brothers Mario and Lorenzo – whose looks and size testified ill to the loyalty of their mother: Mario being short, fat and extraordinarily blond with pale-blue Ligurian eyes, while Lorenzo, the elder, was massively tall, swarthy and almost entirely covered in thick black hair – swore a pact on an open wound to share whatever gains they made through wooing Valentina. They had given the child years of free rides and suffered entire afternoons of playing peg doll and hoopla to gain her affections. Knowing that they sought her as a wife, they had both restrained themselves, waiting for the girl to grow. Mario, the plump blond brother, had just launched the first phase of his courtship when the peasant interloper came along. Mario swore that his attentions were being well received. The brothers' dream of owning the carousel that their family had so diligently greased and painted for as long as they could remember began to fade. Consequently, they hated Alessandro Mezzanotte, and they began to stir up as much hostility to him as they could in the camp. They paid old women to say strange incantations around his name. They stole his handkerchief and used it to set the evil eye to watch over him. Behind Valentina's back, they spoke ill of her lover at all times.

As the summer passed and the grapes began to ripen on their vines and the fair progressed in its slow dusty procession to Castello and San Giustino, Sansepolcro and Poppi and back down behind the hills to Arezzo and Cortona and the Lake, Alessandro became a man. He began to find his way across the cat's cradle of the railway lines. By the time the fair struck camp for the worst of the winter, sheltered outside the town of Castiglione del Lago, he knew his way round the system so well that he had begun weaving his own web of journeys made and remade, crisscrossing the countryside in gossamer threads. His father beat him and his mother begged him, but to no avail, he lived for his new love. He became stronger than ever before, he worked like a tamed beast in the fields, adding almost as much as the oxen themselves to any day's labour. No one could criticize him for neglecting his duty, he worked in a frenzy as though by the sheer force of his energy he could push the week

119

forward, rolling it like a giant bale of hay from Monday to Sunday so that he could set out again and find the Maestro Rossi's fair.

Both his enemies in the fairground and his family were sure that Alessandro would be defeated by distance. Even Valentina had allowed herself to be swept off her feet believing that certain escape was hers as soon as the fair moved beyond his walking distance. She had allowed sides of her character to show that she might otherwise have kept hidden. Like a very superior species of fly, she was held within his web.

'In those days I was immune to cold. When I was a little boy, when winter came, I remember crying over my chilblains. Once, when my lips cracked and bled and my whole face felt as though it had been flayed, Aurelio Venturini told me to eat straw to make it better. I did and I can still remember the feel of the dry stalks spiking my cuts and the taste of blood, and my foolishness. I didn't speak to Aurelio for years after that. I didn't forgive in those days. My feet were warm in my olive clogs and we put straw in them in winter, but my hands and my head suffered in the wind and rain, I suppose I was a delicate child, I grew strong later. When I first started working in the fields, I used to pray for the sun to go away and stop tormenting me. Then I thought I was going to collapse and die like old Ferini's mule when the cold weather came. By the time I was fifteen I was used to the cold. I know the journeys were hard because my family went on and on about them, but I didn't ever notice either cold or rain.

'For the first two hours I walked to the station at Santa Lucia, then I bought my ticket and caught my train. Two things enabled me to travel that way. The first was talk I'd heard down at the bar. People said our area had the best wood in Italy. They said the Romans used us to ferry out their wood and also that all the railway sleepers of Italy came from us. They said our ancestors died cutting the oaks that made up the railways. The further the tracks were laid, the more woodmen died for it. So I knew that there was a railway and I knew that under its tracks were my people; my dead ancestors were paving the way across the entire country. So no soil

120

was foreign soil to me, contrary to what my family said, for so long as I stayed on a train there were people from my village under me. I rode over their bones. They kept me company through many otherwise lonely hours.'

Mezzanotte stopped talking as abruptly as he had begun. He shook his head slowly so that his grey hair shuffled across his forehead. After a long, uneasy pause, he said, 'I didn't feel the cold on my way to Valentina, but I do now.'

Stefano stirred and then rose to fetch a rug to wrap around the old man.

'Where are you going?' Mezzanotte demanded.

'I'm just getting a rug from the chest.'

'No, let it be, Stefano, the cold is inside my head now, it cannot be eased by rugs. It just froze my thoughts for a moment. Don't worry, I'll pick up where I stopped, I hardly ever lose my thread. I've been feeling my way through my life and my past for so long now that I know my way around my memories. I'm just not used to talking. Sometimes, I think my life is like one of my grandmother's misshapen socks; I unravel it, undoing all her laborious work, and I come back to a beautiful ball of wool ready to be used again.

'Do you know how I paid for those trips?'

'No,' Stefano murmured.

'Guess,' Mezzanotte urged him.

'I don't know. I suppose you worked extra hours.'

Mezzanotte smiled. 'There would never have been hours enough in a year to pay for so much as one train ride. The system took care of that. We never had any money, only debts to the *padrone*. Our debts grew like puffball mushrooms in a wood, they swelled and inflated depending on the size of our wages. Whenever anything happened to enable us to get some ready money, then the puffball exploded and spread its spores for miles around to grow again.

'Sometimes we could gather wild things and sell them, but that was mostly forbidden too, and to sell in the neighbourhood meant risking being denounced and either flogged or sent to prison for poaching on private land.

121

'It was the Maestro Rossi himself who saved me. The Maestro Rossi had a huge leather belt with an enormous silver buckle which he claimed had been hand-beaten in Argentina. When he sat down to eat a meal, he said he only ever felt satisfied if he had to release his buckle and ease his belt a notch. Despite the relative squalor of his life on the road, traipsing around with his convoy in tow, living without any kind of sanitation, the Maestro was a gourmet. He lived for women and gastronomic delicacies.

'There were boys in his fairground who could steal a chicken or a duck with such alacrity that I hardly saw the animal disappear or heard it cluck its last muted protest. The Maestro never went short of food, but he balked at paying the prices asked for in the fancy shops, and his tribe of urchins moved too often and worked too hard on the fairground to have the time or the knowledge to know a patch of countryside as well as the least of us village boys. The land was our work and the woods were our entertainment. We knew every inch of both when it came to truffles, be they black or white, and the finer, rarer *funghi*, if the season was right, I would always know where to find them. I could bring the Maestro snipe as it migrated across our hills, I could take him wood pigeons of a succulence that set him dreaming, I could take him leverets gorged on wild salads. I could take him partridge and quail and clutches of their eggs. I could take him fruits from the *sottobosco* of a quality that astounded him, and such was his gratitude that he financed my meetings with his daughter.

'At first, making my way on foot, I would take Valentina and her father and the gypsy Agata little offerings from the countryside as presents. Gradually, the Maestro began to show his preferences. He had a weakness for crayfish which bordered on gluttony. Well, there were crayfish up in the pools above the Nestore and none of us liked them. My father once told us he'd rather eat the clippings of other people's toenails than start chewing on such a collection of alien cartilage. I noticed a little heap of discarded claws outside his caravan, and asked if they had been used medicinally. Imagine my surprise and joy when I heard that the Maestro ate the things.

'For four years I fed him weekly with all manner of strange

122

creatures. He ate land crabs, frogs, snails and a number of other things I failed to recognize. Sometimes I would get over-ambitious. For instance, having seen him eat snails and not being able to find any one particular week, I presented him with a small jar of slugs. He was so disappointed he nearly banished me from the site. It wasn't often I played into the hands of my detractors, but when I did, they were ready to take advantage.

'Mario and Lorenzo, as well as manning the carousel, were cowboy and Indian in chief. On the cavalcades, Mario donned his sheriff's uniform and led a posse of gunslinging boys from town to town, while Lorenzo dressed up as a redskin and led a war party of under-age braves comprising all the naturally dark boys born to the troupe. The brothers grew so used to their roles that they adopted them for every day as well, addressing each other in Wild West vocabulary. No matter how many times Valentina told me that the two were in fact brothers and as Italian as myself, I never really believed that they hadn't somehow managed to stow away or go steerage on a cattle boat from America. I was so fascinated by their feathers and holsters, arrows and spurs, that I didn't notice the malice with which they looked at me. I suppose I thought cowboys and Indians were notoriously mean, they were meant to be, and their vicious stares and sneers just added authenticity.

'Meanwhile, the more I failed to respond to their dislike and their challenges, the more enraged they became. Valentina once told me that I owed my modest popularity with the fairground people largely to those two boys. She said that they spent so much time maligning me and attributing such deformities and perversions to my character that the fair, made up as it was of so many freaks, began to regard me as one of them. So far from muddying my name, they gave me a character reference instead, and the spider-woman, the fat lady, Nando and several others began to welcome me quite openly.

'I sat in the balance and I lost and I gained. I lost some of the closeness to my own family. I grew away from my brothers; missing all their outings and jaunts. Our free time had always been spent together. Marco had a girl, a *fidanzata*, and he spent a few hours a week with her, but he too joined the other boys when they went out hunting and nesting. Elio and I had been inseparable. I listened to his music and he listened to my ramblings. After I met Valentina, although we still slept in the same bed, Elio, Marco and I, head to toe and head to toe as we had always done, I became a stranger at home. It was mostly my own doing. I became jealous of my thoughts. I wanted to save everything up to tell Valentina; to spill any of my ideas or impressions seemed to be to betray her, to short change her. She needed a great deal of attention. I hoarded up thoughts during the week to present to her with my offerings of flowers and pretty things each time I saw her. I racked my brains trying to come up with good things to say, I began to sift everybody else's conversation for sweet words and pretty adjectives. The language I had always spoken became suddenly inadequate. It failed to express my love. Particularly in the early days, before I was able to speak with my body, I felt a need to name everything, but much of what I needed to name was new and so had no name in my dialect.

'The more I escaped, the more my brothers felt the need to keep me. They set traps for me and when they failed, they began to bribe me. Words took over our ways. Things that we did and had always done, wordlessly and by an instinct inherited from generations before us, were verbalized. In order to entice me to join him, Elio began to describe his outings; he lured me in the fields and he lured me at home. He began to talk to himself, like the gypsy Agata, he kept up a commentary on events past, present and future. He would start early in the morning as the first shafts of daylight found their way into our room.

'"I'm going to start where the river dwindles at the first curve past the bridge and then I'm going to make my way up to Zeno Poggio through the chestnut wood. My nose is itching and I know that means those patches of thyme are going to be freckled with fat *funghi*. Marcellino said he saw a meadow full of *biette* under the crest. We'll take a pan and light a fire, a tooth of garlic, and we'll fry them up with a twist of salt. Aah. I can almost taste them, I can smell them as light and as delicate as a pan of larks. Perhaps I'll get

124

Marcellino to set up one of his stick spits and we'll roast a songbird or two, a thrush maybe, to dip our *ciacia* in. Mother and Elenita will be making it fresh for our trip . . . That little taste of ashes left from the flat stone."

'Elio would do his best to tempt me, and I was tempted, but one choice was my pleasure, and one was my love.

'I have been an exile to both taste and smell and yet one of the tastes that I miss the most is the ashes from my mother's bread and one of the smells will always be the indelible scent of the underwood, the first whiff of a *porcino* when the layer of thyme and dead bracken is first disturbed around its hiding place.

'We would all rise early on Sundays – earlier than on other days to extend our freedom and squeeze as much time out of that day as possible. By five o'clock we would all be up and ready to go, so we'd set out, they to their way and I to mine. The hills for them and the station for me. So I'd walk the long road alone, accompanied only by the peeling wafers of paper that lined the village walls announcing deaths, funerals and memorials. Black-rimmed snakeskins discarded by the noticeboards named the known and the unknown until the sun and the rain wiped them from the walls.

'I remember one Sunday in particular, it must have been late October because the grapes were in and the wine was in the making, moving towards its first fermentation, so everyone was purged by the grape juice or bloated, depending on their age and constitution. I myself was light-headed from the emptiness it had wrought in me. Elio had been working on me all week, trying to get me to miss a Sunday by the lake and go with him instead into the woods. I felt myself walking away from the village, unravelling my childhood like a spindle of thread, reducing myself, getting smaller and smaller as I hastened away. I had a train to catch. I caught so many trains in those days that I scarcely noticed how I was losing my roots, cutting the filaments one by one. But that day, I felt my nerves and my muscles being pulled out of me and left like a snail's glare to mark the dusty track until such time as dew or rain should smudge them into the dirt.

125

'That was the first time I became aware of what I was doing: making my choice. I became a voluntary freak, an honorary member of that fair, cut adrift from all that had been mine. This was what Elio and Marco, my mother and my friends, were complaining about. Children by the wayside ran out to gawp at me. Mating dogs looked up from the scorched grass to eye me disdainfully. The Signora Graziella, widow of a war hero who had a pension almost twice as big, it was rumoured, as the widows of ordinary soldiers, eyed me strangely, as she did every Sunday morning as I went on my way, preened like a cockerel for a fight. And I watched the willow stumps growing back in the vineyards like soldiers growing back their limbs after the war, and I passed the vines stripped of their grapes standing forlornly in their straggling lines. And in those days, Stefano, I kept noticing the blueness of the fruit trees painted with copper sulphate in the spring. Blue trees poisoned for their own good, blue trees in green fields, strangers on the earth.

'I used to run along the last part of the road; the bit before the train and after the comfort of my village. I was afraid only of that part of the journey. Even before the war, my family spoke of the outside, the beyond, as though it were all enemy territory, but I was afraid only of the no man's land of the bleak dustbowl in front of the station, a yard where not even hens would dare to scrabble. Once the train embraced me I felt safe. I was a flea riding on its articulated limbs, a worm in its metal gut.

'I once overheard someone telling my mother that she thought I'd been blinded as a divine punishment for abusing my eyes. She was whispering so that I wouldn't hear, but whispering carries further, it adds its own wind to carry its hushed words. She said I had sinned both by ingratitude and visual gluttony and my blindness was a penance. It was in the early days when my heart was still bitter. The temptations of the flesh have been easier to renounce than the temptations of the soul. I have had to drag my mind out of a maze of dark tunnels. I have had to smother grudges and build up a resistance to bitterness. I have had to mummify my heart.

'Are you tired, Stefano? Am I rambling? I have become an old man. I see myself still as a young boy, but I hear myself, since you

126

came, as an old man milking my memories and then churning over the past to make rancid butter. I don't know if I can bear to get much older. I have lived for so long like a moth trapped in a winter curtain that the effort of this flight is using me up.

'My head is full of stations, of oleanders and palms in pots, of water pumps and fountains, ticket offices and waiting rooms, platforms and signals. My memory is circulating slowly through all the capillaries of the central railway system. It stops at every little station, releasing passengers laden with food and shopping. Chickens tied together by their feet and held upside down are clutched against cloth bundles, cardboard boxes, the canvas kitbags of conscripts. Men in their Sunday best sit stiffly in their seats as though strapped to them, their hand-me-down funeral suits shine from generations of use, making no concessions to the size of the present wearer. A few of the peasant travellers wear shoes, but most wear wooden clogs carved from olive or willow. Shoes were an unbearable penance and a wild extravagance, clogs were for best, bare feet were for much of the year. If a man didn't have any clogs, then he stayed in, or borrowed someone else's. It was a point of honour not to admit to our poverty. We all kept a little coffee so that on the rare occasions when the priest or a visitor from the villa or someone from outside came by, we could serve them a sip of it in one of the two china cups we owned and kept locked away like sacraments from the chaos of our own meals. When we drank "coffee", it was toasted barley, and when that was short we would burn breadcrumbs to eke it out.

'Valentina and her father drank real coffee. It was one of the smells of the fair. No matter what time I arrived there, I could smell fresh coffee hovering over the caravans. Valentina lived like a lady. She had three different dresses made out of three different materials, and in winter she had a black-velvet coat with a fur collar, and her clothes had hardly any mends or darns. She washed her hair with potions and creams that the gypsy Agata prepared. She had wonderful hair and she was proud of it. When we lay down anywhere, I had always to put a rug under her hair so that no twigs or insects could catch in it. Then she would spread it out

127

around her like an Egyptian princess: a halo of paths leading to her head. Black tracks to her. Railway lines on our own map, cutting through stations, ignoring the world on my way to her. I had a head full of stations. They ran through my mind as I fell asleep each night, the scent of rosemary-flower water, candyfloss, coffee, the taste of her tongue and a litany of stations: Castiglion Fiorentino south to Camucia, Terontola, Castiglione del Lago, Panicale, Chiusi, Orvieto and Orte. And then there was the line to Poppi, lunging northwards from Arezzo to Giovi, Marcena, Capolona, Subbiano, Rassina, Bibbiena . . .'

——— IX ———

There was snow everywhere. The geese had to be plucked for
Christmas, but it was so cold that the women couldn't sit in their
usual spot together on the bald land behind the school. So they lit
their fire under the cover of Marcello's lifting garage roof. Stefano
saw them transformed from the sophisticated housewives they had
become, with their kitchens full of gadgets, to a huddle of women
unchanged by centuries, dressed in rags with their hair tied in rag
scarves, circling a massive cast-iron pot, poking the twig fire under
it, while they singed, plucked and gutted dozens of geese, scattering
their white feathers in the sludge. He saw them make a carpet of
feathers and down, stained at its centre with blood. He had seen
these same apparently meek women strangling the geese just a few
hours before, twisting the shuddering necks hand over fist, ignoring
the flapping and squawking in their hands.

The village was preparing for one of its annual feasts. There was
to be a banquet, a dance and then fireworks. Only the village
invalids and their nurses abstained from these feasts, Mezzanotte
among them. He said that he hadn't the heart to go, he preferred to
be alone. Banished, Stefano spent a quiet Christmas and a quiet
New Year in Castello. As soon as he could, he left his apartment,
finding the emptiness of his mother's and Fabrizia's rooms unbearable. Afraid to sleep, he lay awake and worried about them and
their many years of loneliness. His uncle Andrea and all of that
family were away skiing. Stefano had been invited and refused. He
was unwilling to distance himself from his charge, the village creed
had sunk in; there was no safety and no comfort beyond the confines
of the parish boundary.

When he returned, the Christmas trees and the wreaths of laurel
and holly and the baskets of fir cones were all still in place. They

129

would stay there until the spring elbowed them out. These evergreens gave the village a northerly air, changing it, together with the snow. It settled so deeply that he and Mezzanotte were forced to stay in. The towers of Rocagnano and Ghironzo stood out above the snow like ancient sentinels as inaccessible as the moon. One night, a blizzard blocked the road and Stefano was obliged to stay with Mezzanotte. He telephoned home to tell his father.

The bare room had filled up a little over the past few months. There was now a rug and an electric heater, a curtain and an extra chair and a large poinsettia which Stefano himself had brought at Christmastime. For the Epiphany he had taken Mezzanotte a shirt and a bottle of *cynar*.

'Well, thank you,' Mezzanotte had said, shuffling with embarrassment. Then he had added gruffly, 'Better this time too; I can't see the flower.'

'No. I'm sorry about that one, I . . . er . . . forgot.'

It was the best thing he could have said. It pleased the old man so much that the corner of his mouth crinkled up, forcing the scar tissue back across his cheek and bringing a flash smile that could relegate the needlework on his face to a backdrop.

'Do you know what Capodanno means to me?'

Stefano shook his head and then mumbled that he didn't.

'It was my last long leave. I hadn't had any free time since April when I got a weekend pass to go to Bologna. We spent twenty-two hours together. The rest of the time was wasted in trains and stations, except that it wasn't wasted because it took me to her. It was spring, but it was cold. Bologna was like that, all extremes when it came to the weather. We would have had nowhere to go except that Valentina found us a place. It was like a little *cantina*, it smelt of spilt wine and must, and it was colder inside than out.

'I told her I would see her again soon, but the fair was halted for security reasons, and she was afraid to travel on her own. She never came to visit me, not in the barracks, and not when we were posted further north up by the frontier. I had my passes, but they never amounted to more than a day at a time and she was always further

130

away from me than that. Besides which, I was never sure where she was, she'd begun to get vague about the locations of the fair. One minute she said they were confined to Reggio Emilia for the duration of hostilities and then she would announce that they had been in Tuscany for three weeks. I could have run away, I suppose I should have run away to find her. Several other boys from our company deserted. One of them was brought back and shot.

'I was never particularly brave. I didn't fear being shot, though. That was not what kept me in the army and away from her. It was worrying what would happen if I couldn't find her, knowing that she had only my battalion and company numbers to write to. If I stayed put, eventually she would find me. If I deserted, we could be separated for ever.

'I took to taking my free time with Gavarini, Massimo Gavarini. He was my best friend. He was a Socialist. He believed in a lot of things I never even used to think about. Half of what he talked seemed like so much nonsense, but some of it was tempting. I used to worry because he believed so strongly in what he said. I thought, you can believe in people, individual people, because you know them, but to believe in strangers is to ask for trouble. Ideas are all very well. But the first thing you have to do with an idea is test it, bit by bit. That was the sort of thing that farmers knew, *contadini* knew, but city folk like Massimo had no idea.

'I listen to the wireless and I hear all the politics, the comings and goings, the endless confusion. It seems to have got worse since Massimo's time, not better. The only thing that has remained the same is that there is still no common sense in it. Most of the time, though, we didn't discuss politics. We talked about our futures, what we would do when the war was finished. We talked about our families and I talked about the village, he talked about his home. He was a Bolognese. He took me back to see his family once. They lived in a tenement on a street called San Petronio Vecchio. He thought he was poor. I thought he was rich.

'He told me his dream was to study science at the University. He was studying at night school before the war. I told him that my dream was to bury myself between Valentina's thighs and never

131

have to move for more than the space of a working day. He used to laugh at me, but I didn't mind. He was three years older than me, but he wasn't in love.

'After they moved us up to the frontier, we never got back to Bologna again. It worried him that some cities had been bombed and he kept imagining that San Petronio Vecchio would be hit. I told him that even if they did bomb Bologna, they were unlikely to target a church, so the apartments behind it should be safe. He worried all the same until each time a letter reached him from his mother.

'The fair had left Bologna, and nobody knew where it had gone. It had left in August. Letters, like whiplashes, continued to reach me. These letters drove me mad. She wouldn't tell me where she was. She said, in each of them, "My darling, we shall be together again at Capodanno."

'From the end of November I had a fever. I couldn't sleep at all. They even took me to the hospital for a few days, but the beds were needed for the wounded, so they sent me back again. It was the strain of waiting. I think I would have died without Gavarini. He kept me afloat in that pond of slime. He said, "We have five days at Capodanno, we'll go together and find your Valentina. Who knows, maybe I'll find myself a girl as well." His girlfriend had left him when the war broke out, she was afraid of his ideas. He always held a candle for her; Rina, he called her. So he didn't go to the brothels with the other men. That was something else we had in common.

'The night of 31st December we were to spend with his family. A house in their street had burnt down just before Christmas and some of the buildings around were declared unsafe. He had a married aunt who lived in Sant Arcangelo near the coast and all his family had evacuated there. So we took the train to join them. It didn't matter how far we had to travel so long as we had the time, our military passes ensured that we travelled with the compliments of the Leader.

'I never really knew what war was until I looked on that landscape, like a scarred face gashed by the train. The north had all the contraband from Switzerland; the further away we moved from

132

the frontier, the greater the suffering. *Contadini*, like my family, suffered, but I think they suffered more in the towns. I saw the face of hunger which I had never seen before. It was not the familiar face of hardship and want, it was a gaunt, sick, ravaged face, honed to the bone by months of not eating. Even in Sant Arcangelo, with its pillared square and its bandstand and its triumphal arch, there were gypsies and beggars desperate for food.

'I wanted to turn back and search for Valentina. I imagined her starving somewhere, too weak to come to me, too weak to live. Massimo would have none of it.

'"Courage," he said, prodding me in the ribs so hard that I nearly toppled off my kitbag. "We have come to share Capodanno with my family. As soon as the New Year dawns, we'll drag our drunkenness back to this station, in strict defiance of the curfew, and we'll catch the first train out to scour Tuscany. You'll be better off with me than without me. Remember that, and I'd like to remind you that there is a war on for everyone, including my mother and my aunt. I am their Valentina; so no moping, please, during the festivities."'

Mezzanotte twisted his face into a smile, then he shook his head fondly as though to savour the last dregs of his memory.

'What a dinner that was, Stefano. What a feast!'

There was a long silence and then he cleared his throat painfully and noisily.

'I was a fool, I was so happy that night. For all my earlier worries, I was happy. Massimo and I and his father and brothers and uncles all got drunk, so drunk we lay in a heap in front of their log fire and slept until the dawn broke over us, not at the station but there in the knot of friendship. I was so happy, I should have known that God would mock me.

'I want to tell you what happened on our trip to Tuscany. I have never dared tell anyone before. I would have told Valentina perhaps. I have often thought I would have told her, but soldiers shouldn't tell tales. So you see, we go to war, and we see things and we do things too horrible to recount, then we come home and we grow silent and that is all. Tact is the enemy of civilization. Massimo

133

used to say, "What boy in his right mind would fight if he knew what was in store for him? They'd all run away. People talk about a soldier's duty. A soldier's duty is to talk, to expose the truth and admit his shame."

'I don't know what is right or wrong, tact or truth. The suffering was wrong, arming brother against brother was wrong, yet mostly what one hears is lies. I listen to the wireless day by day and hear the contradictions all the time.

'I want to tell you what happened in Tuscany, but I'm so tired, I'll have to lie down. The winter has moved in beside me. It lives in my back.'

There was a longer silence. Mezzanotte had fallen asleep.

X

The snow was falling outside, burying the village under its pristine weight, stealing its features until it was virtually a uniform white and unrecognizable. The Giulianis had lent Stefano a camp bed and some blankets. They had offered him their spare room, but he preferred to stay in the relative discomfort of Mezzanotte's. Assunta brought down a tray of dinner which he gratefully accepted. He would have liked to have dined with Mezzanotte, but the old man had not awoken. There was ravioli and roast chicken and a bowl of salad and some cake. There was enough to feed another four.

After he had finished, he began to feel restless. He crept out to the bar and drank two tumblers of local wine at Concetta's. The snow was over forty centimetres deep and had already drifted to well over a metre in places. There was an air of excitement in the village. It rarely snowed in the valley, hardly ever enough to gather and throw. Groups of men and women were playing in the streets. Muffled and zipped and buttoned into anonymity, they were chasing the children with a barrage of snowballs, slipping and skidding as the snow drifted down from the night sky. The laughter turned to shrieking as the fight intensified.

Stefano was hit behind the left ear as he tackled the last steps of the bar. He couldn't see where the frozen missile had come from, but he joined in the fight, pelting whoever happened to be nearest. The schoolteacher came out to announce that the school would remain closed because of the snow, news had just reached her from Castello. She too was drawn into the battle, bombarded with snowballs as she made her way back to the schoolhouse with its acned façade.

By the time he got back to Mezzanotte's, Stefano was chilled and wet. There was melting snow inside his jacket and his ungloved

135

hands were swollen and blue. The smell of his steaming clothes drying over the radiator awoke Mezzanotte.

'Stefano?' he called. 'Is that you?'

'Of course it's me.'

'For all these years my nights have been a blackness all my own. I'm not used to company. Why are they screaming out there? What is happening? And where will you sleep?' Even as he was speaking the outdoor sounds deciphered themselves, turning from alarm to merrymaking.

'It's the snow. I've got a camp bed from Assunta. Were you wheezing? Your breathing sounded odd in your sleep.'

'Eh, *si*, eh. I swallowed my lungs when I went blind, and half my face. It doesn't make for easy breathing, you know.'

Mezzanotte picked over his supper. He didn't say so, but it was clear that he would have rather had his macaroni with tomato. The food brought him no pleasure. He chewed and winced and swallowed with far more difficulty than he had ever shown when eating his own simple diet.

'What was Massimo Gavarini like, your friend?'

'He was like a child,' Mezzanotte told him, answering without hesitation. 'He was so full of enthusiasm and high spirits he was like a child. An infant philosopher. He had a theory about everything. But I really mean everything. Drink; it had to be *cynar* because *cynar* was not only cheap, it was a serious drink, and he would tell you why. Food, every piece of food, had a philosophy behind it. He took each day and he tried to live every minute of it, he said we had to. "Think about all the poor bastards who can't. Do it for them."

'And to look at? I forget that side of things sometimes, but I can still see him, so I'll tell you. He was dark, dark-brown hair and dark-brown eyes and curls all over his arms and legs and neck. He was hairy, smaller than me, and not so wide on the shoulders. His skin was pale like a lady's skin so he looked quite delicate at times. Girls found him very attractive, they used to flirt with him a lot. He had the looks and the city ways they liked. He used to say, "I can milk myself, thank you, I've got two hands and plenty of time.

136

I want something more than that." Sometimes the girls would look at him as though he were a pervert, but they were mostly prostitutes, so some of them would offer him the weirdest services then and there. He was talking about friendship, though, he wanted someone to share all that enthusiasm.'

Outside the snowfight had ended. The only sound left was the *intercostale* chorus of dogs. They yapped and barked all through the night, calling and answering in a high-pitched dialogue. Stefano surmised that Mezzanotte must be used to these small-voiced dogs because he seemed scarcely to notice them. Despite the addition of his own camp bed and the extra chair, Stefano sat beside the old man on his high bed. They were drinking bittersweet *cynar*.

'We took the train to Florence. It was New Year's Day, 1942. We all believed that the war would be over by the spring. We passed through Forlì to Faenza. I knew the railway stations well. I had travelled through them before in my pursuit of the fair. When there were stations that I hadn't been to, I still knew their names from all the time I spent learning the timetables. At Faenza we had to change. Our passes weren't stamped for anywhere other than Sant Arcangelo and Castello, but Massimo said what with broken lines and everybody celebrating the New Year, we could get a lot of leeway out of our routes.

'Florence was like Bologna, it was full of Germans. The last I had heard from Valentina was a letter postmarked Colle Val D'Elsa in the Province of Siena. She didn't say that was where the fairground was, but I remembered that they had been there before, in '38, and I too had been there. She said, in her letter, that she did not tell me her whereabouts for fear of my deserting to find her. She said the war would be over soon and we would be married. "It isn't worth spoiling our future for the sake of a few hours of love."

'She had changed towards me, she had lost some of her ardour. I had travelled through dozens of curfews for her during our years of courtship. I had defied the Leader's stipulations on travel. I had risked internal exile and even prison, crisscrossing the country to get to her. She used to egg me on then. She used to encourage me. "They won't catch you," she'd say, as sure as though she had seen it in the gypsy Emiliana's crystal ball.

137

'I don't blame her for changing, I'm just saying that she did. I loved her so much, it didn't matter if she changed, I never wanted to thwart her. If she needed to grow a little this way or that, my love was big enough to bend with her. It was the not giving any address, not letting me see for myself that she was safe and well, that worried me. It seemed to point towards some trouble. I felt she was hiding something from me. From April to the end of the year I had managed without her, believing that at Capodanno we would be reunited. I took that as her personal guarantee. I refused to accept the power of the war to interfere with and destroy ordinary lives.

'Massimo understood a great deal more than me. In all things it was he who was my leader. I just worked out our railway map, he worked out all the rest. We were lucky to leave Florence quickly, they were rounding people up on the station: deserters and Jews.

'There were no Jews in our village and no foreigners, except for the two sisters who married in from San Severino and poor Rosina's mother who came from somewhere outside Castello. If I had married Valentina and taken her home, she would have been the most foreign of all. Massimo had told me once that they were rounding up gypsies too and sending them abroad in cattle trucks. There were no gypsies on the station. It had not occurred to me until then that they might arrest Valentina and the Maestro Rossi. It was possible that they were in hiding to protect the gypsy Emiliana and the gypsy Agata, but it was hard to hide a convoy of their proportions. I became convinced they were at risk.

'When we finally reached the line for Siena, it was getting late and most of the day had been wasted. I felt bad to be using up Massimo's leave. I suggested that he return to his family. He said, "We're friends, I would just as soon spend my time with you. I don't mind where we spend it. We're enjoying ourselves, we're away from the camp and nobody's bothering us."

'In fact, we were asked to show our papers all the way to Poggibonsi, and a woman sitting opposite told us that boys from all over Tuscany were dying in Greece with their feet frozen to the ground. Soon they would have no sons left. Her own grandchildren would be orphans.

138

' "What business have you to be parading up and down the railways enjoying yourselves while our lads take the brunt of the war? Get back to your battalions and fight to protect us. A fine bunch of nancy boys you are," she said. She was trying to rouse the other passengers against us, but no one took any notice of her. It seemed the more they ignored her, the more outspoken she became.

' "Shame on you, shame, stuffing your faces and larking around on holiday." On and on, grumbling to the rhythm of the train she went, all the way to Poggibonsi.

'When we finally reached Colle Val D'Elsa it was getting dark. The town was garrisoned with Germans. There were a few of them wandering about in the square, sheltering from the cold wind under the arcades. We hadn't enough money to sleep anywhere but in a barn. Despite the approaching curfew, the town seemed full of itself and bustling as though with news to tell. The bar across the square from the station was full of Blackshirts and their fur-trimmed ladies. Massimo wouldn't let me go in and ask for the fair. Instead we walked to where the fairground had been last time. It was deserted but it showed signs of having been used at some time recently. It was a threadbare patch of grass below the city wall. The fair always left a pile of debris behind: used containers of grease, remnants of fodder, rotting food and animal clippings. There would also be dents and grooves in the earth where the convoy was dragged in and out.

'The moon was nearly full. It spotlit the hillocks of rubbish. There were still some families camping out on the site. As I ran towards them, I could not see who they were, such was my excitement at the thought of being reunited with Valentina again. They did not share my enthusiasm. A sullen group stood in front, armed with knives and broken bottles. Massimo grabbed hold of me and pushed me back.

' "Sorry," he said very loudly, "sorry, friends, he's looking for his family. He thought they were here. It's the emotion, it's gone to his head." As soon as I stopped running I saw that these were poor jobless people and refugees. Their clothes were in rags, their tents were made of tin, plywood, cardboard and anything else available.

'Some of the men moved round behind us, so we were encircled

139

by these outcasts with their menacing eyes. We had some food in our knapsacks; left-overs from the dinner. Massimo gave what he had in his to a woman who was standing sneering at him with a spindly stretch-eyed baby staring out from the piece of bloodstained blanket she was using as a sling. Those nearest to the proffered food fell on it and swallowed it in snatched handfuls. There was nothing like enough to go round.

'"Listen!" Massimo shouted, holding up his hand for quiet. "We've been posted to the bakery. Tomorrow we'll bring you bread. Do you hear? Tomorrow we'll bring bread for all of you."

'This was a blatant lie, but as Massimo said to me later, "They might all die in the night and at least they will die hopeful. Anyway, there are truths and truths. These people would have killed us, and none too pleasantly." The mention of the bread worked like a miracle. Massimo took advantage of the change of mood.

'"My friend was looking for the funfair. The Maestro Rossi's funfair." As soon as he asked a question, everyone looked down in the prudent way of greeting questions that years of living under the Dictatorship had taught us.

'"I can't decide how many loaves to bring tomorrow, that's what I'm thinking," Massimo told the silent group. They had a fire burning. Those of them who had been huddling around it before were growing cold. Hunger had lowered their resistance, forcing them to stamp their feet to keep their circulation going. They were all dressed in a great variety of clothes, and although most of these were reduced to tatters, they still showed signs of having been pillaged from fine shops or private houses. A haggard middle-aged man swathed in shreds of faded yellow watered silk, spoke up.

'"It's gone. It came and went."

'"We're looking for it."

'"Well, it's gone. I just told you."

'"Where did it go, where is it now?" I asked, unable to keep quiet any longer. There was a moment of silence which I interrupted. "I'm worried. If they were rounded up, tell me, please, I ask you in the name of all that you hold dear."

'"There's not much left to us to hold dear," a new voice

140

answered bitterly. "I've only my life to lose now. I've already lost my family down in Taranto." This new voice was a man standing in such shadow that I could not see him. His voice choked as he spoke. I appealed to him.

'"I am looking for *my* family. Won't you help me?"

'"I don't know which of those fairground people is your family, but it can't be old man Rossi himself because you don't seem to know him very well. Rounded up?" the first spokesman laughed. "That one would sell his own grandmother before anyone rounded him up. If there used to be anyone controversial in his entourage, you can be sure there isn't any more. He wears a black shirt and you can be sure his papers will be stamped up to the minute."

'"And what of the daughter, the Maestro's daughter?" Massimo asked for me.

'"And what of her?" the first spokesman said, turning back to his fire.

'"Is she all right?"

'"That she is."

'We learnt nothing more from the refugees. In fact we learnt nothing more at all there. We scoured the hills and roads around Colle Val D'Elsa, heading now towards the ruined San Gimignano and on towards Siena, but we found no further trace of Valentina. On the fourth day we walked to Casole D'Elsa, following the river, skirting its flooded banks for signs of the Maestro's camp. A basket maker outside Casole told us that the fair had been through on its way to Colle. It had stopped, he said, for two nights some time before Christmas. He showed us the site near his croft where they had camped. He remembered the Maestro Rossi himself with his high boots and his drooping moustache, and he remembered Valentina. He said she had played cards with an officer and won twenty lire. He said he thought she had cheated, but no one else seemed to notice. He said he thought the Maestro a lucky man and he wished one of his own useless daughters could bring in such a fortune at such a low rate of exchange.

'That night we wandered from the road. Our funds were almost exhausted and we had to beg for a slab of polenta from the basket

141

weaver. He had hardly any for himself, but he gave us enough to let us sleep that night and we made our way back towards Colle across country. We found ourselves an abandoned cottage where we could shelter for the night.

'On our way through the fields I had caught a blackbird with a catapult. We lit a fire and roasted it in the kitchen fireplace. There was nothing else to eat in the entire house, but we found things to cover us with, and we made ourselves comfortable in the wrecked remains of the upstairs kitchen. Part of the roof was missing. We could see the clear winter sky through the jagged hole. We burnt bits of wood, broken furniture and school exercise books. The fire smoked so much we had to douse it, and then it was so cold we held each other to keep warm.

'Massimo told me about his girlfriend and a trip they had made once to the beach at Rimini. He described the sea to me. He said he would take me there one day to feel sand on my bare feet for myself and to watch the tides of froth rolling in and out across the shore. I fell asleep while he told me his story. His army coat smelt of sweat and straw, there was a heavy fog of woodsmoke in the room and the lingering scent of coffee. Massimo could produce coffee wherever we were. He pulled it out of his pocket, he took it out in twists from the lining of his cap. He was like a magician providing for our needs. I felt as safe as I had felt with Valentina.

'I was safe from the raw wind outside, safe from my anxiety and safe from the distant lights of aeroplanes dissecting the Tuscan sky. In the small hours, a barn owl flew into the roofless kitchen and woke me. Massimo was a deeper sleeper than I, he shuddered in my arms and then slept on. Shortly afterwards, there was what sounded like a skirmish over towards Colle. I could hear the muffled whining of sirens and the thud of explosions far away in the town. I fell asleep to the sound of distant violence.

'In the morning I woke up early, feeling very well. Massimo was already awake, he was lying staring up at the sky. His face was an ashen colour. There was some fallen rubble lying around us. I said, "We have been lucky not to die in the night, the whole roof could have fallen in."

142

'He said, "I dreamt about Valentina. I dreamt she came to me and said that her father had thrown the gypsy Emiliana on to the streets and that she had left her crystal ball behind. She said, 'You are a friend of Alessandro's, take it, it is for both of you, but I don't know if you should look into it, it can be very grim at this time of the year.' I thanked her and took the ball, and she disappeared. When I looked into it, I saw that between us we had but one future and it was very dark. A frog which had been crouching in my pocket leapt out and began to polish the ball with its webbed hand. 'There,' it said, when it was all smeared, 'your life is over now, I hope you enjoyed it.'"

'"O Massimo," I told him, pulling at his coat to try to shake some humour into him, "don't let a dream spoil your day." He was very serious, he spoke with a voice that sounded distant and unfamiliar.

'"I am not sad because of the dream, I am sad because I have wasted my life. I have left everything for later and now my time has run out. If I got up and scratched a mark into the smoke and plaster of this kitchen wall, it would be the only mark I have made, the only trace I'll leave. I am full of regrets, Alessandro, my memories drain through me as though I were a pasta sieve. They slip away."

'He was quiet for a moment, then he rolled over suddenly, heaving the weight of his makeshift covers on to the floor, and sprang up. His voice was loud and enthusiastic again.

'"I need a woman," he said massaging his groin, "I need some coffee. Come on, Private Mezzanotte, the tap's downstairs. You bring the water and I'll light the fire."

'The night before we had found a trickle of water from a spring some ten yards from the house. It gathered in a stone tank covered over with a slab of stone. There had been another frost in the night and the ground was brittle and white. Fallen leaves from the fruit trees around the cottage were crisped and frozen into standing shapes. Although I had slept exposed to the elements inside the house, the gush of cold air that greeted me as I picked my way through the ruined stable and out into the garden was such that I felt my bladder about to explode. I crunched over the leaves,

143

crushing them into muddy stains, and eased myself against the tree. I remember that I felt strangely embarrassed at pissing over the pristine whiteness of that frosted garden, so white that it looked virginal, like new snow.

'When I was a child, there was a woodman called Ferini. He scraped a living by gathering bundles of kindling and hawking them from door to door all the way to Castello. Only the rich bought kindling, and it was worth very little. He would rise hours before dawn so as to be offering his dry sticks and broom twigs just as the cooks and maids were struggling to light their morning stoves. All afternoon he would take to the woods, gathering the next day's supply. He lived with his wife and two children in a tiny hovel here in the village. He was famous for being the greatest blasphemer in the neighbourhood. Every day he would take his mule up to the church, bringing it right into the doorway, and he would stop in front of the statue of Our Lady and shout at her:

'"What a fool you are, a fool and a tart and a dirty whore! Here I am, Ferini the blasphemer. You have allowed me to live for another miserable day. I shit on you, I piss on you, I rub donkey's droppings into your hands, and you who have so much power cannot stop me. Pigs and dogs to the Virgin, pigs' balls, dogs' genitals, toads' slime in the holy water; look at Ferini, a miserable sinner living unchastised."

'I don't know why he was allowed to carry on, sometimes he would even interrupt a mass to shout his obscenities. The priest denounced him as a desecrator. That was what I felt like, splattering the perfect whiteness: spoiling it. I thought of Ferini that morning, the desecrator. Then I shook my sudden guilt away and tackled the icy water for our coffee. As I leant over the trough, I heard a growling, rumbling noise. I turned round to see the cottage crumbling to the ground. As it sank, buckling inwards, a cloud of white dust rose up around it. Stumbling back towards the wreckage I heard an explosion, or so it seemed, but the explosion must have come first and just had a slow fuse in my brain.

'At first, I could see nothing through the dust. Then I saw Massimo lying like a baby in an enormous stone manger lined with

144

rubble and broken beams. He too was white, covered in dust and lime. He was laughing nervously but he did not talk. When I reached him, I saw that the main joist of the roof, the backbone of the house, was lying across him. He blinked some dust from his eyelashes and then looked up at me.

'"So, give me some good news, Alessandro, tell me something nice."

'"Wait for me," I told him. "Wait for me and I'll get help. We'll get you out of there."

'"Don't be silly. Sit down, talk to me."

'"Then I'll shift it myself."

'I had already assessed the beam, made from an entire chestnut some half a metre or more in diameter and wedged down at either end by fallen stones. It was unliftable. I knew without attempting it. I might be able to saw through it and release his trapped body like that.

'"Don't be silly," he repeated, reading my thoughts. "I'm already dead, I'm just talking for a bit because I feel like it." As he said this, his mouth filled with blood and it ran from the downmost corner into the dust. "When I die, Alessandro, leave me here. Cover me with stones and just go back to camp. The authorities will make trouble for you out of this explosion. Do you understand?"

'His fingers were fluttering in the dust, floundering like a fallen bat in the masonry. I took them in my right hand.

'"What a thing to happen," he sighed. "What a nonsense of my plans . . . Hold my hand, Alessandro, until I'm gone; and then, will you live a little bit for me? Live a little bit for me too? Will you?"

'The blood and a pale yellow trickle from his mouth were choking him, so his words were distorted. His fingers, which had been jerking in my hand, moving like caught fish between my own, dug suddenly into my flesh. My hand was far bigger than his, but his fingers clawed at it as he struggled to breathe and speak. There were tears in his eyes which tracked across his dusty face to join the growing string of viscous blood. More than fear, the expression in his eyes was of regret. After he died, his eyes still showed that clamouring sense of loss. They didn't glaze over like most dead

145

eyes do, they didn't get that fixed fishy stare. They stayed looking up at me, begging for that extra bit of life.

'I buried him as he had said I should, covering him with stones and tiles, but I left his eyes open. I couldn't bear to close them.

'There was a north-easterly wind that morning. It bit into my face and hands, hampering my work. It took the tears from my face and froze them. It put a tight band around my skull and crushed all my thoughts into ice. After I had covered Massimo, heaping more and more debris on to his broken bones, I began to be afraid. It was lonely there without him. While his body had been visible I had had company, but now that he was buried and out of sight I felt only the searing wind and the desolation of that place. It was the cold wind that drove me across the fields, and the cold wind that lashed me back into the town.

'I returned to our company stunned and numb with my loss, and with that cold wind locked inside me.'

—— XI ——

Stefano stared at the old man, too rapt to feel the cold, too sad to speak. Mezzanotte appeared to be in a trance. He sat silently, minute after minute, and when he abruptly resumed his narrative it was as if he was unaware of having paused.

'I went back to the war. I didn't know what we were fighting for, and I didn't know why, but I knew that deserters were shot and we were watched constantly for signs of what they called alienation. Massimo always said that the war had nothing to do with us. He said if we won with Fascists in charge it was the likes of him and me who would suffer any bad consequences and get no more than a tin medal for it. He said it would be the same if the enemy won so far as we were concerned, except that we might get carted off to prison for having served in the Fascist army.

'He said the only way out was with the Partisans and the Resistance. He had been turned down when he tried to join them. Apparently they had far too many recruits around Reggio Emilia and there was a great deal of confusion and bickering. They told him to join the army and stand by to defect when the time was right. I suppose I should have brought him back here and got my brothers to take him up into the hills. He might not have felt so useless then.

'When I think about him sometimes I feel as though he gave me something with that last squeeze of his hand. It was as though he was passing on his life to me, depositing it in my hand. He had fine, intelligent hands like an artisan, not like my big peasant's paws. It was his last will and testament, that pressure in my palm.

'He said he wouldn't leave a trace, nothing visible, nothing permanent. Even the hand that he clawed at has gone now, thrown away somewhere. I have often thought, if he had taken my other arm, he would be more alive.'

147

Saying this, Mezzanotte lifted his good arm and let it fall as though it were weighted beyond his meagre strength.

'Stefano, Stefano,' he called out.

'Here I am,' his companion reassured him. 'I'm sitting beside you. I've been here for hours.'

'I feel things where my eyes were. I feel them tonight. I feel rough cloth grating the surface, dull green like a trampled leaf. The other has sparks against it, orange sparks fading to the pallor of a winter sun. I think in colours. I see them all. I feel my eyelids hurting. Soon I must bathe my eyes, they are burning.'

The old man's voice had become plaintive. Stefano stood up from the bed, his knees were stiff from so much sitting.

'It's late, let's go to bed now.'

Mezzanotte ignored him, talking on to himself, raking through the memories of his early years.

'I didn't give up sleep, it was taken from me. I exchanged it for pain, swapped it like we used to swap eggs for other things. Eggs were our currency. We had no money. Lire were always extracted, at source, to pay our debts, but eggs had a value.

'Sleeping and waking, night and day, are irrelevant to the blind. Sometimes my memory rests. That is all.

'Massimo Gavarini gave me the strength to live on past my accident and past all the disappointments of my life. He gave me so much strength that I have outlived my entire family. I have almost outlived my generation. There are not many left of the class of '28.

'I have lived through so much, I have often wondered whether I am indestructible, but I know now that I am not. I shall not hold any hand. I know how shortlived such comfort can be. Instead, I am giving you the contents of my head. I am scooping out its corridors, taking the melon from the skin, sucking the honey from the comb.

'It was dark before I ever went blind. There are strips of colour where my eyes once were.'

Outside, the snow was still falling. It had filled up the glass of the one small window, blocking the draught and sealing Mezzanotte

148

and Stefano as in a tomb. The old man had arranged himself on his bed, lying across the embroidered white counterpane as though he had no intention of falling asleep. Within seconds of settling into this position, his voice had stopped abruptly, and he was dreaming, wheezing regularly and painfully in and out of snores.

Meanwhile, the noises of the village kept Stefano awake. Dogs yapped, trees sighed, a screech owl screamed, the wind teased, the old man wheezed, and between them they kept his brain skating across Mezzanotte's memories. He kept the bright bare bulb of the light on all night long. It was nearly morning when he finally dozed, and he dreamt of the blasted shell of the cottage near Casole D'Elsa where Gavarini lay crushed. He dreamt of the cruel wind freezing Mezzanotte's tears. He awoke to feel the same wind wrapped around his shaved head like an icy turban. Mezzanotte was standing in the doorway, pissing into the snow. Stray flakes were blowing into his face and settling on his blanket.

'I can feel you watching me, Stefano,' he said, without turning his head, as he fumbled to close his fly. 'There's not much left of the old marriage tackle, but I've kept it intact, inviolate. I've kept it for her. If desire ruled it would look like a bull's pizzle, but I am prey to old age. Age is shrivelling up the few parts left to me.'

He closed the door, pushing hard against the wind and then holding it. Stefano looked at his watch, it was not yet five o'clock. His eyes stung from the bright light and his sleeplessness.

Mezzanotte shuffled slowly across the room, missing the new camp bed as though by radar. He edged his way to the sink, where he began to dismantle and refill the coffee pot. Every movement he made with his one good hand was both delicate and efficient. From time to time he pressed something into his plastic hand, using the useless limb as a wedge or lever. He lit the Primus stove, sending a whiff of gas across the room, then he stood impatiently over the coffee pot, waiting for the coffee to gurgle up through the filter. He began to talk again, this time speaking towards the bare concrete wall, which muffled his voice so much that Stefano felt obliged to get up if he was to hear what was being said. He took a blanket with him and wrapped it around himself, and then sat on the far side of Mezzanotte's bed.

149

'It was June, five months later, when I had my accident, so you see I had plenty of time to do some living for the two of us. We'd been posted to Ravenna. I met a girl there who was very kind to me. I think she was the sort of girl Massimo wanted to meet. She followed me once when I was walking about the station looking for the timetables to Tuscany. She offered to help me and from there we made friends.

'I could tell she wanted to make love and it wouldn't have been what Massimo used to describe as milking time. She liked me. I even thought one time, perhaps I should do it for him. I was burning up with desire for Valentina, sometimes the desire seemed to escape from her and just leave me aching for anything. But I kept remembering Massimo's last morning and all his regret and I thought, when I die, I want to have something to believe in. I have never really done anything in my life but love. I love Valentina, then and now. She is my country, my religion, my faith. I believe in that true love and in its purity.

'I told that to Liliana once, she was the girl I'm talking about, and she said she would do anything to have such a romance. I think it made her the more willing. But nothing came of it. You see, one day Valentina may come back to me, and when she does it will be to a man who has loved her for over half a century. It will be to a man who sees her as she was, a girl with speckled eyes and silken skin.'

The coffee began to bubble up, filling the room with its heavy aroma.

'Eh, *si*, eh,' Mezzanotte said, smiling to himself, 'not all the disfigured faces were shot. Some of them got away, like Mezzanotte. Some of them are waiting.'

The smile fell from his face as though he had dropped it and was replaced by a shudder. He turned away from the coffee and leant heavily against the painted iron frame of the bed, covering the scratched and crudely painted seascape of the footboard. He felt his way round the bed and then sat down carefully on the edge of the mattress. As he did so, it struck Stefano that Mezzanotte was treating himself more carefully in the last few days than he had used to. He was also wheezing more, far more.

150

'Are you ill?' Stefano blurted out, more abruptly than he had meant.

'Just old. I'm a war veteran, remember, that is why you are here.'

Stefano got up to rescue the coffee. The pot was glowing on the Primus stove and he burnt his fingers on the handle. When he had dealt with it and poured the coffee into the two enamel mugs, he found that Mezzanotte had once again drifted into sleep. He switched the light off and went back to bed himself. He didn't wake again until ten o'clock, when Assunta was knocking on the door.

'O Mezzanotte!' she called, tapping continuously. 'O, are you all right?'

The old man was sitting erect on the edge of his bed. He had changed and shaved.

'Thank you, Assunta, thank you, I'm here,' he called back gruffly, without making any move towards the door.

'I've brought you some fresh bread.'

'No, no, thank you, but bless you for the thought.'

Assunta lingered outside, stamping on the snow and muttering about the weather. It was obvious that she wanted to be let in. She even tried the door, covering herself with a hasty apology when she found it bolted. Eventually she left.

'Life is ruled by petty things, Stefano. The bits of me that are left still line up and do battle over matters of no importance. It is as though my body will never learn its lesson and insists on fighting on for some misguided heroism which turns out to be sham.

'Take Assuntina, with her four children and seven grandchildren, her husband pollarded by arthritis and her own damaged hip grinding her down. She has known hardship all her life. She has money now, like the rest of us, enough never to want again, so much she doesn't know what to do with it, but it cannot buy her exemption from accident or illness. The world is changing too fast for her. It has become like a motorized carousel. She has chosen to whirl round on the gaudy horse that was put under her, but sometimes

151

she likes to make contact with the gentler pace of her past. She limps down the steps to me, as if it were her ticket of admittance to my sickroom. She needs to see that past and she needs to touch it, to shape me to her needs.

'She believes in doctors as she once believed in God. She still goes to mass now and again, but her real faith lies in the hospital in Castello. She has educated herself so that she can understand and speak in medical jargon. She collects analyses the way other people collect stamps or vases. She knows the exact levels of her cholesterol and her albumin, her platelets and her red corpuscles at any given moment.

'Seeing me so maimed, she wants to discuss snippets from our mutual past, our schooldays, and then she wants to spread the good news of her doctors. Her faith is such that I am sure she believes there are operations that could make me see again. She has the fervour of a crusader. She dreams of getting me into her care and taking me to see specialists. She loves specialists, consultants and surgeons. She knows their names and drops them like a socialite. Get dressed and washed, Stefano, and then go to her. Be my emissary, accept her bread and reassure her. Tell her that I have grown cantankerous with the cold. Tell her I'm sorry I didn't open the door.'

The scars on Mezzanotte's face were glowing, as though lit internally. His high black glasses still obscured the centre of his face, concealing both the front and the sides. It occurred to Stefano as he straightened his clothes and combed his shorn head with his fingers that he had never seen Mezzanotte's eyes. He began to wonder what they looked like. Would they be dead and glazed, would they be open or closed? Would they be screened by white cataracts, or blue? Would they have lids? He felt so curious he decided to ask, later, when he returned from Assunta's.

His uniform was crumpled. He looked down at himself and decided he looked a mess. He'd also ask Mezzanotte to lend him a clean shirt when he got back. It would be a bit big, but he felt unclean.

'I'll go up and see her then, shall I? I'll wave my handkerchief and say it's a white flag.'

152

'White flags breed bitterness.'

'Eh, it was a joke.'

'I'm sorry, I'm wandering again. My mind was on Sebastopol. All these years, I have struggled to keep control of my thoughts, to order and make sense of them, and now they have escaped and are in confusion.

'I left the Military Hospital in Perugia because of Sebastopol. All the beds were needed for those new amputees. There were hundreds of armless soldiers on the retreat from Russia. There were legless soldiers too, but most of those joined the thousands who died. All through that winter of '42 to '43 people talked about the Russian Front. At first there were only rumours, whispers in the corridors that the Front had collapsed. Then it became accepted, the glory was amputated from the word army, and sad stories, true stories, began to filter through. The nurses talked about it, the doctors and the patients, the visitors and nuns all talked about it too. The treacherous north had frozen men's feet to the ground. It was eating into their bodies, starving and whipping them with its savage winds.

'We of the long-term wards who had previously been considered incurable or in need of constant attention were miraculously cured and our beds made over for the victims of frostbite. I stayed longer than most of the others on my ward. They put a boy in the bed next to me. He was my age, he cried all through the night, every night, sobbing noisily with no attempt to control himself. The nurses used to come round and tell him off. "You're alive," they used to say. "Thank God for that. Think of all your comrades in arms who died there. At least you've come home." Nothing they said comforted him. One of the nurses told me he had lost one arm at the shoulder, the other above the wrist.

'One night just before I left, the night nurse held me up as an example. "Look at Mezzanotte here," she said. "He has lost an arm and his eyesight, but he doesn't keep everyone awake."

'I had never heard the boy say anything properly articulate, he just sobbed or stayed silent, but when the nurse chided him, he spoke out in a clear low voice far older than his age.

153

'"Then he's a lucky man, this Mezzanotte, for he will never see what we saw on the Russian Front. Perhaps I too would be quiet if I had lost my hands before the battle."

'Then he laughed, a hollow, horrible laugh that managed to wake up the rest of the ward and set them all moaning. He did not speak again in the few days that were left to me there, but I have always remembered what he said, and thought about it. I have been fighting my little battles ever since. The petty side of me wishes to prove that I can fight if I choose to.

'It used to make me angry to think that I had been called lucky yet again. But how many men have had the fortune to pass their lives in reflection? My injuries forced me to think. I had to ignore my grandfather's edict. When you are blind you *have* to think, your whole world is constructed through thought and memory.

'On 6th January the Befana brought us all a present: a present from the Leader to each of his men. I had been waiting for word from Valentina. I was sure that she would write to me for Capodanno. I believed she would come and see me again. Not having heard from her, I blamed the Fascists and their alliances, their war and their heartlessness for keeping us apart. I resented being given that present. I hated having my hand put on to the wrapping paper and made to rustle it like a child.

'One day I'll show you my letters from Valentina, my four letters, and you'll see for yourself how much she wanted to come.'

Stefano had been standing by the door for some minutes. He continued to do so, immobile.

'If you're going, go,' the old man said crossly, as though he had been indiscreet and given away a secret that he now wanted back.

Outside, Stefano walked in the deep fluffy tracks left by Assunta. He followed them round to her door. He delivered his message, and she was mollified enough to take Stefano into her confidence. She sat him down in front of a small log fire and presented him with a glass of homemade wine, a dish of sweets and her theories on the state of Mezzanotte's lungs. Stefano ended up promising to take the old man to a doctor.

'Eh, *sì*, eh,' Assunta told him, rocking her head from side to side

154

as a portent of unspeakable complications, 'and not just a doctor: a specialist. The medical history makes it essential. I can hear him wheezing through the floor. He's taken a shine to you, you know, he listens to you when he won't listen to any of us. And he talks to you.' She bustled back to the big unlabelled bottle of wine on the sideboard, threatening to replenish Stefano's empty glass.

He declined, covering it with his fingers, which she ignored and began to trickle wine over until he moved them away.

'There!' she said triumphantly. Socially, it was of great importance to make a guest eat and drink, regardless of whether they wanted to or not. 'There!' she repeated, and then began to rock her head as further complications flooded in. 'What a tragedy, what a waste! You know, he is the only person in the village with no family.'

Stefano gulped his wine and headed back into the snow. On his right, half-concealed by drifted snow, were the steps leading to the door of his lone soldier. In every other direction there were signs of the tight communal life of the village. Children like iron filings were scattered across the arctic landscape; at regular intervals, as though by the pulling of a giant magnet, they were drawn together. The village streets had been compacted, smoothed by a tractor and then trodden down. Ahead of him, under the ranked hydrangea pots outside Concetta's bar, people were gathering, pulled by the communal magnet. Without really thinking, his feet guided him along the slippery path towards them. He was greeted warmly, hailed as a new member of the clan, and asked many times whether it was true that he had spent the night there. They also asked after the old man, anxious to know how he was bearing up in the cold. A couple of them expressed their regrets that Mezzanotte would probably not enjoy a snowfight. Estelio, who could see advantage in any situation, however bad, tried to argue that maybe he would.

The arrival of the snow had made them almost incestuously close. They patted and hugged each other, shifting their way up the salted steps to the bar like crayfish locked in an embrace. Angling their way through the door without breaking out of the rugby scrum, they held an impromptu breakfast party in the long

155

fluorescent room between the shelf of drinks and the shop. They drank milky coffee and ate doughnuts filled with bright yellow custard.

He felt an unspoken solidarity with the group in the bar. Looking around them he saw three generations of people bearing their various scars, internal and external, and accepting each other for what they were and not for what they looked like. He realized that what set Mezzanotte apart from this village of people whom he so much loved was his need to be separate, not theirs. They were more disturbed by his reclusion than by his injuries. It was not his absence of family that saddened them so much as his refusal to make one. He had cut himself off to think, and they were afraid of his conclusions. They didn't want him to be lonely, they wanted him back; the welcome they were giving Stefano was the welcome for a lifeline, the link between the lands of the living and of the dead.

Thinking of Mezzanotte made Stefano miss him. He excused himself and hurried back. Mezzanotte was sitting in his usual position on the edge of the bed. Stefano felt relief to see him, he had been worried. Stumbling through the snow he had felt a pang of regret that he had left him alone with his memories. It was hot and stuffy in the room, so hot he had to get rid of his coat. His hands had turned clumsy, and he kept dropping it instead. He felt he had lost his spontaneity. He felt a little as he did whenever he needed to say something to the Judge. He was planning opening lines in his head, thinking up a conversation before trying it out. The silence oppressed him so much, he thought that Assunta's acid wine must have gone to his head. He turned to Mezzanotte to try to explain this unease. It was then that he noticed the tears on Mezzanotte's face. It was bathed with them, rivulets of tears finding their way down the uneven course of his cheeks.

'*Oddio!* Mezzanotte, what can I do? Please don't cry.' As he said this, he felt stupid; why shouldn't the old man cry if he wanted to? Who was he to be keeping up appearances?

'I'm not crying, Stefano, I'm not. I can't cry any more. I haven't cried since the months after Massimo died. I can't cry, but I have a fever. I think I'll get back into bed.'

156

Stefano didn't believe him at first, it was only when he saw his thick checked shirt soaked through in patches that he realized Mezzanotte must be ill. He remembered his promise to Assunta and told the old man he was going for a doctor.

'Wait, before you do that. You and I have certain understandings, so I'll ask you this favour. Don't let them take me away. I don't want to go into hospital. Not for anything, do you understand? It is true that I am ill, and more than ill. Like Massimo said, I'm already dead, I'm just talking for a bit because I feel like it.

'I have no desire to live more than a few days, just long enough to say what I have to say. I want to die in this village, in this bed. Do you understand?'

Stefano was afraid and embarrassed. 'Don't talk like that, it's not true. You've got years of life ahead of you. We've only just met. Don't leave me, you can't do that.'

'The wind is inside my head now. It's inside my lungs. I'm not afraid of death.'

As though by some prearranged signal, the wind picked up outside the window and began to hurl snow across the street. Mezzanotte, lying propped up on three pillows, was either sleeping or feigning sleep. Stefano crept across the room, battled with the door and went in search of Assunta. For once her encyclopaedic medical knowledge could have some relevance. He feared it would be difficult to get a doctor into the village with the roads so blocked.

Dr Mearelli lived in the village. He had been born there in the rabbit warren of the *vicinato*, he had done his homework on his quarter of the kitchen table. He had studied for his exams with a continual sense of guilt at using up so much of his parents' hard-earned savings. His father worked in the tobacco fields, his mother in a nearby knitting factory. Since his graduation, ten years before, they had pooled their money and built themselves a new house above the village. It was he who attended Mezzanotte's illness.

'It's nothing to worry about,' he reassured them both, 'you've got a touch of bronchitis. Well, a bit more than a touch, but nothing that some antibiotics can't cure. You'll have a job getting

157

to a pharmacy today. You'd better collect some pills from me and, eh, something for that fever.'

Stefano walked back with Dr Mearelli to pick up the antibiotics. 'Is it serious?' he asked as soon as they were outside.

'I don't believe in telling a patient one thing and his relatives another. The old man has got bronchitis. He'll be up and about again in about a week.'

Stefano returned to Mezzanotte feeling chastened and rather like a schoolboy. The doctor had given him strict instructions to freshen up the room, change the air, feed his patient a well-balanced diet, give him plenty to drink, unstrap his artificial arm and not let him get too hot in bed. Although the doctor had said nothing unkind or treated the old man badly in any way, Stefano felt there was a heartlessness in his efficiency. He wondered how he would have dealt with the amputees from the Russian Front.

As Stefano made his way back, his feet grew numb with cold. Already the lively feeling of the morning had been lost in the glare. He looked morosely at the snow-bandaged village, wandering what went on inside each of the isolated houses. He felt like stopping at each one and asking, 'How do you unstrap a plastic arm against the wearer's will?' or 'How do you feed a balanced diet to someone who has eaten only four things for the last forty years?' Then he remembered that despite his irritation with the doctor, he had just given Mezzanotte a new lease of life. He picked a gloveful of snow up off the low wall he was passing and rubbed it into his own face. As Mezzanotte kept telling him, there were two kinds of problems: the ones you had a choice about and the ones you didn't. The first ones weren't really problems.

——— XII ———

The valley lay wrapped in a quilt of snow, forced into immobility. Certain areas were cleared, the rest was abandoned to the great white weight that froze nightly, offering its still glow to the moon. Nobody went to work and nobody went to school. Expeditions, prepared with polar foresight, set off to all the outlying hamlets and the few isolated cottages in the hills. The entire village began to imitate Mezzanotte, making a daily pilgrimage around the contours, edging their way through the treacherous ice and snow to the various boundaries, crawling up the hill to Concetta's bar and slip-skidding down, clinging like snails to the walls, to the bar by the road. From Nuvole to the main road they patrolled the streets, exchanging greetings and regular bulletins on the parish news.

Meanwhile, also enveloped by the snow, but in the smaller capsule of Mezzanotte's room, Stefano continued to nurse his charge. The nursing was scarcely arduous. It consisted of administering an antibiotic three times a day and supplying him with extra mugs of natural spring water and the occasional tumbler of *cynar*. Mezzanotte, encased in his bed, seemed a much reduced man, but this was partly due to the removal of his plastic arm. This had been unstrapped and placed beside him under the covers like a bedwarmer companion from the first day of the treatment. The doctor said it was important that the patient should rest completely and for some reason he seemed to equate toil with the carrying of this surgical appliance. The doctor had been to visit twice. His duties at the hospital had been rearranged. The weather was so severe that a State of Emergency had been declared and the doctors were instructed to stay on call in their own neighbourhoods if they were the only medical practitioner within a certain radius. So

159

Dr Mearelli stayed at home, venting his learning zealously across the valley. Chilblains and fevers, coughs, colds and throat infections fell to his lot. Elderly victims of strokes and other ravages were wheeled into their kitchens for his inspection. Diabetics and the hypertense were showered with more attention than they knew how to take.

The doctor, with his high brown wellington boots and his grim black bag of tools and pills, calmed his own nerves and his impatience at this enforced absence from the operating theatre by making continual rounds. For villagers who saw the arrival of a doctor at their door as an ill omen, it was strange to keep ushering in his restless figure. The snow had lifted people's spirits and united the already close village to such a degree that the level of *bonhomie* and well-being were uniquely high. Without any emergencies to cope with, without any births or deaths, the young doctor felt confused. He was used to working with a team of surgeons at the civic hospital. He was used to changing into his green sterilized theatre clothes at every summons of his personal phone. He was equipped to deal with catastrophe. It seemed to him that he had left the village to become a miracle worker, it was like a punishment to be confined to this healthy happy valley. To live here was one thing; he returned home elated with exhaustion from his skilled operations in the city. The snow had blocked his ambition and stayed his delicate hairy hands.

Each time he went to visit the war veteran, Mezzanotte, he felt inadequate before him. Touching the old man's mutilated body, re-created and embroidered by other doctors, he felt a jealous irritability. He was aware of this in himself, and ashamed at the unworthiness of his feelings. He returned each time determined to be kinder to the blind man and his young companion, but something twisted the words in his throat, chilling them into the curt remarks that he made. He wanted to return to normality, to return to his fleeting rounds of the post-operative wards at the hospital where he would lean over each patient so that they could focus on his face and whisper words of encouragement and strength. 'Courage!' he would say, kindly imparting the secret of survival to his helpless victims. The number of scars on Mezzanotte's face testified to more courage

160

than he, Mearelli, would ever know or understand. The missing arm, the striated chest, the blind eyes, all defied his attentions.

Each time he left the war veteran, he did so disliking himself and wanting to change, to be gentler and more understanding. In penance, he visited every sick person in the village, no matter how minor their ailment. He forced himself to sit and drink the endless cups of coffee served in the best wedding coffee cups. He massaged twisted ankles and snowfight injured wrists. He tapped backs and dispensed lozenges, good advice and kindness. He wished he could be kind to the old man as well, but meanwhile, he became the guardian angel of the village. He had always been admired for his skill and learning, yet now he won the much greater accolade of being a good man. Previous patients of his who had been the objects of his surgical handiwork were amazed to find how nice he really was; how approachable. They blessed the snow that had allowed them to come closer to this previously somewhat aloof figure. The doctor's wife, who came from Castello and was, therefore, welcome but unfathomably foreign, suddenly became approachable too. The snow gave an excuse for impromptu visiting; and whereas before most of the women had found little to talk about with the doctor's wife after the initial pleasantries were over, there was now a new and mutually acceptable topic: the doctor. So the doctor as saint, saviour and simple soul was bandied over yet more cups of coffee and the village net drew in another generation of Mearellis.

Stefano decided to stay in the village until such time as Mezzanotte should recover from his bronchitis. He no longer felt afraid that the old man would die. The doctor had said he was fine, and the doctor knew best. The decision to stay was not entirely his. To have left would have meant a long tractor ride and then a perilous walk through the snow from the point where the road was still impassable. There were five-metre drifts beyond the village. Mezzanotte's was about the only household not stocked against a siege. Everyone else had enough food to last them at least until the summer.

'Eh, old habits die hard,' they told him at the shop. They were all proud of their thrift and foresight. The hundreds of bottles of

161

tomato purée that they had made at the end of the summer could come into their own. The hams and salamis, the cheeses and the sacks of potatoes and chestnuts no longer seemed like silly hoarding. Stefano was offered so much food that, had he accepted it all, there would have been no space left in the room for him and Mezzanotte to live in.

During the first night of his illness, Mezzanotte was fractious, he spoke very little, and when he did, it was of his room and his belongings. It seemed that he wanted to exorcize the doctor's presence from his territory. He insisted on having only his pasta and tomato, refusing the chicken broth that Stefano had procured. He complained that Stefano was interfering with him. He fell silent when his arm was removed.

'Are you sure you want it off? You don't have to, you know. You can have your arm back whenever you want.' It made Stefano feel uneasy and sad to see the thin hanging stump. It looked like a turkey's elbow, plucked and boiled. It was more than naked, it was stripped, vulnerable and abused.

'It's not my arm, Stefano, it's a bent piece of plastic, an articulated doll's arm. It moves for me, it does for me, but it isn't a part of me. I am the sum total of the flesh and bone that I have left, and my memories. I am not an appliance.'

He complained at intervals that his bed was too hot or too cold. Outside, the wind was beating against the door, rattling the window shutters of the rooms above.

'O, Stefano,' he called to him at regular intervals through the night. 'O, Stefano, go home now, go away.'

Each time Stefano explained to him that the snow had cut them off, locked them in, Mezzanotte would find this hard to believe. Eventually he said, 'What luck,' and fell into a sleep until the morning.

He was already awake and stirring long before Stefano awoke.

'You should be in bed, you know the doctor told you to stay there.'

'So, did the doctor tell me to piss my sheets? You unstrapped my arm, not my bladder.'

162

'You should have woken me,' Stefano told him apologetically.

'You city folk aren't easy to wake. How did you manage at the barracks? Or did they bring you coffee in bed at ten o'clock in Udine?'

'It's not ten o'clock already, is it?'

Stefano struggled out from under his blankets. He felt an almost overwhelming desire to drink a bottle of champagne. He washed and changed into some of the clothes that Assunta's sons had lent him, and by the time he returned to the sickroom he was feeling half-human again.

'*Oddio*, Mezzanotte,' he said, 'you are having your affair with *cynar*, but sometimes I pine for a gulp of champagne.'

'Have it,' the old man told him. 'Go and buy it, drink it. If you are really pining for so small a luxury, then indulge yourself. You are lucky if you long for something you can have. Have it. I have so much money in the Post Office I don't know what to do with it. The Government has rewarded me well for the loss of my bits and pieces. They pay me handsomely. Have it, go on.'

'No, it's all right, it's passing, and I don't think I'd find any real champagne here. It was just a joke, a notion.'

The two of them sat in silence, Mezzanotte propped up on pillows in his bed, his wheezing temporarily appeased by an inhalation of aromatic herbs that filled the room with a steamy fragrance of eucalyptus, and Stefano in the lone chair. He was staring at the space between him and the old man as though it were an uncrossable sea. A barrier of depression had descended between them, a stubborn silence put out by the change in their routine.

'Are you sad, Stefano?'

'Not really . . . I don't know.'

'I feel your presence near me, it pleases me. I am not used to talking for more than a few minutes at a time. I'm not used to saying anything out loud any more. My world happens inside my head.

'When you came with the fair I felt like a bird released from its cage. I have been flapping and singing a last song. I have heard music in my head; choir music, and my brother's accordion, and fiddlers playing the dance tunes I was hard put to follow as a boy.

163

'They tried to teach me braille in Perugia. There was a therapist there, a nurse, I suppose. She told me it would stop me from feeling lonely if I learnt how to read on paper graters. I never found school easy, and reading in particular meant little but trouble to me. We used to have to read and learn the Dictator's speeches. I can still remember a few. They never made any sense to me at the time, just a string of meaningless words. I see now that they were not meaningless at all, they were carefully chosen weapons; they were the whips and sticks that goaded us into his war. The words were his enchanted music, they led us everywhere he wanted. We danced to his tunes. I didn't get very far with braille. I wasn't willing and then the soldiers returned from Russia. I could have gone to a teacher in Castello, but that would have meant leaving the village and I couldn't have done that during the early years of my blindness. I was a poor pupil, I'm afraid. I had no heart for it, not even for the basket weaving classes. The therapist gave each of us a bundle of withies to bend and twine. They were freshly soaked and wet to touch. I was squeamish. I thought those severed shoots were too recently alive. I thought of someone somewhere being asked to twist my own flesh into something useful. I didn't know then how to put that idea into words. I don't suppose it would have helped much if I could.

'I was like an insect, for a long time I was as raw as any larva. My mother and my sister spun a web around me, a protective chrysalis, a skin to wear into the world. Even the sound of my father sucking on his empty pipe was comforting. I heard him sigh, and imagined him thinking about his ruined fields. He thought of his crops as an extension of himself. Their failure was his failure. If they thrived, then so did he. The year the beetles ate his entire potato crop, he told me that he felt as though his own skin was covered with its slime. Before I went away to war, I used to think that he should shake off his lethargy and his regrets and play cards again or join in with the serenades round the village. It was only when I lost my arm and my eyes that I realized how hard it is when you feel incomplete.

'In those early years, I wanted to move, but I couldn't. It was as

164

though part of my will had been blown off with my arm. I grew fond of my father in his last year. He sat by the fire. He must have been staring into it, because he always did. I sat in a wicker chair in the corner between the sink and the window. Every time anyone needed a wash, they would splash me as they tipped their buckets of water into the sink. The spilt water made me feel like a plant. I even imagined that the water, gathered from the village well and tipped into the familiar chipped stone sink in my own home, would have the power to regenerate my flesh.

'It healed me in other ways. It rinsed away much of my anger and my bitterness. I felt cheated when I came home, not just by the Leader and all his blackshirted minions, I felt cheated by life itself. If I had had the strength to walk to church, I would have stood in front of the statue of the Madonna and cursed like old Ferini. My throat was still choked by scars or I would have denounced the world for swindling me. I came of age. My brother Elio died, and then as though by a miracle I began to see without my eyes.

'I always blamed other people for what happened to me. I always had done, even when I was a child. If I fell out of a tree, it was always somebody else's fault. If there was no one else there to blame, I blamed fate. My mother interpreted her life differently. She assumed the blame for everything like a true daughter of the Church. Every year, before the war, when we had all followed the procession of the Madonnuccia down to the bridge and back to bless the fields and save them from harm, the entire congregation would follow the priest with his prayers and responses. The Latin was a bit tricky for some of us, but there were certain easy bits that we all joined in with. *Mea culpa* was one of them. So we would wind down the dusty track, following the small painted Madonna on her stretcher. The monks of San Crescentino used to erect a scaffolding around the Madonna and cover it with broom flowers so that they and the priest could stand under it while the mass was said. The rest of us would stand out in the scorching sun, fidgeting the further back we were from the prayers and the sermon. They would also put up a scaffold that looked like a gallows and hang a bell there to call the faithful to the service. Every time we had to thump our chests and say *"mea culpa"*, I could see that my mother said it with pride, with fervour, convinced that everything really *was* her fault, and more hers than anyone else's. She would stare at the bell-gallows transfixed, as though imagining herself punished for all her manifold and unpardonable sins.

'I often heard her say that my blindness was a judgement on her for having neglected her household. When we were children, she made a special exception for my father: a lot of what was going on was his fault. Later, though, she seemed to reassess the damage and she decided that even his depression was her fault – other women didn't have husbands who moped and stared like hers did. When Elio died, shot by the Germans in the hills somewhere around Umbertide, she felt inconsolably guilty. She would sit for hours sobbing in the kitchen.

'We lived in a space no bigger than this room. It was divided into an upstairs and a downstairs. When we were all together, there were six of us shoving into each other like a colony of rabbits. When we sat in the kitchen, mother sobbing, father staring and sucking into the fireplace, Elenita cooking or sewing and me sitting motionless in my chair, there can't have been more than an arm's length between us and yet we ignored each other. It sounded as though my mother would drown herself in her tears, she made terrible noises like some of the patients on my ward in the hospital at Perugia. I started to talk again so that I could talk to her. I wanted to explain about blame. I wanted to tell her what a fine mother she was and what a fine woman, and that her mere proximity was healing me.

'I often think of the dresses she could have bought with my pension. She could have had a house built to her dreams and all the things she'd ever wanted or imagined. I have been indemnified for my loss. I have been paid for the war damage, so much for an arm and so much for a gut and an extra pension for my eyes. I have been indemnified by fate. I have had four decades to sit and think. If I hadn't been in love, I would have died of loneliness long before now, but I have had Valentina with me in my mind. My mother died as poor as she had lived. They were sorting out a pension for

166

me in Castello, but it didn't come through until after she died. I suppose they didn't want to decide on the amount until the war was over, in case they had to multiply it by millions.

'I think of Elio. I wonder if he suffered when he died. Did he know it was coming or was it just like a knock on the neck? I think of rabbits in cages, struggling to find room for their babies, losing them so many times that you would think they would just give up breeding. I think of the frightened look in their eyes every time a hand reaches into the cage to pull out supper by the neck. Sometimes, there isn't so much between us and them.

'I think of Elio missing his accordion. What music did they have up in the hills? They probably couldn't even sing, for fear of giving themselves away. I've still got his accordion somewhere, under the bed, I think. You can have it.'

Stefano was protesting that he could not accept such a gift when there was a knock on the door, and without waiting for an answer to his brusque 'May I?' Dr Mearelli was upon them and between them, wielding his black bag.

When he had gone, Mezzanotte said a little sheepishly, 'Don't leave me alone with the doctor, will you.'

'Not if you don't want me to, of course not.'

'Thank you. I'm afraid of them, they see the cracks in my shell. You must lock the door when you go so they can't get in.'

'I'm not going anywhere, I'm staying here with you.'

'Even tonight?' Mezzanotte asked anxiously.

'Yes . . . What's so special about tonight?'

'It's like an anniversary. I'm glad that you're staying. It seems fitting in a strange way. I'm keeping you from your home, though.'

'Isn't that what the army is all about – making men out of boys?'

'I always sympathized with the deserters. They did the right thing. Why did we have to fight for the lords of the cattle trucks?

'That's sleep coming now . . .' he announced, and it came as abruptly as the doctor pushing his disfigured head into the pillows.

XIII

'Massimo said we were not prepared for war. He said our army was a joke. At the time, I didn't understand all that he told me about such things. We came from two different worlds. He was a worker and I was a peasant. He said all the Alpini had to combat the bitter wind in the mountains of Greece were cardboard shoes and thin coats. I didn't even know where the mountains of Greece might be. I had heard talk of the mountains of the moon towards the lands of the Irregni across Le Marche, but not these other Greek ones. I was better on cities and towns: anywhere that had a railway terminal I could place and picture. I knew in what direction Nice, Paris, Calais, Zurich and Vienna lay because they were timetabled on the railway boards. Countries were more difficult.

'There were no trains to Africa but I knew something of it because of the news bulletins on the radio. All through the winter of '35 the announcements would blare out through the loudspeaker at the priest's house to the upper curve of the village. The news was always of victory; battles and victories, day after day. Six months later, we were an Empire. There was talk of chariot races and triumphal marches. There was talk of lions and wild beasts in the Colosseum again. I never knew there was so much to talk about until then. I had never heard the radio until about that time, and then, suddenly, there it was talking and talking. Elio used to play 'Faccetta Nera', it was one of his favourite songs. When the radio wasn't talking, it used to sing that too.

'I never thought much about the war. We had our own battles to fight. There was hail and there was drought. There were the beetles that ate my father's potatoes. There were weevils that ate the corn. There were fevers and accidents, and then there was the continual fear of the future. Everyone feared the future, experience had shown that it never brought anything but trouble.

'I suppose if I had to say then what a war was, I would have described it as a great many people talking, some battles as quick as flick cartoons, some songs, and then a lot more talking, louder and faster. Victory is short, the whispers are saved for defeat.

'I never thought a war could be lying in a barracks fighting off a lot of stupid teasing. I spent most of the war waiting. We waited to hear if we would be sent to Africa. But it was other soldiers who were shipped to Libya. Everything was so far away; it dulled and blurred. Even the air raids were always elsewhere. I saw no bombs crash over roofscapes, or buildings collapse like mud dams. They were never near, they lived as hearsay, stokers of fear. Men from our battalion deserted by the dozen. And I knew that a lot of deserters were shot. We heard about it all the time. I am not sorry to say that I never served on a firing squad. I met someone who had, but that was all. It is not that I miss having seen the war, it is just that I missed it. I never saw it happen. I lived in a barracks, I slept in a uniform, I slept in ditches, I lost my best friend and I lost all these bits of my body, yet I never saw battle.

'It is a strange paradox that no one here in the village wants to talk to me about the war because they see me mutilated and they remember how terrible the war was here for them and they think my war was worse. The atrocities I saw were all in my dreams after I was sent to the hospital. I have heard people being reprimanded in whispers for referring to my injuries as an accident; and yet it was an accident, in a way. I was the victim of a random attack. No one bothered to take a gun and shoot me, no one caught me with the whiplash of their machine-gun fire. No tankman fired a cannon or plane dropped a bomb. I . . .' Mezzanotte interrupted himself with a dry cough followed by a deep grating breath.

'Forgive me, Stefano, the day is passing and you must need some air. I find it eases me to talk. No wonder we all loved the radio: it was just like us, saying what we had to say, talking, if need be, to an empty room. A fountain of words controllable by a switch. An electric monologue, a talking memory, a rewriting of the truth to suit ourselves, relayed with an official stamp. Like me, Stefano – I have an official stamp, I am a registered war veteran, a registered

169

mutilated person, registered blind; my sister told me that even my artificial arm is stamped "Government property". So you might think my memories of the war would be the official memory, the official version. In which case I could recount them in two sentences. After an air raid over Colle Val D'Elsa, a ruined house exploded and killed my friend, Private Massimo Gavarini. Then I could say that from the time I joined the army until my accident, I lived in a state of mild confusion and the last thing I saw was the sea.

'At home we didn't consider the sea. If anyone mentioned the sea it was really Lake Trasimeno they were talking about. We were landlocked; the sea was not only distant, it was incomprehensible. It was more incomprehensible than the moon. We saw the moon every night. We planted our crops by its phases. We pruned the vines and transplanted our seedlings at its dictation. Its face was a familiar face and its name was familiar both for itself and for its mountains, which showed themselves on clear days from the crest of Muccignano.

'I followed Maestro Rossi's fair all over the country, but it was an inland fair trading on the meagre earnings of peasants and the richer pickings of the inland towns. They had an understanding between them in the fairground world, the inland fairs never so much as smelt the sea. Their rivals stuck to the coastal routes. So I travelled and travelled but I didn't see the sea at all.

'They moved us to Ravenna in the spring of '42. There was talk of the war being over soon. Some talked of victory and some of defeat, but either way no one thought it would last for long. We knew very little of what was actually going on. We were bombarded by radio announcements, calls to duty and endless congratulations. We heard of the loss of our battalions like so many setbacks on a chessboard. We were the pawns, touched with glory by our service to the Leader. We were the inevitable sacrifices, offered like careless moves by a child in a game against a grand master. We lost whole countries like pieces. It had long been necessary not to see things, to pretend not to notice what was going on and to do it so well that certain things ceased to exist. At home, we had survived for

170

decades, probably centuries, by limiting the world to the known world of our village. Anything beyond was threatening. To leave was to draw attention to the nest, to attract the predators and lead them back. My traipsing around after Valentina before the war had filled my family with dread.

'The radio talks a lot about Regionalism, but it misconceives the regions. I come from Umbria and I understand my region as a name. When I meet someone from Le Marche, I know that he is an Irregno as surely as I am to him a Papalino: again, they are names that we bandy about and understand. Yet my region lies within the boundaries of this village. It rises to the east with the crest of Zeno Poggio then it skirts down towards San Severino to the north, climbing to Rocagnano and Muccignano and Sant Agnese, stretching far across the hill to the west from Bolbina to Nuvole, and travelling along the facing crest through the pine woods with their cypress trees that stand sentinel over the patchwork fields and woods that drop down to the heart. The two hilly streets are the arteries that run from the two churches: the parish church and the monastery church, with their competing bells. Either side of the river the fields stretch out like opened fins. The road and its various tracks lie like crooked spines. To the south the village draws together into a head pointing open-mouthed towards Castello.

'My compatriots are those who were born and live within these frontiers. Our language is the dialect of these hills. The dialect of San Severino is not the same. Old men from either village cannot understand each other well. Our loyalties were never to the Leader or the King, or to the Christian Democrats or the Communists. They were to each other. We voted for each other without the palaver of elections and ballots. We supported each other, growing like vine and tree so intertwined that separation was a physical impossibility.

'The war wasn't really our war, so a victory would not have felt like our victory. But when it came, the defeat was our defeat. Perhaps that was why soldiers who had taken little interest in the war took an interest in the peace. There were men in our unit who were far more confused than I. There were soldiers who still didn't

171

speak Italian by the time we moved to Ravenna. They learnt to decipher a few essential orders, enough to keep them out of trouble; for the rest, they were locked in their own languages. Massimo and I understood each other, more or less. There were words and phrases that we had to explain, but we communicated well. Mind you, Massimo spoke to me in Italian. When we went to visit his family, he used a different dialect and it was much harder to follow what he said.

'There were boys from the south in our unit who might have been speaking German for the sense it made. There was a Sardinian man, older than me by a few years, who used to whimper in his sleep. He always tried to speak to me. He gave me cigarettes and he would tag along when I had free time. He kept telling me something, but it always came out as gibberish. He had very black eyes which gave out no light. They swallowed you up, they drew the light in. They were worrying eyes. At first he had acted like an animal, pacing and charging at the fence. He spent some time in prison. When he came out he seemed tamed and broken. It was rumoured that he had tried to shoot himself with his rifle when he first arrived but he couldn't make it fire. When he came out of the cells, he stopped following me around. I didn't notice him any more, and then he hanged himself on the barbed wire enclosing our compound. They didn't send his body home. They sent a letter, it was said, to his family in Sardinia saying, "lost in action". It would be hard to imagine less action than the apathy of our camp.

'I was used to rising at five and working in the fields. My body grew heavy and my mind grew dull living through the monotony of those days in the army. Reveille was the most exciting part of the day and the busiest. We had to get up, dress, make our beds, clean our equipment and go on parade. After that we would just sit around. If it was my turn for guard duty I would take it; if not, I'd play cards. A lot of the time I thought about Valentina. I used to write to her and a lot of the time was spent waiting for her reply. I monitored the post far more closely than I did the war.

'After the New Year she wrote me a card every month. She always posted them on the 15th of the month, but they would take

172

several weeks to arrive. They were picture postcards of cathedrals from the cities she had visited. Each one had the same message: "Remembering you, your Valentina". Each one was postmarked from a different town. The picture and the postmark did not tally. January, February, March, April were all months of the same message. Valentina had a strange way of doing things, she was very complex. She used to play games. She always had, she would make up situations and they would seem more real to her than her own life. I know the war distressed her. She was terrified of insects. Anything that came out of the air and stung frightened her. Wasps, bees, horseflies and hornets were her pet hates. She had once been stung by a wasp and been in a coma for an entire day. The mere idea of aeroplanes and bombs filled her with horror.

'I could well imagine that she had invented an alternative me, created a different play with her at the centre. She was ignoring the war, pretending perhaps that I wasn't a soldier. Her cards were to tease me. She had teased me before. She had a slightly cruel streak. I know she was very fond of some of the animals in the fair. When one of the monkeys died, she cried so hard her head puffed up, and she would dose the dogs herself when they were ill. For all that, she used to tease them when they were chained, she'd poke them with a stick and irritate them until they'd snarl at her.

'I knew that eventually she would relent, because she always did. Eventually she would come back home as sweet and pliant as the best of loves. She played with me, but I didn't mind, I knew that she was like a wild animal that I had tamed with my love. Her playing was a ritual, a strange mating ritual that I imagined belonged to her tribe.

'Meanwhile I wrote to her at all the places and collection points I could think of. I told her of Massimo's death, I told her of our move to Ravenna; I told her of the desire that consumed my nights and the longing that consumed my days. But most of all I told her that I loved her and I always would.

'On 10th May she rewarded me with a letter. Valentina had never been to school. She had learnt to read and write from the gypsy Agata, who was far from being the harridan I had taken her

173

to be. The gypsy Agata loved poetry. She taught it to Valentina, dozens of lines about love and beauty. When Valentina bothered to, she wrote beautiful letters. They sounded like poetry. She used words so soft they felt like little caresses.

'You know, after she came to see me in the Military Hospital she wrote me four letters. I have them still. I have always treasured them. They are a balm to my wounds. They are a vision, an arm, a touch. They mean more to me than all my life. I never get them out nowadays. I used to touch them and sniff them, but the paper is rough now from my fingers, and the smell is my own. They were read to me as they arrived and I memorized each one, just as she used to learn Agata's poetry. Four kisses. Four miracles, Stefano.

'I wanted to tell you about the sea. I started off and then the wind got inside my head. I am confused. What shall I do now. What shall I say?

'I can smell blood in the room. There is smoke on my tongue. I am thirsty.'

Stefano was glad of the interruption. He felt restless. He had been fidgeting for the last several minutes, pulling at a loose thread in his borrowed cardigan and playing with it. He felt very aware of Mezzanotte's own restlessness. He had come to rely on the old man's calm.

'I'll go to the bar,' he volunteered.

He was gone before his offer could be refused. He rushed out without his coat, grabbing a scarf on his way to the door which he wrapped around his neck four times so that it covered his mouth. The chill outside was such that it instantly cracked his lips. He breathed into the damp wool of the scarf, inhaling deeply as though to free his lungs from any contagion from Mezzanotte's wheezing. Out in the brilliant glare of the rounded, bluish mounds of snow, he felt elated and slightly drunk. This made him think of actually getting drunk, something he had not done in weeks.

At Concetta's he stocked up as though for a party. Several people asked him, 'How is he?' to which he would invariably reply, 'Fine, fine.' Each time he repeated the word he felt a slight nausea, as

174

though he knew that Mezzanotte wasn't fine at all. His rational mind believed Dr Mearelli, but his intuition was locked into Mezzanotte's claustrophobic world.

Stefano sensed that the old man had told him all the incidental details of his life. The two things he had not explained yet were the outcome of his love and what had caused his 'accident'. He knew that Mezzanotte was struggling to tell him now. Everyone saw him as a dark, enigmatic figure, a stronghold of secrets. What would be left of him once all these secrets were told? He was emptying himself out, preparing to rid himself of all thoughts and memories. He was handing on his past and his dreams, he was giving away his anchor and his roots. Once they were gone, broadcast like so many handfuls of seed, what would be left to stop him drifting away?

The illness and the snow had bitten into Mezzanotte's routine. The support system of half a century had been taken away. Stefano returned through sculpted lanes of snow. On either side of him were shovelled walls of whiteness. He felt a vicarious sense of vertigo. It was so slippery he had to feel his way along the frozen corridor. It seemed much further than the hundred metres he had run so many times before. His steps were slow and unsteady.

As Stefano turned to tackle the deeper snow of Assunta's garden, he realized that the street was deserted. Apart from Concetta at the bar, there had been nobody around. He looked back at the bright dazzle of the drifts and he shivered, more with fear than cold. The street had never been entirely empty before. The village had never seemed so devoid of friendly faces. He hurried back into the dark womb of the sickroom. Once inside, he bolted the door.

All through the middle of the day, despite the apparent desolation of the village, visitors came and went, providing constant interruptions. Dr Mearelli came, carried in on a draught of irritable concern.

'So, how do you feel now?' he asked. The words transformed themselves on the way out of his mouth into a veiled challenge.

'Fine, Doctor, I have no complaints.'

'Good, good,' the doctor answered, giving the impression that whatever reply his patient made, his own would be the same. The

175

doctor looked down at Mezzanotte and his gaze stayed there, pinned like a captive butterfly to a board. He felt as though someone had sneaked up behind him and anaesthetized his capacity for thought. He realized that he had never seen the blind man's eyes. He wanted to take the dark glasses away and examine his eyes. He wondered, after seventeen years of practising medicine, that he was so unprepared for such an act. He was embarrassed to find himself behaving more like a witch doctor than a medical doctor. He was willing Mezzanotte to remove his black shield.

'Would you strip a snail of its shell?' Mezzanotte asked.

Dr Mearelli blushed and stammered.

'Well, I can't stay here all day. I'll look in again later.'

'I sleep early, Doctor,' Mezzanotte lied. 'Perhaps it would be better if you came tomorrow.'

'I'm sure your companion can let me in,' Dr Mearelli insisted.

'Stefano goes off duty at six. He's tired and he'll be sleeping early too.'

The doctor made his slow way through the snow. Thick flakes were falling again, adding to the existing mounds, whitewashing the occasional stains, covering the surface scrapings of hungry birds and plastering over the holes of human tracks. The sky was a uniform white. He thought of the linen room at the hospital with its hundreds of starched, stacked sheets and runners, and he thought of a first communion. He had wanted to make friends with the blind man. He had always thought of himself as a delicate man, more skilled than those around him. He was the wielder of innumerable scalpels and blades, his art was one of delicacy, *par excellence*. And yet, trudging through the snow, with his rubber boots sinking occasionally into the edges of hidden drifts, he felt the boundaries of his own existence less defined. He felt clumsy for the first time in his life. He punched his gloved hand into a coping of snow, sending a shower of icing sugar into the field beyond. He looked at his padded fist with scorn, as though it did not belong to him. He was used to the fine rubber gloves of the operating theatre and to the balletic movements of his profession. He brought his offending hand down to his side and let it hang there rigid and disgraced.

176

Something about the blind man and the conscript threatened him. The further away he got from the beehive of the village and the troubling cell of the blind man's room, the happier he felt. By the time he reached the edge of the vineyard with its limbless tree trunks jutting forlornly out of the covering snow, he had decided to go back the next day and make amends to Mezzanotte. He hit on the plan of taking his elder son, Roberto, with him, to keep him from succumbing to the confusion that overcame him every time he entered that particular sickroom. Meanwhile, there was a blizzard threatening. The snow was tickling his face in a rush of tiny kisses. Flakes were spinning around his head like summer butterflies.

After the doctor, Assunta came, bearing a tray of food and a further basket of provisions. After Assunta, Rosina arrived with a freshly baked loaf of bread. After Rosina, Estelio came with his wife, bringing a bottle of *cynar* with a large gold bow around its neck and a bunch of flowers, both presents from the village. After Estelio, the blizzard began to wrap its white bandages around the village, binding everyone to their firesides, muffling every sound with its orchestra of wind. The wind rattled window shutters and banged doors, it snapped the snow-laden branches from frozen trees, it took the snow and whipped it into powdered glass to hurl at men and dogs. Once it had cleared its domain, it worked with a more creative hand, sculpting the drifts, erecting primitive statues and carving smooth ridges in the white landscape. It sealed the door of Mezzanotte's place, piling up snow as high as the handle, locking him in, holding him hostage to the biting cold and the desolation of the snow storm.

By evening, the village had been stripped of its distinguishing features. Concetta, who was an avid cinema-goer and knew, via the screen, the face of every landscape in the world, telephoned all her cousins in Castello to tell them that her village had been transformed into the Russian Front. Later that evening, she wanted to phone them back to tell them that since the blizzard, the landscape had changed again. It had become the Antarctic. From her bedroom window she could see along the valley to the north. Moonlight reflected in the voluptuous curves of the drifts. When Generale

177

Umberto Nobile flew to the South Pole, the newsreel had shown just such a landscape. There had been frozen bodies trapped in the ice that had lain there for thirty years. But she could not phone, the telephone was dead. She supposed the snow had brought down a line. It was romantic to be so isolated. In the morning she would help her husband to dig their way out of their cocoon. Meanwhile, she felt an arousal goaded by the snow. The bleaker the outside world, the more sensual she became. At ten o'clock she awoke her husband from his fireside sleep to share this unexpected echo of her youth.

Twenty minutes later a low moan reached out across the valley, elongating into an anguished howl as years of frustration and unresolved dreaming escaped like caged birds shaken into the night. A hunting barn owl picked up the sound and carried it into the weighted branch of an umbrella pine. It called sporadically through the still hours. It wakened Mezzanotte from a troubled sleep and his companion from a dreamless stupor.

Inside the capsule of his room, time had become meaningless. They had slept intermittently from daylight to darkness and the room was lit only by a glint of moonlight heightened by the snow. Mezzanotte's breathing had quickened in his sleep. He wheezed now with a regularity that made it seem normal. There were no more raspings or gratings, just the regular wheeze like an engine running somewhere in the background.

'The night has lit a fire in each of my eyes, Stefano. By one, my father sits staring, sucking at the pipe he cannot afford to fill. The other is blazing, the kindling has burst into flame. It was broom twigs, they crackle and splutter and sparks fly out, singeing everyone and everything within range. There is a queue of people outside our cottage, waiting for their turn to blow on the leaping flames. Elio has taken a pair of bellows. He is leaning through the kitchen window fanning the fire into a furnace. He was always impatient. My eye has taken in the wood below Muccignano on the scarred triangle where the forest fires always begin. My eye finds its way to the driest saplings and the patches of shrivelled bracken to fan the flames. My mother would like to riddle the ashes and

178

extract the pieces of hot clinker and press them into her breast; but this is a furnace that cannot be controlled or contained. The ashes will heap up of their own accord and then scatter in the wind.

'My mother is mortified by her failure to cull the clinker from my fire. She sits down at the end of the battered table and sinks her tired head on to her arms. She remembers the day she culled lilies from the riverside and took them to the *camposanto* to her mother's grave. She remembers that the cemetery ladder was already in place. She remembers using the ladder to climb up past the layers of slotted coffins in that giant and macabre chest of drawers to deposit the flowers in the tin vase beside her mother's photograph. Once she was down, she removed the ladder, but a voice called out from inside one of the tombs: 'Don't take the ladder away or I can't get out.' She screamed and ran, too terrified to see the tousled head of a vagrant emerge from one of the empty slots.

'In the kitchen, she holds her head, remembering what fear and tribulation she has known. She has been spoken to from beyond the grave, and she has seen bombs falling on her village, gathering her friends to their graves. She has witnessed too many things. She is tired. The flames swallow her up, licking around her pinned grey hair.

'My left eye is transfixed by my father, it aches with the cooling embers of his despair. My right eye burns. Low flyers drop bundles of propaganda on to it. My eye consumes them and reaches up for the planes. Grey English aircraft break through the smoke. They open their hatches and drop hot coals. My eye catches them, darting backwards and forwards in its socket like Annibale D'Agnano, the juggler at the fair.

'I could have dipped my hand in and taken out a nugget of clinker, but the time has passed. I must tell my mother that the time has passed. She has been here today. There is a scent of lilies in the room. She has been here to gather sacking. She is making herself a new apron. She draws thread from the sacking. It catches fire and burns like a piece of string, slowly as a fuse.

'The wind has been hiding in my head. It is a north-easterly. It

179

leaps out of my other eye and makes a tunnel of flame. Somewhere near the base, there is a blue streak at its heart. A jet as blue as the Adriatic at the beginning of June.

'Water beats fire. So the fire has gone hissing under the petticoats of spume. My lids roll backwards and forwards, propelled by the tide. It is washing in. It is dragging out. There are worm casts in the sand. It seems as though thousands of thrushes have stood in line and smashed so many snail shells that a ridge of their debris has been left behind. The sea takes this ridge, forcing it to dance with the insistent edge of the waves, bobbing a polka along the shore while gulls shriek and circle in the sky. The sky is blue with the blue of the robes of the Madonna. The sea is a grey-blue and dull in places, like the chipped paint on the scroll of Valentina's caravan. The shade is the same chalky shade of that faded paint. Where the sun singes the water, it sparkles a burn. The sand is the pale yellow of ground corn. There are no husks. This is the first time that I have seen the sea.

'Although we have nothing to do in Ravenna but pretend to be extremely busy every time an officer or outside observer approaches, we are given very little free time. Our passes are for hours, not days. We are told that our brothers in arms are fighting for their lives and the glory of our Empire in the desert and on the plains. There is talk of garrisoning the Greek islands. We are told that we must stand by, permanently ready to fill the gaps that might arise. There are rumours of breaches so wide that the entire population of Italy couldn't fill them. There are those who follow the war closely. They gather in their free time to listen to the radio from London. I have two strands of thought that I twist together and separate. I play with them like a penitent with a rosary. One strand is for Massimo and one is for Valentina. I brood over his death and her life. My love is monstrously selfish, so selfish that it often elbows grief out of my heart. I live for Valentina.

'We have orders today to lay rolls of barbed wire along the beach. We have been told that the Resistance receives arms from Yugoslavia via this stretch of sand. Night craft have been observed. The last unit before ours has started the work. The idea is to make

180

a minefield out of this apparently innocent swathe of sand. The coils of barbed wire will act as a deterrent in the meantime. We have been told that the Communists of Reggio Emilia must be crushed. I feel like a vandal defacing the sea. A lorry has brought the rolls of barbed wire. We have a pair of wire clippers between every three soldiers. We are working in teams. The rolls of wire are too heavy to move, the lorries do not tip up. Part of the unit is deployed in heaving the wire into the sand. The rest of us have nothing to do but look away.

'I am a fish breathing the salt water through my gills. I dip my fingers into the cool shallow water and feel the exquisite tug of the Adriatic pulling me out, beckoning, calling. I feel tempted to run after the disappearing wave. I envy the gulls their freedom. I long to throw myself into the water. Sand sticks to my hands as I rummage through it. I imprint the wistful beauty of the water on my mind. I breathe in the tang of it on the air. I inhale deeply. It is like a drug. I feel elated. I long to bring Valentina here to show her this miracle. I decide that we will spend our honeymoon on this beach, when the war is over and the barbed wire has been rolled back. We will lie in the sand together with the grains sticking to our bodies. We will lie under the water. We will swoop and shriek like the gulls. Massimo had wanted to show me the wonder of sand filtering between my toes. I feel my blood race.

'We spread out across the beach, a line of soldiers parallel to the shells. There are low dunes behind us. I have eyes only for the sea, so I turn away from those dunes and the land behind them. We pace across the sand, dragging barbed wire with us. There is a great deal of cursing as hands and uniforms get torn. We stop. Orders are being relayed along our line like Chinese whispers. The waves and the gulls drown words. The sea ripples back to the horizon. It is a never-ending lake. I gaze across its silken surface entranced. A seagull with a black hood swoops down and settles on a wave. I looked into it and became its black head. It dived under the water. It dived and never came up.

'We didn't know that the beach had already been mined.

181

'I don't remember the next month at all.

'Then I spent six months in the Military Hospital in Perugia. Six months of hell.'

V

VALENTINA

———— XIV ————

'Stefano, Stefano!' the old man called, knowing he was there but wanting to say the name so that he could hear it because it had grown dear to him. 'Stefano, have you ever felt an insect walking across your face? A praying mantis? Have you ever opened an eye, cautiously because of the creepy tickling of spiky heels, and seen the orange glow of a praying mantis with its hands clasped in prayer over the bridge of your nose?'

'No, I can't say I have. I've never even seen a praying mantis.'

'At the end of every August, when we brought in the corn, they would hover in the long grass and the bulrushes at the edge of the field. It was hard work but mostly it was hot work. Every time there was a moment's break, when we stopped for water or for lunch or for a slug of wine, I used to throw myself down among the cut cornstalks and lie under their striped shade, and a praying mantis would come to investigate. They were as curious as the monks themselves. The priest was never curious; he didn't need to be, he knew more about us than we did ourselves. He gleaned all his information from the confessional.

'Just think, the priest knew who everybody's real father was. But the monks used to trudge around the village making detours on their way up and down to Muccignano and to their church at San Crescentino. They would flap their brown habits and slap their open sandals on dust or ice and they were, some of them, the most inveterate scandalmongers. Mother said that because they couldn't have a woman themselves, they liked to hear about what everyone else did. They adored gossip. On Sundays they would go to mass at our church and stand or kneel with their necks craning around the congregation, straining to see who was who, to match faces to stories.

185

'Like so many things, they were here in the valley before the war and gone by the time it was over ... Where was I?' he asked abruptly.

'The praying mantis,' Stefano reminded him gently from his horizontal position on the camp bed.

'Eh, *si*, eh,' Mezzanotte commented. 'If this night were any longer than it's going to be, I'd be senile by the end of it. Shall we have a drink? What do you say?'

'Of course. I'll get it,' Stefano said, rolling out of bed on to the cold terracotta tiles.

The *cynar* bottle was already half-empty. He wondered aloud if the antibiotics could work with the sticky artichoke juice. Perhaps they would react. His uncle Andrea had a thing about interacting drugs, it was one of his pet themes.

'There are enough chemical deposits in my body to float a mining company,' Mezzanotte snorted. 'When I'm dead, if you have any initiative, you should shovel for chemical salts in my veins. Dig for minerals. I am a sack of old newspaper pieces and ashes, a stitched-up sack of old newsreel and salts. The famous salts of the earth. Salts as pure as the crystals we cycled back with from Volterra are interred in me. A simple man, a harmless old man, and so skilfully sewn!'

As though by some chemical process, Mezzanotte's humour had turned to anger and was now transforming itself into his more habitual nostalgia. Stefano had poured out half a mug of *cynar*. For the first time ever he was afraid of the old man. They were shut in by the snow. There was no escape. He took a long swig from the bottle and shuddered as the bittersweet liquid burnt his throat.

'Here you are,' he said, taking the two steps necessary to get him from the so-called kitchen to Mezzanotte's bed. It was dark in the room. Too dark to see what he was doing, but the space was limited and his movements few, so Stefano manoeuvred himself around the room as though he too were blind. He could have turned the light on, the switch was as near as everything else, but for once he feared what he would see in the light more than he feared the darkness. He lay back on his mound of blankets, low to the floor beside the much higher bed.

Within minutes his fear had passed and the darkness felt soothing. So did Mezzanotte's deep husky voice.

'I would have swum in the sea. I would have returned to the Adriatic and let salt water lap over me. I would have gone there with Valentina. I would have gone, but I never did. Nor have I ever swum in a lake or a river. The most water I have ever known, after my christening, was buckets of water tipped over my head to wash in, and water was scarce in our village, it was not to be wasted. I have heard that people even immerse themselves in rivers for pleasure. That was not our way. We were all wary of water.

'One of Assunta's brothers once swam across the Tiber in Castello. The ferry was there but the ferryman was missing, and the river was swollen and unfordable. He had his wife with him and a young child with a fever so high they could do nothing. He sat his wife on the planks with the screaming baby in her arms, and tried to push the ferry to the other side. His desire to save his baby was greater than his sense. Like any of us, he had never been in water. It was January and nearly freezing. The current took him and he would have drowned had not a soldier seen him from the bank and rescued them. The baby died and no one else ever swam again.

'And yet, sometimes in the hospital I woke up drowning. I was tied down to the riverbed. The water was so cold it burnt me. Sometimes it froze me and sometimes it burnt me. The chains of the ferry caught and tore at my flesh as they grated back and forth over my weighted body. If I tried to breathe, my mouth filled with water and links of that rusty chain. My mouth was not my mouth and yet I was my mouth; a raw pulp entrance to that tunnel of death.

'Sometimes I woke, and I saw myself, bandaged from my head to my groin, swaddled in blood-stained cloths. I saw myself choking and struggling on a white metal horse. A black fist encased in an armoured glove had pierced through the trunk of my body, it had punched off the front of my head. It came out of my mouth like a puppet. It squirmed in my throat like a giant snake's head, stinging and biting only to reappear more powerfully. It reached out and turned the handle of the carousel, a massive cranking handle beside

187

my horse. It turned that handle with such speed that the hurdy-gurdy music turned into a scream. It turned the handle so hard that the horses on the carousel flew round and round, a red froth pumping over them. I was tied to my white horse, strapped to its back and kept rigid by the gloved hand.

'Sometimes the hand wasn't there and I would be strapped with bandages to the metal horse and then made to turn at lightning speed past all the faces of the Maestro Rossi's fair. Valentina was there, hanging upside down like a bat with her beaded bag cut in half and stuffed into her eyes. As I passed she would reach out for me with tiny brown claws sawn off and dripping at the knuckle. The gypsy Agata and the gypsy Emiliana were there, and the Maestro Rossi with two monkeys with their necks twisted stuck over his mouth for a moustache. The spiderwoman and the fat lady and Annibale D'Agnano were all there too, hanging upside down in a human pelmet around the edge of the carousel. Instead of arms, though, they all had brown bats' wings. The horses rode up and down and round and round until smoke came out of the central axle, then a flame leapt into the air, shattering all the horses in a series of great explosions. At each, the bats would squeak and flap and fly away. Then my father would come with his worn truncheon of cypress wood and he would hit me around the head, shouting, "Don't you know we must save all we can, even the bad ones?"

'His blows would force my head down and I would see slime oozing through my toes. It was the slime of his ruined crop, the slime of rotting potatoes. I was standing in a strip of field full of putrefying tubers. My father beat me with his cypress stick. He was so sad and so angry he showed me no mercy. He made the blood run from my head. He forced me to pick up the rotting lumps and put them in the sack I was carrying. Each time I bent to pick up another, there would be blood on it. I thought, "This is the blood from my father's stick." But it was the blood from pieces of meat, pieces of me cut up and scattered in the mud.'

—— XV ——

Mezzanotte paused only long enough to take a swallow from the mug of *cynar*. He seemed agitated, hurried, as if now that he had begun to tell the last of his secrets, he was anxious to be done.

'I was not a man or a boy, I was an animal. I was not myself, but a part of me was trapped inside that wounded animal, choking on its blood, drowning, tormented by its pain. The pain was everywhere, chopped and pounded and ground into everything. I ceased to exist. I swapped my body for pain. Only sometimes I rose above that delirium, hovering under the vaulted ceiling of a bandaged ward. I wanted to leave. I could see a long palace with rows of shutters outside the hospital window and I could see through a narrow alleyway beside it the bell tower of a church. I saw a corridor of funnelled sunlight and my will yearned to go down it, to follow its bright warmth out of the pain. But the pulp on the bed was stronger, it dragged me back time and time again. It dragged me back into its nightmare, smothering me with its slabs of skinned meat, flaying me with its torn nerves, its jutting bone splinted and bundled back, pressed into a shapeless concentrated block of pain.

'Just as I divided and became both myself, high above the bed, and the body below me in the bandages, so I struggled to subdivide, to become many things and thus by cunning to escape. I was too strong. I heard a doctor say so. I was floating up by the ceiling when three doctors came round, escorted by a troop of nurses. Some of these were in uniforms of the Red Cross, others were sisters of mercy rustling in their white robes with starched white butterflies on their heads. One doctor was like the Leader. Everyone bowed to him. He stood beside my bed and he turned back to his minions, smiling.

189

'"Incredible, eh. I would never have believed anyone could survive in that state. Medically, this boy should have died within a couple of days of the incident. Eh, these peasants are strong – too strong, perhaps, poor lad. It looks like he still might make it. He's like a beast of burden, only his instinct keeps him alive."

'I grew more cunning, I divided myself into fragments. I pulled from more than one direction. Once, I got to the brink of the light, I was so close to getting away. But the sisters of mercy showed none to me. They held me down. They forced me to breathe in pain. They wouldn't let me leave the ward. After that I spent a lot of time underwater learning to swim. My arms and legs mutinied against me, and endless times when I was drowning, they brought me ashore and rubbed sharp sand in my wounds.

'When I began to ride on the carousel, I knew that if I managed to speak to Valentina she would help me. Each time my metal horse whirled past I tried to call to her. All I needed was one word. I tried to say her name. For weeks and weeks I tried to say her name, but it had sharp edges and they caught in my throat. Then I had more cuts and more pain. I could not deal with the razor edges of her name. Eventually I understood that, I had to adapt. To escape across to her I had to adapt. The tunnel was made from the walls of my own body. Each time I passed Valentina hanging on to the carousel, I called, "Help." It didn't come easily from my lacerated throat.

'Once I had seen Annibale the juggler play with fire. He dipped a stick in petrol and set fire to it and then he opened his lips wide and kissed it with a lover's kiss. I saw him repeat this several times and then, quite suddenly, he pulled the stick from his mouth and threw it to the ground and began to dance around it. Then he stuck his head in a barrel of water and came up howling like one of the Maestro's monkeys. He had burnt his throat, burnt his tongue. Somewhere in the explosion there must have been just such a stick: a firebrand that fate had rammed down my throat. I moved the hole where my mouth used to be and I whispered, "Help." Sometimes I managed to make a sound, sometimes not. I didn't manage to make a word. I didn't manage to shape any words for

190

some months. No wonder Valentina didn't hear me. She didn't know I was there. That world was alien to her, the underworld; she belonged to the field of light. She had her own field of light, independent of death. I had lain there so many times, sheltering her black mane in the crook of my arm, shepherding her spent body into sleep.

'Had I been capable of it, I would have said or done anything in that time of torture. I would have confessed to all the crimes of history and assumed the guilt of the entire world if it had meant easing the unspeakable weight of that pain. When gradually it eased, I had long ago given up hope. I had delivered myself, devoid of any human qualities, to despair.

'One day I woke up from another night of having my skin picked by the waves, to find my sister, Elenita, near me. I recognized her voice. I felt bathed in sweetness and relief, and then that too turned to pain. I heard her voice again, soothing and kind. Her small rough fingers were in mine. I squeezed them and then I heard her cry. I thought, "I have become pain, even my touch transmits it. I have hurt my sister." Her sobs came like gasps of surprise. They always did. She had cried like that as a child. Then she stopped, and she spoke again. She said she had been to see me many times. She told me that she had sat by my bed for many hours. I squeezed her hand again, more gently.

'She asked, "Are you still inside there, are you still Alessandro, my brother?" I squeezed her hand twice, then the waves began to call me back. The tide was going out, washing the debris from an explosion in the sand. The sea was struggling to drag bits of twisted iron out with it. There were seagulls circling and screaming overhead, dipping and perching on the wreckage. The curls of spume at the crest of each wave were beige, the colour of the pulp of boiled chestnuts. It was the colour of Valentina's winter skin. Strips of her skin had been beaten like meringue and then strung out along the lips of every wave. I tried to say her name but my mouth filled with salt water and flakes of rust. I tried to think her name, but my mind had already drifted out to sea. It was floating somewhere near the grey horizon.

191

'I drifted in and out of stupors, in and out of delirium. Elenita came to see me every week. She sat by my bed and described the world to me: the immediate world of my bed, the ward, the hospital and the parts of Perugia nearest to it. I had never been to Perugia, although I had been to so many other places. I had been to the station of Ponte San Giovanni because I used to change trains there, but I never had time to travel the extra few minutes into the city centre. The fair never stopped there. It had camped on a field beyond the railway station. So I had never seen the Etruscan capital. Perugia for me had been the village of San Giovanni and illicit hours stolen from prying eyes in the cemetery. When we couldn't find anywhere more private, we used to hide in the *camposanto*.

'I have no fear of cemeteries. No fear of death. After the explosion I tried to die. I wanted to. I wanted to be put down like an animal. Since then the strength of my love has kept me going. My conviction has sustained me. As you see, I need very little food. It disturbs me to swallow. It is not exactly pain, it is worry. I think when they put me back together, they muddled up my senses. Food and fear are associated somewhere in the back of my throat. They are distantly related. You see, I do have some relations after all. I should have told Assunta, she worries so about my lack of family.'

Mezzanotte paused, filling the silence with his sibilant wheezing.

'Are you afraid of death, Stefano?'

'I don't know. I don't think so . . . I haven't thought about it. I used to be afraid that my mother would die. She died when I was seventeen. I used to be afraid of the dark. That was my real fear. It's dark tonight, I have kept the light off, and it seems fine to me.'

'Come back and sit on my bed, then, like you used to do. I say I'm not afraid to die, but I keep feeling confused. I feel there is something else that I would like to say. I have spoken so much, I have taken all the newspaper stuffing from inside me, all the torn-up pieces, and I have pasted them back together and left them with you. How can there be anything left to say of one life, one man? Eighty per cent of a man, some would say. What I am, though, is the love I feel, and that is undiluted.

'I'm in a hurry now. "If thy right hand offends thee, cut it off."

192

My hand never offended me. I hardly knew it. We were like strangers. When we went our separate ways, my right hand was dear to me. It had touched half the satin of my lover's skin. It had tangled its fingers in her hair. It had held her hand. It was my right hand that accompanied Massimo to his death. My right hand had a hundred messages for me. Perhaps that is why we have never truly parted. The ghost of my fingers signals to me.

'The edge of the riverbed in June has come to sit with us. There are a few trout in the centre stream. The river is running low, the heat drinks from its banks. There are lilies growing wild in clusters under the alder and the acacia trees that overhang the water by the bridge. We pass them in the procession of the Madonnuccia. The priest stops with his following monks and parishioners and he intones his prayers on the bridge. He is asking for the protection of the crops. We listen carefully. Our life depends on it, without the crops we would starve. "Save them, O Lord, from hail and lightning . . . Save them, O Lord, from plague and drought. Save them, O Lord" from so many things that the voice becomes monotonous and a boy's attention is prone to stray. I see the lilies, white trumpets with long stamens licked by sunlight into a pale gold. The scent rises up through the leaves to the bridge. The scent lodges in my nostrils and sends a sudden delirium to my head. The beauty of the lily captures me and holds me ransom to its cloying perfume. Then the procession moves on.

'There is a lily here in the room. There must be one in the flowers Estelio brought. Bring them here, Stefano, to my bed. Lilies are the flowers of the dead. No one ever picked these river lilies and took them inside, they were for cemeteries. Lots of sweet things are reserved for cemeteries: the sweetest flowers, stolen kisses, rest. Can you see the flowers?'

Stefano had just got comfortable on the bed, his head wedged against the footboard with its crude chipped picture of the sea. A beam of moonlight had found its way through the only uncovered piece of glass in the window. Its eerie shaft cut the room in half diagonally. It provided just enough light to see by. He brought the jug of flowers across to Mezzanotte, clearing a space on his cluttered bedside table. There were pills and balms and empty glasses there. Sure enough, there was a large waxen pink and white lily in the vase.

'Lovely, eh?' Mezzanotte whispered.

Leaning so close to the old man, Stefano noticed that his face had changed. All the colour had drained from his skin, leaving only the hairline scars, set like fences on a surveyor's map. The rest had the translucent waxiness of a votive candle.

'I have seen people so old, when I was a boy, that it seemed that if they were carried away from their firesides and into the light they would turn to powder like stored silk that disintegrates in the sun. It would do me no good to revert to such frailty. No good to be utterly dependent again. My body was wrecked in its youth: it is a blessing to be spared the ailments of old age. Remember that.

'It is natural to covet time. Something in me hankers now for a few more hours, a few more days. I feel rushed, despite my years of preparation. Remember, though, that I am content to go now as I am. I believe that a love as true as mine will be rewarded. It has been, literally, the light of my life. It has obliterated darkness, and kept my mangled body alive.

'In my mind's eye I am always a boy of twenty who still feels nineteen for having passed a year away from home and not received congratulations either on my twentieth birthday or my saint's day. In my mind's eye I look as I did then: a big, broad-shouldered country boy with a clear skin and curly hair. In Ravenna, on my evenings off, I used to meet Liliana at the foot of the monument in front of the railway station, then we would walk along those grand streets, me in my uniform, she in her raincoat, to the main square. We would weave through the granite colonnade, always following the same route, like ants to their nest. In this case, a small café behind the strange-shaped Church of San Vitale. The walls of the café were lined with gilt-framed mirrors. There would be other soldiers on dates, perhaps there were even others like me who took one girl out to talk about another one. Well, I used Liliana as a listening post, and all the while, I could see the back of her head in the mirror and my own face. Even as I talked, I imagined Valentina in her place.

194

'Elenita said that Liliana came to see me at Perugia, in the early days. It seems a long way to come to be shown a piece of meat covered in bandages and told that that bellowing heap is your friend. The me that she knew had gone. The me that I knew never left. I am still the same frank-faced young man with the crack-bridged nose and the wide brown eyes.

'If you ask me to describe my face as it is now, I can, although I have never seen it. I see my face as I once knew it although I know that there is a fine patchwork on my skin like an old map of the village. I have the cheeks of divided fields: a strip for corn, a strip for flax, a strip for potatoes, a strip for barley, a square for vegetables, a patch for melons, a bit for pumpkins along the edge of a ditch, and all between them, the lines of vines.

'Do you know that Valentina came to see me in the hospital? . . . It was 8th November, the week I got my new arm. They gave it to me for my morale. The bandages had been removed and I assume they were moved to pity by the sight. They never did understand that at that stage I could not see or feel what was there, so my morale was the best it had been since the explosion. Valentina was coming to see me. She had written to say that she would be coming – on the 8th, at four o'clock.

'It was Elenita who had tracked her down. She heard where the fair was from a returning soldier, and she wrote. I don't know what she wrote, but I fear it did not prepare my darling for the shock. I should, of course, have kept my bandages. The anonymous face of injury is so much more bearable than the reality of welts and scars. I should have covered my face. I thought so much of her, and so much about her, I still find it hard to credit that I was stupid enough to believe she could bear the shock.

'I have tried to imagine her dear sharp features annihilated by scars, and then to imagine the effect those scars would have on me. Knowing her vanity, I would ache for her, but I would not love her any less. I don't think it is possible to love her any more, but if it were, my pity would extend to that. I thought, like a stupid selfish dolt, that she would want to recognize me. My hair, at least, had grown back. The doctor had persuaded me to wear the plastic

195

arm, he said it would give me confidence. It didn't. It confused me. It felt like a clawing, grasping lump of lead pulling me down. I wanted to take it off, but it was too late.

'Elenita was there. She said, "Here she comes." Then she stood up, dropping something metallic on the floor. There was a click of high heels tapping down the ward, a delicious noise that other patients responded to as well. I felt the tension, the aroma of sex, fill the long room. Then the tapping was louder, it came to the end of my bed and it stopped. I waited for it to come round to my side, but it had stopped. A waft of rosemary-flower water stung my nostrils. My heart had stopped beating and was growing so large I thought it would burst out through my chest and mouth simultaneously. Then the blood began to race in my veins, pounding in my ears, cracking like machine-gun fire, drowning out almost every other sound. There was a buzz on the ward, a hum like a dislodged swarm of bees. Elenita was speaking, she said words that slurred and caught in the drumbeat of my blood. I thought I heard the word "outside" but I could not be sure.

'My tongue was like a dead fish in my mouth. I struggled to release it, to make it move. I had called her name so many times. I had slept repeating the syllables Va-len-ti-na, and I had woken innumerable times mouthing them still. They were my prayer, my chant, my life. I struggled to pronounce them. The sea flooded over the dunes I had erected against it and flooded my head again.

'I heard her voice, her soft melodic voice. It was higher than usual, it was awkward and stammering. I knew she was crying. I hated myself for hurting her. I had had five months to deal with the shock, she had had only these brief minutes.

'I forced myself to speak. I called out, "Help." I had meant to say, "Valentina."

'I heard her blow her nose. She said something I missed and then, "I'm so sorry, so sorry. O Alessandro. O my God!"

'I wanted to get up and comfort her. I had been up before. I could get up very slowly with a little help, easing myself this way and that so as not to pull too heavily on my internal injuries. I could walk too. I cursed myself for being supine and helpless to

196

assuage her grief. I cursed myself for being so overcome with emotion as to be virtually paralysed.

'I forced myself to speak. I called her name. I heard it reverberate around the high ward. I heard the shuffle of the sisters of mercy coming towards my bed. The strong hands held my thrashing body down. I felt hot breath in my face. A staff voice said, "Come on now, calm down, be good."

'Another hand touched my new arm. I felt it jolt on the stump. I didn't know if it was a nun or Valentina. I felt it had been touched but I didn't know by whom. I try to remember it as her. Who knows?

'Much later, Elenita came back. She had a bag of things that Valentina had brought for me. There were postcards of Florentine paintings, some biscuits, a pack of cards, a tie and a photograph. She had told my sister that she needed some time to adjust to the way I was. Elenita said that she, in turn, had explained that I was over-excited and really much better than I seemed. Valentina had promised that she would be back for Capodanno. She sent her love and she said that things would be better next time.

'Some people say that you can't die of a broken heart. I don't know about that. Perhaps what one dies of is failure. My father died of that. If it hadn't been for the letters, the four letters that followed after the New Year, I think I too might have died of failure. How could I have lived if I hadn't had the chance to tell her of my love? I dictated my own letters to Elenita. It was Elenita who read me Valentina's four.

'"Alessandro, my love, my love, I shall be with you soon." Her words were the sweetest words, sweeter than any medicine and a better healer than time itself. Time numbs and replaces. It fades, I don't know that it heals. "May nature then restore to you the grace/That you owned formerly..." Elenita only read that letter once and yet I knew that sonnet off by heart. It was the one poem I did know off by heart. It came from the only book we owned. When Valentina used to write such fine letters before the war, full of lines of poetry, she bought *The Sonnets of Michelangelo* and Elenita and I had learnt that poem to try to

197

share some of Valentina's passion. It was Elio who helped us in the end, he turned it into a song.'

Mezzanotte began to smile. '"Alessandro, my love, my love, if only you knew how I have missed you. I have been so afraid for you . . ." You see, inside this wrecked carapace I am the same man I ever was. I have had a chance to arrange my thoughts, to order my ideas. Some little things have changed. I feel neither bitterness nor blame. I have known loneliness but I have been saved from desolation. I have become a man. I have witnessed every emotion, but my love is undiluted.'

Stefano waited patiently for Mezzanotte to continue. The wind banged on the windowpane, dislodging a slice of snow, drawing his attention outside. An owl called somewhere far in the distance, and then there was silence again.

'Mezzanotte,' he whispered, 'are you asleep?' There was no answer, so he eased himself off the old man's bed. The silence continued and began to oppress him. There had not been such a silence for days. Then he realized what it was that was missing and he reached out to take Mezzanotte's hand. He was on the wrong side, Mezzanotte's good arm was further away, there was only a space where there should have been flesh under the covers where he was feeling.

'O Mezzanotte,' he called, 'Mezzanotte.' He touched the old man's chest, trying to bring back the wheezing that had been like a slow motor in the room. He thought, 'If I go to sleep, it will be back in the morning.' Then he lay down on his camp bed and pulled the covers up over his head, trying to recall some of the old man's monologues to keep him company.

It was still dark when he awoke an hour or so later. He turned the light on and as the single bulb dazzled the room, he found himself believing for a moment that he had been mistaken, and that Mezzanotte was still alive. He looked very much as he had always looked. The waxen quality of his skin seemed to have diminished. The old man's face was set at the exact moment before a smile lifted one side of his mouth up to ripple his scars.

198

'O Mezzanotte,' he whispered. He twisted his own mouth, willing himself on, knowing inside that the blind man was dead.

Stefano felt a division in himself. One part of him wanted to cry, the other part refused. Instead, he straightened the blankets across the body and he rearranged the room. He had never had any dealings with the dead. He knew from films that someone was meant to close the corpse's eyes. He realized with some apprehension that he had never even seen Mezzanotte's eyes. He told himself it was better for him to do whatever needed doing than some stranger. So he removed the black deep-cut goggles that Mezzanotte had worn day and night in his company. He had braced himself to see anything. He was prepared to see eyes in any state of disfigurement. What he saw shocked him more than that. What he saw were no eyes at all. There was smooth skin growing over the sockets. There seemed to be no scars, just skin and a sense of emptiness. He looked down at the naked face and tried to imagine it as Valentina must have seen it so many years before. Now it was like a piece of marquetry made by a skilled hand. It was a patchwork stitched as neatly as any nun could wish. Then, forty-eight years earlier, it must have been swollen and misshapen, raw and grisly.

He decided to wait until the morning before calling the doctor. It was too late anyway for anything Mearelli could do.

Once again he lay down on his camp bed. Every time he closed his eyes he heard the sea sucking out its tide, sucking out the ashes of Mezzanotte's eyes. The sea that had put out the fire, the fire that had put out his sight. He found himself staring around the room, trying to memorize everything about it, drinking in the details. Under the bed, more prominently, he was sure, than it had been a few days earlier, he saw the dusty box of Elio Mezzanotte's accordion. He pulled it out by a black leather strap that snapped in his hand. He opened the box, feeling as ashamed of his curiosity as if he had been a graverobber. He found himself explaining, 'He said I could have it.' It wasn't the having, though, that made him uneasy, it was the touching, the violation of relics.

Inside, there was a white rosette in stained satin of the kind boys used to have for their first communion. There was a lock of child's

199

hair, the light reddish-brown of fallen needles from a Christmas tree. There was a small wooden knife carved roughly out of olive wood and there was the squeezebox with its battered keyboard and black leather sides. As Stefano picked it up it let out a low wheeze which startled him. He put it back, noticing, as he did so, a small bundle of letters wrapped in a piece of blue ribbon. Tied on to the ribbon was a luggage label written in a girlish old-fashioned hand. It said, 'Please do not ever read these letters to my brother, Alessandro. They would break his heart.' It was signed, laboriously, 'Elena Mezzanotte, 1943'.

Stefano unwrapped the package. His hands were shaking and the knot was old and tight. There were four letters, each in its original envelope. The postmarks were still clearly legible. The first came from Massa-Carrara, all the rest came from Modena. They were written on lined paper torn from an exercise book. The first letter read:

Dearest Alessandro,   March 1943
                    I cannot come back and see you. I cannot bring myself to do it yet. I was engaged to somebody else, something else. I am so sorry that this has happened to you and that you are blind. I am afraid of illness. I am afraid of you, but I'm sure we can be friends again, someday

> May nature then restore to you the grace
> That you owned formerly, but may it be
> Celestial beauty now which lights your face
> And shows your tenderness and charity . . .

My affectionate regards to Elenita, with best wishes to you and your family for the New Year,
                              Yours,
                              Valentina

The second letter read:

Dearest Alessandro,   April 1943
                    I have been thinking about you. I am sorry I was unkind last time. I was very shocked to see what a terrible accident you had had. I was frightened that you would try and hold me to our engagement, or come after me or something. Now I know that I was being silly.

Your letter was so nice, but I'm sure you will understand when I tell you you mustn't write like that to me again because I have a new *fidanzato* now. He is called Domenico and he is very jealous. When I told him I had a friend who was crippled in the war, he said the Party would look after all its heroes, so you won't need to worry too much. He works for the Party here and so he gets quite a lot of perks; which means you mustn't worry about me either because I am fine. I get new shoes and clothes, and when I am married, the Leader will give us most of what we need to set up house.

My father is being difficult, but you know what he is like. I have been lonely since Agata left the fair. One of the Cotechini twins has run away and the act is ruined.

I am glad you are back home now. The hospital was horrible! I can't wait to leave this fair. It gets worse every day. The war has got inside the camp and everyone is bickering. I don't have many friends left here.

My affectionate regards to Elenita and your parents and to you,

Yours,
Valentina

The third letter read:

Dear Elena,   July 1943

I was too cross to write before, but here you are: there is no point in writing to me. I won't accept any more of your letters or your brother's, so stop poking your nose in. If you want to marry a monster, then go and find one, there are plenty about since the Americans started bombing our towns. If not, and you care for your brother as much as you say you do, then you must nurse him.

He can't find me anyway because I'm not with the fair any more. I ran away when it left Modena. Well, actually, it left and I didn't, but it's the same thing. Domenico and I are married now, and I am expecting a child.

Yours,
Valentina

The fourth letter read:

Dearest Alessandro,   December 1943

Tomorrow is Capodanno, and it makes me think of you. I remember all the times we were together and the times we were apart. I'm sorry if I hurt you. When I was with you, I loved you, maybe not as much as you loved me, but still a lot. I want you to know that I did love you when we were together. I couldn't bear the separation, and worse than anything I couldn't bear your accident. I'm sorry. I hope you don't hate me. I have made another life and found my feet. We have a son now, Alessandro Benito, born three weeks ago. I am very happy.

Please accept my New Year greeting, with best wishes,

Valentina

Stefano put the brittle letters back into their brittle envelopes and then shut them back into the accordion case. He walked around the high bed and sat down on the empty side. He touched Mezzanotte's rigid hand locked in the stiffness of death. Outside, the church bell began to toll. It must be eight o'clock, the priest was calling the faithful to mass. Not many would go, the snow was virtually impassable. He decided that he would go himself and tell someone less hostile than the doctor that Mezzanotte was dead.

Stefano was divided differently now, the warring factions inside him had called a truce: all of him wanted to cry except his eyes, which refused to release their tears. He unbolted the door and opened it on to a wall of snow nearly as high as himself. The blizzard had drifted in the night, enclosing them in a white cocoon. He wanted to call the priest to begin the arrangements for the burial, and yet the north-easterly wind had already locked them in a tomb. He would have to wait in the funeral chamber like an Egyptian servant interred with his dead lord. He looked around the room at the scant belongings that would have to serve to accompany Mezzanotte to the other world.

The bells had stopped ringing. They would ring again before the day was out, to toll the death knell for Mezzanotte.

Down towards the road there was a distant rumbling like the sound of a convoy of approaching tanks. The snow plough was out. Soon they would be dug out of their isolation, excavated by prying hands.

—— XVI ——

For a day and a night Stefano sat with the inert body, yet he still
half-believed that Mezzanotte would wake up. Stefano was used to
seeing deep sleeps. He had been the occasional witness to his
mother's trance over a period of years. He had seen her at home,
apparently dead to the world, locked away from all his own questions and caresses. At first, when he was four and then five, when
he had sat with her, defying his father's orders to leave his petrified
wife alone, Stefano had lain on the bed with his mother and
whispered endearments and goads to no effect. He had found
comfort in her presence. He had not been afraid of her until other
people began to interfere. Nosy friends of Fabrizia would tell him,
'Leave your poor mother alone, you mustn't go near her, she's very
ill.' He hadn't understood. Why was she ill? She wasn't ill, she was
just sleeping, she'd been sleeping ever since he could remember.
She could pass from coma to laughter in a matter of minutes, and
she could pass as easily from laughter to tears. She was afraid of
being taken away in her sleep, of being locked up, and he was
afraid of losing her in the night, of waking up and finding her
gone.

Once, when he had come home from his nursery school and seen
her being carried away on a stretcher, he had bitten one of the
ambulanceman's hands. After that, his mother had been ferried
away under cover of darkness. Over the years he had thought
about that darkness, fought it off, and had nightmares about it. He
had accepted the official story: that in the end she had felt nothing
and was better off in the Lombardy clinic where she eventually
died. Twice a year he had been taken there. Twice a year he had sat
and listened to her gentle breathing. Sometimes he had watched the
drops fall down the transparent tube of her drip. He had studied

203

her still, beatific face for any signs of recognition and, finding none, he had watched the large clock over the door for the minutes to tick into an hour, when one of the nursing sisters would come and rescue him. Each time, he felt afraid he would be unable to last out the hour. When his ordeal was over, Fabrizia would escort him shaking through the silent corridors of the clinic and usher him out into the grim northern sunlight, with its pale sickly fingers.

During his vigil with Mezzanotte he had felt no such fears. By some strange paradox, when his mother had slept, he had feared she was dead; but now that Mezzanotte had died, Stefano felt sure he was merely sleeping. After the snow plough had liberated them, many of the villagers came to pay their last respects. The austere room had never looked so richly furnished. Mezzanotte had been laid out and prepared and placed in a chestnut coffin on a trestle table draped in black crêpe. There were four fat candles on brass stands like guards around his coffin, and the room was full of flowers. There were lilies so powerful they could have woken the dead, there were white carnations and chrysanthemums, but mostly there were lilies drenching the room with their heavy scent.

Stefano felt numb. The cloying flowers were smothering him. People came in and out, they patted him on the back, they spoke to him. There were tears shed for Mezzanotte. The villagers talked about him more as he lay dead than they had ever been able to talk to him when he was alive. Drinking cups of coffee heavily laced with *mistrà*, and tumblers of wine, they lamented his life in stages, like the stations of the cross. They lamented the hardships of his childhood, and the error of his straying from the fold. They lamented the war that had carried him away, and the war that had sent him back in pieces. They shed tears for the loss of his eyes, and the loss of his love, and for the loss of his family. They lamented his inability to bury his scars, as they had done, and build a new life over them. They lamented their own inability to cope with his loss and his loneliness any better than they had.

Knowing that Mezzanotte and Stefano had shared some mysterious pact, living the last months in a state of complicity, they wanted to reaffirm their own allegiance to the dead man and also to acknowledge their inadequacies.

204

'*Dio buono*,' Estelio sighed, 'all those years of silence.'

'Eh, *si*, eh,' Gelsomino agreed.

Estelio and Dr Mearelli were arm in arm, both looking down at the scarred waxen face framed in the coffin by satin cushion.

'We all knew him for a fine man, a serious man. We used to tease him about his diet, but we all knew he fed on dreams and dignity. Do you think he knew how much we would have liked to have been close to him? He was one of us, you know.'

Estelio stopped, his throat closed by tears. Mearelli released his arm and gave his shoulder a squeeze. Then he stepped back, at a loss for words.

Mezzanotte was buried the following morning to the sound of the bells of Santa Maria. Although it had not snowed any more in the night, the snow was still lying in thick dunes over the entire valley. The surrounding woods were lost under its load. The outlying roads had all been cleared by the municipal snow plough, and the streets of the village by tractor. But the road to the cemetery was slippery with compacted snow and ice. The priest had asked for salt to be sprinkled ahead of the funeral procession, but it was a slow and laborious climb none the less to take Mezzanotte's coffin from his room to the *camposanto*.

Unlike other funerals, for which relatives and friends came from beyond the village, this was a very private affair. Stefano carried the coffin together with three of Assunta's sons. The ice hindered them all the way. They stopped at the end of the path that led up from his basement and then again at the steps to Assunta's rooms. They slipped at the curve where Rosina's bread oven jutted into the street, and they slipped again at the hump in the road above the schoolhouse where Mezzanotte had learnt to recite the Dictator's speeches. They paused to rest where the road forked down towards the new houses. One of Assunta's boys lost his footing at the corner of the vineyard and had to be relieved by his father, who was a head and shoulders shorter and caused the entire coffin to tilt perilously.

They paused again by the water trough in which Gelsomino

raised seedlings in the spring. At the point where the road turned off to the new sports field, they readjusted the weight. Their feet slipped and they stumbled by the cypresses in front of the cemetery. At the gates they stopped to reassemble the struggling cortège: several of the followers had fallen in the snow. Stefano halted the pallbearers beside the monument to the war dead, and then took the coffin on to its place beside the cabinet of coffins which reached up five-high along the side wall of the cemetery. Here Alessandro would be cemented in beside Secondo, Agostina, Elio, Elena and Esmerelda Mezzanotte, as their names and photographs testified. Not far away, in another stack were his grandparents on both sides, his sister-in-law with a photograph taken on her wedding day and with her right arm seemingly amputated where the picture had been cut to exclude her husband, Marco. In a corner of the cemetery, by the del Campo vault and the gate, there was a crèche of small mounds and a litany of unbaptized babies' names, among them Lucia, Quinto and Giacomo Mezzanotte. The snow had left only their small crosses above its smothering pall.

Despite the severity of the snowfall, the next day brought a watery sun that weakly tried to loosen winter's grip. The land under the snow seemed to stretch itself, breaking the deep crust that encased it while the trees wept quietly from their branches.

Stefano trudged towards the cemetery along a path turned to sludge by the passage of yesterday's funeral and the light thaw. He carried an armful of lilies for Mezzanotte's grave. They were pure white in contrast to the speckled mush underfoot. The bell of Santa Maria in Alto was ringing with its heavy clank, echoed across the valley by a duller, slower toll which in turn was taken up by the smaller bell of San Crescentino. The muffled thud of Muccignano joined in to announce the hour. It was noon – *mezzogiorno* – but it was Mezzanotte that caught in Stefano's head. As he walked towards the dead man, he felt only the quickness of his friend's life. Rosina and Gelsomino, Concetta, Rosanna, Mario and Luisella all noticed that his mood was not that of a mourner. He seemed to emanate a sense of calm assurance.

On the night after the funeral, Stefano had found himself adrift. He had stayed in Mezzanotte's room, purportedly sorting out his scant possessions, but actually to delay the inevitable hour of his return to Castello. His usual fear of sleep increased to such a degree that he warded it off until his eyes stung and finally betrayed him. He was relieved to find that for once the darkness had been soothing.

Rosina, watching from her vantage point on the curve of the steep road by her still warm oven, saw Stefano reach the cemetery gate, then the cypresses swallowed him from view. Stefano pushed the heavily rusted, spiked iron contraption and then paused, surprised at the ease with which it swung on its oiled hinges, eerily noiseless, and as strange as the gentle voice spoken by a monstrously scarred mouth.

Stefano had woken up that morning resigned to feeling his habitual sensation of the loss of hours from his life, time amputated as from an amnesiac after an accident. Instead, he was overwhelmed by fleeting images, clips from a film about passionate love. Images as clear and as miraculous as visions stayed in his mind, and later he realized that he was remembering dreams. It was the first time in his life that the void of unconsciousness had been peopled and alive. He knew that he had been one of life's abstainers, someone who moved on the surface of things like a moth on a mask. That morning, with his first dreams still in his head, he remembered, as a boy, standing on a rock looking down into a pool in the hills outside Castello. The water was so still and clear that it was difficult to tell if it was there at all. Perturbed by this, he had picked up a stone and thrown it down, making the water reveal itself, folding and wrinkling its unblemished skin. Mezzanotte had been his stone; dashed on to his own blankness, it had released in him a spring of life.

He stepped cautiously along the still slippery paths between the stacked drawers of the long dead with their photographs sepiaed like the snow. When he reached the newly cemented grave of Mezzanotte, a third-floor slot with a vase of flowers and a heap of wreaths made transparent by the cold, the small empty frame where

207

the black and white image of his friend should be seemed to stare out in its own kind of blindness, the only blank frame in the *camposanto*. He imagined Mezzanotte himself would have wanted a piece of newspaper in the frame, a snippet in black and white of the kind that collaged his life.

Stefano put his flowers on top of the previous day's already dying ones and he stood and stared at the otherwise anonymous resting place of his friend. As he stood, shuffling his feet in the salted snow to ease the cold, a wind began to blow, tapping twigs against the outer wall of the *camposanto* and tipping over unstable vases. The wind rose and wrapped itself around Stefano's head. It was hard to stay there, but somehow harder still to go. As the minutes passed, he began to remember more clearly the details of his dream.

A young man in uniform was walking on a beach, he had a wide back and a youthful gait. He stopped and turned his head. He had dark curly hair and he wore sunglasses. Seagulls flew up from the sand like an expanding puff of smoke. Stefano recognized the young man at once as Mezzanotte.

The sea was rough and the rising wind carried his salutation and threw it over the bare dunes, but he saw Mezzanotte smile and wave his right hand. It was not a plastic hand but flesh and blood. Mezzanotte was walking in the surf and the breakers were pounding in Stefano's head. Mezzanotte seemed to be performing the steps of a complicated dance, splashing his feet in and out of the surf, and the water had divided into lines of embroidery, fine white stitches with fragments of paper fluttering along their edges like pieces of torn-up letters. Overhead, the seagulls reappeared and began to fly in a strange formation. Stefano turned his head with the slowness of a drunk and saw an enormous wave gathering.

He called to Mezzanotte, warning him, shrieking like a gull. Mezzanotte had turned to face him, he was staring at him. The huge wall of water was moving closer and Mezzanotte still had not seen it. Stefano waved and shouted. Mezzanotte waved back, with a slow mechanical wave, a windscreen wiper on the edge of the sea. Stefano began to run, stumbling in the sand. He was shouting

208

frantically but his words were shredded by the wind. The wind increased and the wave built and between them they drew out Stefano's nerves, filling him with fear and pain as they unravelled him like a coarsely knitted sock, covering the beach with threads.

The seagulls shrieked in unison and Mezzanotte turned to see the wave begin to break over him. He raised his hands to cover his face as the roaring water exploded over his body. It tore him off his feet and somersaulted him in the spume. The water churned and Mezzanotte disappeared. The bubbling water settled and receded, leaving the prostrate body of his friend covered in a lace sheet far out across the beach. Stefano sprinted across the sand and knelt by Mezzanotte's battered body. He turned him over, struggling with the weight. Mezzanotte's face was scratched and bruised, his sunglasses were gone, his eyes were shut. There was a shot as if from a starting pistol and a skylark fell into the sand. Mezzanotte pulled himself away from Stefano and grimaced, then he coughed and spluttered and hauled himself to his feet. He smiled at Stefano and then he ran past him, beckoning him on with his arms. Where there had been wool on the dunes there was now a barbed-wire fence and inside it there was a carousel of metal seagulls spinning round.

Mezzanotte turned back and called to him, 'Come on, hurry.'

The wind rose again and blew against him as he followed Mezzanotte to the fair.

The wind rose in the cemetery, channelled through the alleyways of high graves to an arrowhead that drove Stefano out past the many tombs with their urns and vases and the terracotta angel with a broken wing stolen long since from the ruined *palazzo* and the marble tablets with generations of names inscribed on them. At Mezzanotte's funeral, the parish priest had said in his sermon, 'The ship of death leaves no wake and no gulls follow it.' Yet Stefano could still hear the gulls and he was following in the wake, knowing that Mezzanotte was there to ferry him through whatever darkness and light awaited him. For how long this would be, he did not know, but he felt that it would be for long enough until he could make the journey alone.